THE TALHOFFER SOCIETY

Michael Edelson

This is a work of fiction. Names, characters, places and incidents are either the products of the author's imagination or are used fictitiously. Any resemblance to actual persons, living or dead, business establishments, events or locales is entirely coincidental.

www.michaeledelson.net

Foreword and Translations

Although this is a work of fiction, the fighting depicted herein is based on the research, understanding and skill of an accomplished historical fencer (the author) and contains translated excerpts from centuries old European and Japanese fighting manuals. The underlying meaning of each excerpt is relevant to the happenings of the chapter it prefaces.

These translation excerpts are used with written permission from the translators, with the exception of public domain translations.

Anonymous Gloss, Codex 44.A.8, "Von Danzig Fechtbuch," 1452, translated by Cory Winslow

Sigmund Schining ain Ringeck, MS Dresd. C 487, "Ringeck Fechtbuch," 1440s, translated by Cory Winslow

Salvatore Fabris, Lo Schermo, overo Scienza d'Arme, 1606, translated by Thomaso Leoni

Ridolfo Capoferro, Great Simulacrum of the Art and Use of Fencing, 1610, translated by Jherek Swanger and William E. Wilson

Miyamoto Musashi, Go Rin No Sho (Book of Five Rings), 1645, public domain translation

Acknowledgements

I normally like to list everyone who contributed to a project in this section, but I can't do that for this one because the list is too long. Instead I will name the primary contributors, those who have profoundly impacted the book and made it what it is. First and foremost, I'd like to thank Sarah Yake of Frances Collin Literary Agency, who was the driving force behind the idea for this story. I'd also like to thank Cory Winslow, Jherek Swanger, William E. Wilson and Thomaso Leoni for allowing me to use their excellent translations of period sources.

The test readers who have had the biggest impact on the evolution of the story are Tristan P. J. Żukowski, Cory Winslow, Jessica Finley, Jake Norwood and Angela Baker Galindo. The rest are too numerous to list, but rest assured, I know who you are and I am grateful to you. Betsy Winslow deserves special mention for her excellent editing services.

Bill Grandy of the Virginia Academy of Fencing was instrumental in teaching me about rapier fencing. I practice and teach KDF, a medieval German system that focuses on fighting with the longsword, and so I knew very little about the rapier. Bill was able to give me enough understanding to write about it intelligently.

The person to whom I owe the most thanks is Jessica Finley, who contributed a wealth of knowledge and experience about what it's like to be a fighter living with multiple sclerosis and the incredible strength of character it takes to persevere and thrive under such a heavy burden. Her invaluable insights allowed me to write about a person who, while not lacking in strength or character, found the weight of her condition too heavy to bear alone.

Finally, I want to thank and acknowledge Sang Kim, who taught me what it really means to fight with a sword. This book, and my career as a historical fencer, would be significantly poorer if not for his influence. Not to mention that this story would be missing one of its most pivotal characters.

Chapter 1

Every father, in order that his children should acquire standing, procures for them a place in some noble court, and seeks to place them under the protection of the highest ranked.
- Ridolfo Capoferro, Great Simulacrum of the Art and Use of Fencing – 1610

The tub was almost full. Droplets of condensing steam rolled down the bathroom's yellow and lavender tiles. In the bedroom, her laptop's monitor glowed with the white background of a search engine screen, revealing the cream colored invitation that lay on the keyboard. She stood in the hallway, a crossroads between realities. Her reflection through the fogged mirror was faded and distant, as though she had already caught a ride with the ferryman.

She clutched the knife in a practiced hand, her grip strong and firm. So it would remain, as long as her medication lasted. Her body trembled, the strain of holding back tears was wearing, but she would not give in, not before making her choice.

The tub, or the computer.

The tub was the easy way out: certain, final, almost painless. The heat would aggravate her symptoms, but by then it wouldn't matter. She would sit in the warm water, close her eyes and fade quickly and peacefully into oblivion.

The computer—the invitation—was also a way out. It offered a painful, difficult death, but also hope. It was struggle and torment to the bathtub's serenity and solace, and she was tired of fighting, tired of hoping and of being let down.

She took a step toward the tub, but her gaze lingered on the bedroom doorway. Just past the laptop she could make out the shadow from her rapier hilt where it hung on a wall hook.

Her rapier. An elegant and deadly weapon, and the only thing left in her life that mattered. She loved reading the ancient texts, teaching others, receiving recognition from her peers. But all the while she had to hide the truth, retreating each night to the murky depths of her reality. The rapier was now her only chance, if not for life, then for dignity. But did she have the strength to take it?

She walked to the tub and leaned over the steaming water, savoring its warmth as the vapors caressed her bare skin. Reaching for the crank, she shut down the flow, then set the knife on the adjacent sink and walked out of the bathroom.

Once at her laptop, she picked up the invitation and entered the address exactly as it appeared. A blank white screen greeted her, and she shut down her browser. It was done.

Returning to the tub, she lowered herself into the soothing hot water and reached over the knife. Her hand, just starting to tremble slightly from the heat, pulled a towel from a brass ring and folded it into a makeshift pillow to put behind her head as she lay down.

Closing her eyes, she savored the feel of the water suspending her in its comforting warmth and ignored the growing numbness in her feet. She would not take the easy way out, not so long as there was a chance.

Free of the burden of her decision, she let go, allowing her grief to consume her. She wept, her tears rolling down her face and neck and disappearing into the tub, diluted by the great mass of ordinary water, lost forever.

Chapter 2

Young knight, learn
to love God, honor the women,
so waxes your honor.
Practice knighthood, and learn
the art that adorns you,
and in wars brings honor.
- Liechtenauer's Verses, Von Danzig Fechtbuch – 1452

People would sometimes ask Jack why he had no pictures of his wife. He would smile, shrug and change the subject. He couldn't explain. They wouldn't understand. He decorated his loft apartment and the training hall below it more by rote than forethought, but for that one thing, he made an exception.

The training hall was an old dance studio on the second floor of an early twentieth century brick building. Intricate moldings that had survived a century of spackling ran along sagging walls in lines so wavy that at first glance it was possible to mistake the result as intentional. The original plaster was neatly painted but showed its age in the form of cracks, bumps and irregular surfaces, much like the oak floor that was scarred and darkened by decades of hard use. Blunt steel swords arranged in racks gleamed under fluorescent fixtures suspended from a cavernous ceiling. One part of a wall was dedicated to medals. A lot of them were Jack's, but most belonged to his students, past and present. He was a lot more fond of the latter.

Jack had considered renovating but the place had an old world charm that he thought was fitting. The only modern touch was a massive picture window that overlooked the street and let in enough sunlight to let him keep the lights off most of the day. The overall impression was of a warm, happy place, but that was a facade. If there was happiness in these walls, it was not his. To Jack, the place was a tomb.

"That bad, huh?" Will asked.

"What?" Jack looked up, startled. He had been staring at the raindrops splattering against the weathered window panes long enough for his computer to go dark from inactivity. Instead of neatly stacked icons, its blank screen showed a hazy reflection of a short haired man with wire rimmed glasses and several days' worth of stubble. A stack of bills was waiting for him in his inbox and three weeks' worth of students' tuition had to be processed before he could pay them.

"I thought you were on Facebook," Will said. "I took a look this morning. Wow. What a shit storm."

Jack shook his head. "Not me. You should reply, I don't have the time." That was a lie, time was one thing he had plenty of.

"Okay," Will said, the word drawn out, uncertain. Though he was technically an employee, he had been a friend long before that, and more importantly, Jack trusted him. It would be good for him to take over as the school's public face.

"So what's up?" Jack said.

Will frowned. "Terrance. He flat out refuses to listen. I told you we should've kicked him out." Will brushed a lock of his long blond hair away from his eyes, a nervous habit that warned of a tense situation on the training floor.

Jack closed his eyes, lifted his glasses and pinched the bridge of his nose. "It's been a long day. You can't handle it?"

"Not this time. He's gone too far."

Jack groaned, lifted himself out of his chair and followed Will out onto the training floor where several pairs of students were engaged in free fencing. The clanging of swords and the murmur of voices sounded harsh and distant in the large room. Most students wore a hodgepodge of protective gear: lacrosse gloves, homemade jackets, hockey leg guards and such. A few were decked out in the latest purpose built Historical European Martial Arts gear—the acronym "HEMA" was even printed on the labels. The gear was all black and looked very sharp. The fencing masks had protective flaps on the back and sides, the padded jackets were tailored for freedom of movement and the knickers had pockets for protective pads. The best pieces of custom gear were the hard rubber mitten gauntlets that protected the fingers and wrists from the sort of catastrophic injuries a three pound steel sword swung in two hands could inflict. Jack had several broken fingers from a time before such gloves were available.

"Watch him," Will said. "He's going to do it again."

Jack turned to look at Terrance, who was easily identified by his red lacrosse gloves and yellow knee pads. He was squared off against Raymond, one of Jack's senior students. Raymond was short, thin and extremely quick. He was a very technical fencer who used crisp, precise movements and made good use of canonical techniques straight from the pages of medieval fencing manuals.

Terrance advanced aggressively as he often did. Raymond hopped out of range, creating just enough threat with his sword to keep Terrance from backing him into a wall. Terrance retreated to reorient. Just as he took his first step, Raymond leapt forward, blindingly fast, and struck the larger man right on top of the head before backing off quickly, covering himself against a possible after blow.

Terrance shook his head, raised his hand to indicate he was hit, and started forward aggressively. Jack could feel his anger. Raymond attacked again, but this time Terrance cut into the attack. Their swords bound with Raymond controlling the center. This made Jack proud, as Terrance was much stronger and it was only Raymond's superior technique that had given him the advantage.

Raymond moved to thrust into Terrance's face, but Terrance left the bind and struck him on the side just before Raymond's sword point scored on his mask. Raymond shook his head and withdrew. Terrance's cut had been small, not quite edge-on and obviously ineffective, but he didn't seem to realize that.

"There, you see?" Will said. "He does it every time. I told him to stop it, but he just smiles and ignores me. How am I supposed to teach someone who ignores me?"

"I've told him too," Jack said. "Thought he understood. I made him try those cuts on tatami and they never work."

"Yeah, but he leaves gashes in the mats and thinks he'd leave those same gashes in a person. I've explained that tatami is a pedagogical tool, not a flesh simulator."

"What did he say?"

Will grinned and adopted a crazy, wide eyed expression that he used when imitating Terrance.

"Son I've killed men with a knife in Iraq," he said, using his best Terrance voice. "Just to watch them die. You ain't gonna tell me my cut won't drop you like a..." He faltered, trying to think of something witty. He had never liked Terrance. Although he was right about the man's arrogance and obstinance, he hadn't made it any easier on himself with the way he treated him.

"Cut it out," Jack said, trying to hide his grin. "You can't do stuff like that anymore, you're an instructor now."

"Yeah, I know," Will said. "Sorry. But the guy is an asshole and he doesn't have a clue. I don't care how many people he shot and stabbed." Terrance was a combat veteran, a Force Recon marine with three tours in Iraq. Other vets in his school benefitted from their experience and Jack found them easier to teach than most. He wasn't sure why Terrance was different.

"And he flat out refuses to listen to you?"

"Yep. You should kick his ass again. Teach him a lesson."

Jack shook his head. "What would that prove? That I'm better at this game than he is?"

"Game?" Will said, not understanding.

"It's just a hobby, Will. Terrance can play his way if he wants to, just not here." He turned to the training floor and shouted, "Terrance, can I have a word please?"

The big man stopped fighting, saluted Raymond and ran over to Jack. He removed his mask, revealing dampened hair that dripped sweat onto his forehead. He wasn't much older than Jack, somewhere in his early forties, but his hair was almost entirely white.

"Terrance," Jack said. "Will has told you several times to stop that. Why are you still doing it?"

"Doing what?" Terrance asked, adopting his usual half smile.

"Leaving the bind when your opponent has the center and leaving yourself open. It's suicidal double-kill bullshit."

"I hit him first," Terrance said. "It's not a double kill."

Jack looked at him a moment, considering. He thought of a dozen things he could say to try to convince him, but he had said most of those things before. Terrance beat him to the punch.

"Only one of us has ever killed people with a blade, Jack," he said. "I'm willing to learn, I want to learn how to use this sword, but when it comes to telling me what would happen if I hit a man with a three foot razor blade right above the floating rib, I think I'll trust my own experience."

Jack waited for his brain to come up with something to say, and suddenly realized that he didn't have the energy. Despite Terrance's seeming assurance, Jack read the signs easily. Terrance wanted a fight, he wanted to prove himself, to himself. Jack understood that desire all too well, but it was an unattainable goal in the sword arts. No matter what he accomplished, there would always be that nagging doubt, that question: was he good enough? Did he have what it takes? Were his theories correct? But there was no way to know, not in the civilized world. The sooner Terrance accepted that these questions had no answers the easier it would be for him.

"Hang on a sec," he said and went to grab a thick paperback book from a bookshelf by his office door. He returned to Terrance, who was regarding him with a raised eyebrow, and handed him the book. "Read this, or at least a good chunk of it."

"What is it?"

"Firsthand accounts of sword fights, mostly from the 18th century. Not our period of interest, but still applicable. Can you do that for me? You'll understand why we don't attack without covering ourselves, especially if an attack is imminent, and why we train so hard to cut well."

Terrance examined the book. "I suppose." He looked confused.

"Great. Also, I'm going to put you in my advanced class. It's Thursday nights, eight to ten. Will is a good instructor but you two don't seem to get along very well. You're not at that level yet, but I'll make it work. One thing though, you have to listen to what I tell you. No more of this 'I know better bullshit.' Read the book and decide if you want to do that, okay?"

"Yeah," Terrance said, his brow furrowing. "Thanks for the book." He turned around and walked off into the locker room. Jack ignored Will's stare and returned to his office.

* * *

"What the hell was that?" Will said. He sounded angry, maybe even hurt. Jack was back in his chair, trying to decide what chore to tackle before calling it a day.

"What was what?"

"Don't give me that," Will said. "He disrespects me in front of my class, refuses to do what I tell him, and you give him a free book and promote him to the advanced class?"

"I thought I was doing you a favor, getting him out of your hair." Jack decided to sort the mail and picked up the stack of letters from his inbox. "And I only lent him the book." Tossing the bills into a special pile he liked to ignore until the very last minute, he sifted through the remainder: updated insurance cards from State Farm, an appeal to donate money to earthquake victims in some place he'd never heard of and a strange envelope made from high quality textured paper, cream colored and thick. It was addressed to his school but mentioned him by name and had no return address.

Will snorted and sat down in one of the chairs facing the desk. "Well you certainly did that. I guess I should be happy."

"What did you want me to do, kick him out?" Jack cut open the envelope and pulled out a single card, made of a thicker version of the same fancy paper.

"No, I know we can't afford it. But something's up with you, Jack. You don't want to go online and make fun of Todd Marrone for being an idiot. You don't want to beat Terrance's ass for being a douche. You don't practice anymore, I know you don't, don't give me any bullshit. It's like you've lost it. And all this 'it's just a hobby, it doesn't matter' bullshit? What the fuck is that? I know," He hesitated, struggling to phrase it diplomatically. "I know it was hard, but it's been almost two years."

Jack sighed, and looked up at Will and made an effort to smile. "I guess you're right. Maybe I need to get out more, take a vacation or something."

"Do it," Will said. "I'll totally cover for you."

"We'll see." Jack examined the card. On it was an odd black and red symbol and a nonsensical web address of seemingly random letters and numbers. The symbol looked like some bizarre fusion of kanji and the style of writing most often used in medieval German fencing manuscripts. He almost tossed it, but the odd symbol intrigued him just enough to defeat the impulse.

"What is that?" Will asked, standing up to take a closer look.

"No idea," Jack said, handing it to him.

"Looks like Chinese characters," Will said. "Or Japanese, whatever. But weird too. Maybe Kanemori will know."

"Kanemori," Jack said, suddenly remembering that they were supposed to have dinner in just a couple of hours. His spirits lifted. It would be good to see his old friend and mentor again. New York City was less than two hours by car, but tight schedules and fast paced urban life made that a greater distance than it should be.

"You forgot?" Will asked.

"I did. Are you coming?"

"Wouldn't miss it."

Chapter 3

Glaive, spear, sword and knife,
Manfully handle,
and in other's hands ruin.
- Liechtenauer's Verses, Von Danzig Fechtbuch – 1452

"You're a racist," Kanemori said, taking a sip of his Sapporo. They sat at a window table, which afforded Jack a view of the strangely dressed college students strolling towards the waterside, clutching umbrellas to ward off the lingering drizzle. They weren't quite hippies, nor Goths, though they had elements of both. However they were dressed, he was sure it was considered trendy, at least in Kingston.

"How do you figure?" Jack asked. The short haired waitress came back, setting down assorted appetizers. He took a whiff of his Miso soup and his mouth watered. There wasn't much he missed about having a real job, but going out to eat regularly was definitely up there.

"You think that just because I'm Japanese I would want to eat sushi."

"*Do* you want to eat sushi?" Jack asked.

"I guess."

He grinned. "Well then."

"Fine, but you're still a racist." Kanemori lifted his beer, and Aiko and Will followed suit. Jack had to force himself not to stare at Kanemori's new girlfriend. She was breathtaking.

"To friends," Kanemori continued, then turned to Aiko. "And to girlfriends."

"Very beautiful girlfriends," Jack added, raising his own beer, and Aiko blushed. "And actually, it had nothing to do with you. Do you know how long it's been since I had sushi?"

"Last Saturday?" Will volunteered.

"Asshole. Chinese buffet sushi doesn't count."

"It certainly doesn't," Aiko agreed with a smile.

"So tell me," Kanemori said. "How is the school going?

You've had your doors open for more than a year now, so you must be doing something right."

"Pretty good, actually," Jack said. "I can't complain. I wish I had more students so I could actually make some money, but as long as I can keep it open and pay Will, it's all good. It helps to live in your school and have a tiny mortgage. Couldn't afford to run it in Manhattan though. I'd have to teach out of my backyard like the old days."

Will looked away and muttered, "I kinda miss the backyard." Jack pretended not to hear him.

"Tell me about it," Aiko said. "I love Manhattan, but I think that in many ways it's a victim of its own success." She was a doctor, a pediatrician. Or maybe a podiatrist. It had been hard to pay attention to Kanemori when he introduced her. Jack had been too busy trying not to gawk. She looked like a Japanese movie star—petite, adorable and radiant.

"In what sense?" Jack asked, wondering what the connection was.

"Your school," she explained. "And things like it...they enrich a community. Culture, history and all that. You're working to recreate a five hundred year old martial art and everything that comes with it, traditions, philosophies, et cetera. And you can't afford to run such a school paying Manhattan rent, so the people of the city have to do without."

Jack laughed. "Not by a long shot. I would need like a thousand students at the rates I'm charging here. Or I could get cheesy and add in some lightsaber fitness classes. That might do it."

"It's not easy," Kanemori agreed.

"You seem to be doing quite well," Jack said. "What with the new car and all."

"I guess, but I only moved out of the karate dojo last year. And I have one of the biggest schools in the city. It's tough. I envy you your nice big training hall."

"It's not fair," Jack said. "You should have a grand training hall that's like its own building." Kanemori was one of the senior-most Japanese teachers in the US, an unheard of achievement for someone his age. He was younger than Will, though not by much.

Unlike most in the Japanese sword arts, Kanemori was always eager to exchange ideas and compare techniques. When Jack had realized how good he was, he had enrolled as a student in his dojo and trained under him for several years. That was before Allison. Before the accident.

"With neon lights and an orchestra pit?" Kanemori said with a grin.

"And a Death Star. In geosynchronous orbit." Jack turned to Kanemori's girlfriend. "Aiko, if you're into local color, we can take a walk by the waterside after dinner. This is Kingston's trendiest neighborhood, if you can believe it."

"The Strand," she said. "I know. I'm looking forward to seeing it."

"You actually heard of it? It's like a hundred feet long."

She laughed. "A bit bigger than that, but...admittedly not by much."

A waiter came with their food, setting a plate of artfully arranged sashimi and sushi rolls down in front of Jack, who immediately began to mix the entire chunk of wasabi from his plate into his soy sauce dish.

"You know they don't do that in Japan," Kanemori said, pointing at the floating chunks of wasabi. "It's an American thing."

"We won the war," Jack said. "We can eat sushi our way."

"So racist."

"Speaking of Japan," Jack said, remembering the letter. "I got a weird letter in the mail today."

"Oh?" Kanemori asked, raising an eyebrow.

"Not much to tell. It was just a character, like a westernized kanji, on a fancy sheet of paper. And a weird looking web address. Mostly numbers."

Kanemori looked at him a moment, eyebrow arching. "Did you go to the website?"

"No way," Jack said. "It'll probably eat my PC or something. Especially since I haven't renewed my antivirus crap."

Kanemori nodded, then smiled and made a shooing motion with his hand. "Probably just junk mail. You should go to the website anyway, you might see porn."

"I have it here," Jack said. "Maybe you've seen it before?"

"Sure, I'll take a look."

Jack took the folded paper out of his pocket and handed it to him.

"Hmm," Kanemori said, staring at the symbol for several seconds, his expression blank. "I'm not sure. I think it has something to do with food. Probably an ad for a trendy new Asian fusion restaurant."

"Aiko?" Jack said. "How about you?"

"Sorry Jack. I was born here, so I can only read Romaji. But it does remind me of a trendy restaurant ad."

"Oh well," said Jack, feeling a bit let down. A mystery was so much more interesting before the mundane reality was revealed.

Kanemori handed it back to Jack. "Go to the URL, check it out. Maybe you'll like the food."

"Disappointing," Will said, echoing Jack's thoughts.

They ate their dinner, after which the waitress brought the check. Jack reached for his wallet, but Kanemori raised a hand to stop him.

"Jack," he said with a grin. "My dojo is running in the green and Aiko is a doctor. You two are a couple of sword bums. Let me have my moment."

Jack chuckled. "If you insist."

"I do."

"I'm a PhD candidate," Will protested. "Not a sword bum." They all stared at him, and after glaring back for a moment, he gave in. "Fine, fine, I'm a sword bum. I did move here only to hang out with this other loser."

"Wear it with pride," Kanemori said.

As promised, Jack led them down the hill to the waterside, where the casual stroll along West Strand Street lasted all of four minutes before they left the trendy historic part behind and doubled back. There were few people in the streets, mostly young couples and two white haired ladies sitting on the benches in the gazebo between the nineteenth century style storefronts and the boat docks on Rondout Creek. The rain had gone entirely, leaving the warmth of a July evening with a heavy dose of humidity. Traffic on Old Bridge was light, but a sizeable cruising yacht drifting in from the Hudson kept them from feeling lonely.

"Why do they call it the Strand, anyway?" Jack asked Aiko.

"You're the local," she teased.

"I'm too poor to ever leave my school." They shared a laugh.

"It's actually Dutch," she explained. "Or at least its roots are. Strunt means beach or shore."

"You're really into this stuff, aren't you?" Will asked.

"You boys have your long pointy things," she said with a smile and a glance at Kanemori. "I need my hobbies too."

Jack raised an eyebrow. "You're not into the whole sword thing?"

"You know I don't date my students," Kanemori said. "It's nothing but trouble."

"I would date my students," Jack said. "If any of them would go out with me."

"Pervert," Kanemori said, punching him in the arm lightly. "So are we going to fight, or what?"

"I thought you'd never ask."

"Awesome," Will said. "Knight versus Samurai." Aiko just shook her head and muttered something about men and testosterone.

They made their way back to the restaurant and Kanemori's champagne colored Jaguar, then drove to Broadway and parked outside the school. Jack's knees protested as they ascended the long staircase to the second floor, one of the few things he didn't like about the building.

He and Kanemori changed in the locker room and started to stretch on the laminate floor of the training hall. The big window on the far wall let past the lights and sounds of passing cars, but it was hard for Jack to hear anything over the excited pounding in his ears. He had to get himself under control, or Kanemori would make short work of him. Outside of kendo and its limiting stylistic rules, competitive fencing was very rare in the Japanese arts. There was a movement to revive the practice as it existed before the war, but it was still relatively new and those few who fenced weren't usually very good. But Kanemori was the one leading the revival in the United States, and he wasn't just good, he was a prodigy.

"Help me with this, will you?" Jack asked Will, picking up the padded fencing jacket and strap-on plastic elbow pads. It was a bulky garment, but it was designed for unrestricted mobility, as were Jack's rubber fencing gauntlets. After helping him get into his gear, Will brought him his favorite blunt longsword, and Kanemori fetched a rebated steel Katana from his duffel bag. The two swords were not all that different. Both were held with two hands, though both were light enough to be used with one. The katana was more rigid and had a slight curve, making it the better cutter, but the longsword was longer, had two edges and a wide cross guard, giving it more versatility. The techniques for their use were surprisingly similar, but the strategy of the fight was another matter.

Once they were both dressed and ready to begin, they exchanged deep bows from opposite sides of the training floor and took their guards. Will and Aiko retreated to the bench by the far wall, but both chose to remain standing.

Kanemori approached him in Chudan, a middle guard with the point held out before him. Jack raised his sword over his head in the guard Vom Tag, and watched his opponent move slowly towards him. He hated Chudan, it was twitchy and unpredictable, which was exactly why Kanemori used it on him. He loved to complain about Jack's longer sword, but that didn't stop him from creeping right in to his measure.

Too unnerved to play it safe, Jack leapt offline and cut at Kanemori's upper arm. His friend's counter was lightning fast and incredibly powerful, and would have struck Jack on the forearm if it hadn't gotten caught on his cross guard. Japanese swordsmanship was about controlling the center, and they were fiendishly good at it, their shorter swords giving them greater leverage in a bind.

Jack pushed his pommel out to his right so that the point arced left. He hoped to get a thrust in, but Kanemori pressed down, making contact with Jack's forearms—and made a mistake. He forgot to factor in the cross guard. Jack pushed forward, the cross lifted the katana away from his arms and his sword's point bent against his opponent's torso.

Kanemori stopped and looked down at Jack's sword. "Very nice. Damn that cross guard."

Jack couldn't believe it. He had actually scored the first point, and it was clean. "Thanks," he said sheepishly, then withdrew.

The rest of the fight did not go well for Jack, though he managed to barely hold his own and even score a couple of good shots. For the most part, however, he was on the receiving end of some fantastic swordplay, which was to be expected. His friend seemed to have complete control of his actions, never motivated by fear or uncertainty, and he herded Jack like a border collie, forcing him into unfavorable positions, one after the other. His movements were enviably precise and never random: he followed his own motto to the letter—win first, then strike.

Jack was the first to throw in the towel, breathing heavily inside his fencing mask, and Kanemori gracefully obliged. After exchanging bows, they clasped hands and then embraced.

"Outstanding," Will said, coming up to pat Jack's back. "I've never seen such clean fencing before. Well, except the last time you two fought, I guess."

"Thanks," Jack said. "He kicked my ass again, but I had a great time."

"Nonsense," Kanemori said. "You held your own. And let's not forget who got the first hit. You've improved a lot, Jack, and you were no slouch last time."

"Thanks," Jack said. "But the way I see it, you won the last two championships in Japan. If I can get a few points in on you, I'm happy."

"Then you should be thrilled," Kanemori said with a grin.

"That was something to see," Aiko said, coming over to kiss Kanemori. "Very dangerous, as fast as you two were moving, but you both have such control."

Jack, still high on adrenaline, beamed under such praise from so lovely a woman.

They spent the next several hours talking over beers at a tavern next door to the school, then made plans for another get together and waved goodbye as Aiko drove the inebriated Kanemori towards the NYS Throughway.

"Now that the cool people are gone," Will said. "I'm going to turn in. See ya tomorrow." He waved goodbye and stumbled towards his apartment on the other side of the parking lot behind the school.

Jack, finding himself alone, decided to go to sleep before the beer wore off and he was left with only his thoughts, and his memories. He meant to go straight to bed, but he lost a battle with curiosity and entered the URL from the weird letter into his browser. It was a blank page. He hit refresh a few times, wondering if there was a glitch, but nothing changed.

"Great," he said. "Now some fucking virus is probably eating my hard drive." He closed the browser, put the machine to sleep and went upstairs. By the time he got to bed, the strange letter was forgotten, but other memories had stirred and would not let him rest. When he finally fell asleep, birds were starting to sing to the first rays of morning light.

Chapter 4

The moment you first face your opponent in a bout,
you must carefully evaluate his style, his strength
and his size, since it is necessary to mold your tactics
to the peculiar characteristics of the person you fight.
- Salvatore Fabris Lo Schermo, overo Scienza d'Arme – 1606.

The examination room was cold, sterile, devoid of color. It reeked of fresh paint. There was nothing on the walls, not even the medical posters that covered almost every inch of the hallway. She supposed that someone in her position was obliged to check her watch, tap her foot impatiently, perhaps blow a lock of hair off of her forehead, but she wasn't bored. She wasn't the opposite of bored either, she wasn't anything. She could have sat there for the rest of the day and not said a word.

The door swung open and Doctor Prabhu entered behind a clipboard he held like a shield, a subconscious barrier between him and the diseased freaks he tended. Just behind him trailed the familiar and pleasant odor of Indian spices.

"I'm sorry to keep you waiting, Mrs. Dragoste," he said, pronouncing her name wrong, with a long "ey" at the end instead of a short "ah." She had given up on trying to correct him.

"It's Miss," she said without looking at him. *That* she felt obliged to correct.

"Oh, yes," he said. "I'm so sorry." He flipped through the pages of her records from behind his clipboard, as if he would see something there he didn't already know. "How can I help you today?" Prabhu had been her neurologist since she had collapsed in her kitchen for the first time, wondering why she suddenly couldn't move. He was a good doctor, but no doctor was good enough to help her. "Are you here for your regular evaluation? It's not due for some time."

"I need to know..." she started to say, but found it hard to finish. She took a deep breath, and forced herself to continue. "I need to know what will happen if I stop taking my medication.

I…I need to know how long I will last, before it gets worse. How long I will be able to function, to do… what I do."

Prabhu raised a thick black eyebrow that looked out of place on his bald head. "Oh? Why on earth would you stop taking your medication?"

She turned and looked at him. "Because I can't afford it. You know how much Copaxone costs."

"But insurance— " he started, then nodded. "You only respond to Copaxone."

"Right," she said. "The plans I can afford...the deductibles are just too high. The crap I can afford didn't work, so I stopped paying."

He sighed. "Maybe I can help you shop for a better plan? There might be something you can afford that will give you what you need."

She shook her head, not wanting to get into it, and he didn't push.

"Well, then," he said. "I'm afraid I can't really give you an answer. It varies greatly. It could be years, or a week, or anything in between."

She had been afraid of that. "There's nothing you can tell me? You know me, you know my condition."

Prabhu rubbed his chin, still holding the clipboard, and made a show of looking her up and down. "Well, it affects everyone a bit differently, but you're strong, and your progression has been pretty mild so far...your only serious problem is that you only respond to specific medication. You'll have your episodes, of course, and some will be pretty bad. But on the whole I'd say you'd be able to carry on for some time. Years. Maybe lots of them. Of course the episodes will get worse, and more frequent."

"And they can happen any time," she said, half question, half answer.

"Any time," he agreed. "And without warning."

She nodded, thanked him and let herself out, not bothering to stop by the desk to schedule her next appointment. One way or the other, there wouldn't be one.

She walked towards her car and glanced at her watch, trying to figure out how much time she had. Her next destination would be less pleasant than the last, the questions perhaps more difficult.

It was six thirty, which meant she had about a half hour to get there. She pulled out onto 355, heading Northwest towards Rockville. She had only eleven miles to go, but at this time on a Friday all of the business casuals would be pouring into Georgetown to hit the Jazz clubs or wine bars, clogging the roads with their Audis and BMWs.

Despite the traffic, she made it with a few minutes to spare and sat in the parking lot, watching students heading in and out, carrying long bags filled with fencing gear. She didn't have much time before the next class started, so she forced herself out of the car and through the glass double doors. The salle was smaller than she remembered, but still enormous compared to her own school. The familiar smell of sweat greeted her as she walked towards the back, where an open door led to Mark's office.

He was there, seated at his desk, talking on the phone. He looked up at her, and his eyes widened. His hairline was a bit higher, but the hair was still sandy and full, and aside from a slight deepening of the lines around his eyes, he looked just as he had when she walked out of this very door for what she thought was the last time.

"I'll have to call you back," Mark said. "Yeah, there's someone here to see me. Bye." He hung up the phone and looked up at her, a slight frown forming in the corners of his mouth.

"Maestro," she said, managing a faint smile.

"Freddie," he said, his expression blank. "It's been a long time, and I'm not your maestro, not anymore. What do you want?"

Straight to the point, as always. "I need something," she said without apology. "And you're the only one I know who can give it to me."

He stared at her, his brows furrowing in confusion. "You walked out on me. My best student, after years of investment. You just left and opened a competing salle not five miles from here. And now you think I want to do something for you?"

"I don't want to be here," she said, lacking the energy for sweet talk. "You're the last person I want to come to, Mark. But it's important, and I don't know anyone else."

"I'm intrigued by your bluntness," he said. "What do you

want?"

She reached into the pocket of her jeans and pulled out the card, then set it down on his desk in front of him. She saw his knuckles turn white as he clenched his fist.

"You can't be serious."

"I am. And I guess I'm not surprised that you know what it is."

"I won't help you kill yourself," he said flatly, and pushed the paper away from her. "That is why you're here, isn't it?"

"I have my reasons," she said. "I don't want to discuss them. What I need is to fence, to get ready."

"You have your own students."

"I don't need students. I need a master."

"I am not a master of the rapier," he said, leaning back in his chair. He folded his arms across his chest, another barrier. "And I don't think classical fencing is going to be of much help to you there."

"Cut the political crap, Mark," she snapped. "I don't need forum debate, I need to fence. It doesn't matter what you call yourself, you're as close to a master as I've got."

"You mean besides yourself?" he said acidly. "Isn't that why you left?" The door was still open, and a few of the students had picked up on the tension and were hovering nearby.

"I left," she said. "Because you had your head up your ass, poring over the texts, looking for wisdom, instead of finding it with a sword in your hands. The period masters tried to make fencing theory simple, to explain it, not to hide code words in the Latin roots of every third word."

"Get out," he growled, showing his teeth.

She nodded. "It was a mistake coming here." She walked out and slammed the door behind her. People watched her nervously as she crossed the worn wooden training floor, but she only made it halfway.

"Wait," he shouted.

She turned and saw him standing in the doorway.

"For what?"

"I'll do it. I'll fence with you, help you get ready for…" He broke off, looking around, then walked towards her and lowered his voice. "If I say no to you, it's like I'm killing you myself. But you're crazy, and once we're done here, I'm going to wash my hands of you. Never come back."

"I have about two months," she said. "How much time can you spare?"

"Two months is not enough," he said. "But it will have to do. Come in the day when I don't have classes scheduled, every day if you can. After one, but before four. All that time is yours."

She was stunned. She had expected a couple of hours a week at most.

"I don't know what to say."

"The less you say, the better. Now get out, I have a class to teach. We can start tomorrow."

"Thank you, Mark."

He nodded, then motioned for her to go. By the time she got to her car, she was crying, and she wasn't sure why.

Chapter 5

He who goes after hewing,
He deserves little joy in his art.
- Liechtenauer's Verses, Von Danzig Fechtbuch – 1452

"In the 14th century," Jack said, shifting his gaze from one student to the next. "A Swabian named Johannes Liechtenauer traveled all over the continent and learned from various fencing masters. Or so the story goes." He smiled. "He's probably as real as Santa Claus."

He waited for the giggles to die down, then continued. "He put together a system of combat that became the dominant fighting art of Europe and was used for hundreds of years after his death. It combines principles of timing, leverage, geometry, anatomy and more, and forms the basis for later period fencing, including most if not all of the Renaissance rapier systems."

There were four new students in the front row, three men and a thin blond girl with braces, probably a student at the local university. All four looked like college students, which was probably Will's handiwork. It had been his idea to hang fliers on campus.

"But the most important thing you need to know about this art," he continued. "Is that it is just that, an art, a martial art. It is not easy, nor is it free of pain. I am not trying to discourage you, but I'm giving it to you like it is, no lies, no empty promises. Learning this art is largely a waste of your time from a practical perspective. Whether you choose to sacrifice so much to gain what most people would see as so little is a difficult choice, and it is a choice each of you will have to make on your own. Before we begin, I'd like everyone to take a look at your handout." He waited while they examined the paper he had given them.

"It's a strange piece of art, by modern standards," Jack said, glancing at the image, displayed on a poster on the school's back wall. A man with a bird's head, a deer's hooves and a lion on his chest. "This picture is from a manual by Paulus Kal, an overweight

15th century fencing master who commissioned an illustrated fencing manual and had himself drawn into it, nice fat paunch and all. It represents the three virtues of medieval fencing. It says, *I have eyes like a falcon, so that I will not be fooled. I have a heart like a lion, so that I will strive forward.* And finally, *I have feet like a hind, so that I spring towards and away.* Every time you pick up a sword, blunt or sharp, remember those words. Now then. Raymond, get your mask."

Raymond stepped up to the front, put on his mask and took up his training longsword. This one had a rubber stopper taped to the tip. Jack slipped on his coaching mask, a worn rusted thing long overdue for a liner washing.

"Raymond and I are going to show you some fencing so you can see what to expect in your own training. Before that, though, I'm going to show you some fundamentals that I want you to keep in mind as you learn. Now you're all new, so don't think I expect you to memorize anything at this point. Just keep these lessons fresh as you begin your training." He turned to Raymond. "Ready?"

"Yes." Raymond put his sword over his head in the guard Vom Tag and prepared to strike.

"Number one," Jack said as he positioned his sword out in front of him, pointing at his opponent. "Attack the man, not the sword. Raymond."

Raymond struck at Jack's sword, trying to bat it out of the way. Jack dipped his point under his strike, brought it right back up and stuck it into Raymond's chest.

"If you fight the sword, you're not doing anything to me, which means you're wasting your movements. Number two, treat the sword like it's real. If you don't fear the sword, there is no need to defend against attacks. Raymond."

Raymond reset to Vom Tag and struck at Jack's head. Jack ignored it, letting it hit his fencing mask as he cut down into Raymond's thigh.

"It is almost impossible to defeat a fencer who is willing to sacrifice his own life to kill you. Again."

Raymond executed a series of strikes and Jack ignored each of them, either undercutting or overcutting Raymond's line. If he cut low, Jack cut high, if he cut high, Jack cut low. In each exchange, they both hit each other.

"This is the most important lesson in fencing," Jack said. "If you don't understand this one simple thing, you will never learn how to use a sword. Any questions?"

The wispy blond girl raised her hand.

"Go ahead," Jack said, taking off his mask.

"So how do you fight someone like that? Someone who is suicidal?"

"Very carefully." They all laughed. "But seriously, you really wouldn't have to. Our text sources, the Peter Von Danzig Fechtbuch, Sigmund Ringeck, 3227a, they are all very clear on the fact that if you attack someone, that is the man and not the sword, to the head or to the body, then that person must defend. Renaissance rapier systems calls this responding in obedience, because you have no choice. People in period would have been very aware of what a sword was capable of, in the same way that if I were to point a gun at you right now, you'd freak out. They wouldn't take a sword moving at them as anything but imminent death."

"What if the person was crazy?" she asked. "Are you just screwed? Or better yet, what if god forbid you had to fight someone today, and that person didn't understand this, what would you do?"

Jack smiled. "What's your name?"

"Leyna," she said, looking down at the floor. "I'm sorry for asking, I just—"

"Don't be, it's an excellent question, particularly the second part. It's also a very difficult question, because it has no easy answer. The simplest way, I'd say, is to let that person attack first, so that they are committed and can't suicide. If they don't want to attack, you're going to learn ways to force them, to pressure them into doing what you want. That is the highest level of fencing, when you can make your opponent dance to your tune."

"Thank you," she said with a shy smile.

"Anytime. Now then, Raymond, let's fence."

Just as he was about to put his mask back on, the little brass bell on the door jingled and Will rushed in, short of breath and in an obvious hurry.

"Sorry," he said. "Class was held up. You want me to take over?" He unslung his backpack and tossed it in a corner with a dramatic flair.

"Please do," Jack said, then turned to the students. "This is Will, my assistant instructor. He teaches most of the beginner's classes. You'll be in very good hands."

"Oh," Will said. "Before I forget, the UPS guy made me sign for this." He handed Jack a large padded envelope.

"Thanks." Jack took the package and retreated to his office while Will geared up to square off with Raymond. He sat in his chair and tore open the envelope, not bothering with the letter opener. A neatly bound stack of newly printed money fell out onto his desk, and he stared at it blankly, wondering where it had come from. He shook the envelope and another stack fell out. Hundred dollar bills.

He blinked, trying to understand what he was looking at. Had Will ordered fake money for their poker games? Why would he have it delivered to Jack?

He picked up a stack and ruffled the edges. The money wasn't fake.

"What the hell?" He pushed the stacks away from him before realizing what he was doing. His heart was racing as he spread the mouth of the envelope open and looked inside, hoping to find something that would explain why someone had mailed him two stacks of hundred dollar bills. If these were typical bank stacks, there was twenty thousand dollars lying on the desk in front of him.

A piece of paper, thick and cream colored, fell out onto his desk. He picked it up and read the small print below a smaller version of the strange symbol he had found in his mail a few days prior.

Mr. Jack Fischer,
You are hereby invited to a tournament of arms.
You have been selected based on your reputation for skill and innovation in the recreation of medieval European fighting arts. Participation in the tournament is entirely

voluntary, and you may withdraw at any time
without prejudice. The tournament will take place
September 5th through the 25th, which includes travel time.
If you decide to accept this invitation, kindly once
again visit the web site indicated below.
Enclosed please find a token of our admiration for
the work you are doing, which you may keep regardless of
whether or not you accept the invitation.

www.ts16022715.info

Jack read the paper five or six times before setting it down on his desk next to the money. He was terrified. There was only one thing that could make a tournament illegal, and it being illegal was the only reason someone would send that kind of money and provide so little information.

"Holy fucking shit." His hands were shaking. This wasn't real, it couldn't be. He started to get dizzy, his vision clouding. Things like this did not happen to him, did not happen in real life. They were the domain of fiction, of books and movies. The money, the note, they had no place in the real world, in *his* world.

He opened his bottom desk drawer, swept the money, the envelope and the note inside and closed it. He locked it with his key, put the key in his pocket and practically ran out of the office, out of the school and started walking down the street, staring at nothing in particular, his mind racing. Scenarios with possible explanations came and went. Some he dismissed early, others lingered. Someone would come for that money and for him if he refused the invitation. The money was actually fake, he had made a mistake. Kanemori was playing a trick on him and would show up asking for his money back. The police were setting him up, like people who arranged meetings with underage girls who were actually cops playing a role.

He found himself outside Burger King, about half a mile away from the school. He was not aware of enough time having passed for him to have walked that far, but there it was. The smell of flame broiled mystery meat was appealing, and he decided he could use some comfort food. He went in, ordered a double whopper, fries and a chocolate shake, then sat alone in the back and ate quickly. The smell had been better than the taste, and his bill, over ten dollars, started to depress him. He had precious little savings and no income whatsoever—every cent he made running the school went into keeping it open. He couldn't afford to spend frivolously.

But then—couldn't he? He had twenty thousand dollars.

Apparently some idiot had sent him a bunch of money hoping to lure him into some illegal underground death club where rich old bastards would wager on how long he would live while some thugs hacked away at him with machetes. Not unlike a signing bonus for military service in the Middle East. Well screw them. The note did say, in black and white—well, black and cream—that he could keep the money whether he accepted or not.

"Fuck yeah," he said under his breath. They had set the trap, but the mouse would make off with the cheese.

Chapter 6

Your War should not be rushed.
Who enters the war above,
he becomes shamed below.
- Liechtenauer's Verses, Von Danzig Fechtbuch – 1452

They sat on the ground, leaning against the building. They were hidden from passing police by a low wall that divided the sidewalk from the parking lot. Jack wasn't sure which business the lot technically belonged to, but he encouraged his students to use it when necessary.

Will took a long pull from the bottle of Black Label and handed it to Jack. He cringed, gulped down all he could stand and passed it back, trying not to snort.

"You're like a big drinking baby," Will said. "One or two sips and you're running naked through the streets."

"I'm a cheap drunk," Jack said. "Chicks like that."

"Oh, what chicks?"

"Your mom, for one."

Will laughed. "She just might. You can have her if you want, she lives in Sydney, that's like an hour away."

"An hour and a half," Jack said, passing the bottle back. "I checked."

"You did?"

"Yes," Jack said. "When I was going out with your sister."

"Touché," Will said. "But you're still a lousy drinker."

"Indeed."

Jack looked up at the sky, stars mostly visible behind some slow moving gray and yellow clouds. The occasional passing car obscured them for a time with its headlights, casting sweeping shadows across the mostly empty lot as it sped away. One of the best things about Kingston was that it had no tall buildings with glaring window lights to blot out the night sky.

"It's nice out here," he said. "Much better than the city."

"This *is* a city," Will pointed out.

"Hardly." One of his local students had taken Jack to see the Kingston "ghetto" when he had been looking to rent a space for his school. To Jack, white picket fences and stately Victorians, albeit in various states of disrepair, did not a ghetto make, regardless of who lived there. Mermaid Ave, Bedford Stuyvesant, those were ghettos.

The bottle made another couple of rounds while they sat in silence, then Will said, "So do you think it was real?" Jack had been waiting for the conversation to come back to the invitation. It hung over his head like the sword of Damocles, a metaphor a bit too close to home for his liking.

"Of course I think it was real, they sent me twenty thousand dollars."

"Maybe it's counterfeit," Will suggested.

"I went to the bank today," Jack said. "I had them check the bills and even run some of the numbers. They're real, and not stolen."

"So, um," Will said, hesitating as though unsure how to phrase the question. "Are you…I mean…will you go?"

Jack turned to stare at him. "Have you lost your god damned mind? Of course I'm not going to go. Why the hell would I go?"

Will shrugged. "I'm not saying you should. I wouldn't. Just making sure, I guess."

"It's fucking crazy," Jack said. "It's obviously some kind of death match bullshit. If it were a normal tournament, we would have to pay them, they wouldn't pay us. I should take it to the cops."

"You should," Will agreed. "But they might make you give the money back."

"What money?" Jack said with a sly grin. "There was no money in that envelope."

Will smiled. "Yes, of course. So will you? Take it to the cops I mean?"

"I don't know. What would be the point? The local cops would just write a report and put the letter in a file. I'd have to take it to the feds. And you know how I feel about them."

"Fuck the poh-lice," Will said with a goofy grin. "Hey…I wonder if they invited our good buddy."

"Who?"

"The one who badmouthed our YouTube videos. Don't you go on Facebook anymore?"

"I don't have time for that shit," Jack said. The same lie, again."And now I'm glad I didn't see it. Who was it?"

"Todd Marrone, who else?"

"I hate that guy. All he ever does is give people shit unless they do things his way."

"Who doesn't hate Todd?"

"Lots of people, apparently."

Will shook his head. "I don't know, man. Frederica came out on your side. She basically told him to put up or shut up."

"Frederica?" The name sounded familiar, but Jack didn't spend nearly as much time on social media as he used to.

"Frederica Dragoste, the chick from Maryland. She does Capo Fero and Fabris and all that junk."

"Ah yes," Jack said, remembering. "Pretty name. She has the fancy avatar pic, right? Like from a professional photo shoot, with the rapier hilt superimposed? I like the things she posts. Very smart, and insightful."

"That's her," Will said. "Rapiers are gay, but I guess it's okay since she's a girl."

Jack shook his head and smiled. "There are just so many things wrong with that statement, I don't know where to begin. I won't kick your ass because you're drunk."

"You know 'dragoste' means 'love' in Romanian, right?"

"I know," Jack said. "Like the song. Love from the linden trees."

"Oh yeah," Will said. "That was your wife's ringtone. The thing used to go off like ten times a day." His eyes widened, and he looked away, embarrassed. "I'm sorry, I keep forgetting."

"It's okay," Jack said, his grin seamlessly shifting into a melancholy smile. "Sometimes I forget too." Sometimes, but not often enough.

"So yeah," Will said, quickly changing the subject. "I wonder if they invited Todd."

Jack chuckled. "I bet they didn't. And I can't believe I'm now officially proud of having been invited to a glorified snuff shoot."

"We're so sad," Will said.

"Yep, a couple of grown children." Jack leaned back, his head hitting the wall a bit harder than he intended. He wanted to cry out in frustration and pain, but what came out was, "God, Will, what the hell am I doing with my life?"

"What do you mean?"

"Come on, you know exactly what I mean. I'm forty fucking years old, and I teach college kids how to play with swords."

"Raymond is no college kid."

Jack glared at him. "Stop fucking around. Raymond has a job, you're getting a PhD, what the hell am I?"

"You're a sword Mozart, that's what."

"Kanemori is the sword Mozart."

Will shrugged. "He certainly is, but that doesn't mean you can't be one too. I think you sell yourself short. Kanemori is almost half your age. You are old, tired and fat, and you can give him a run for his money."

"Shut up," Jack said, but without much enthusiasm. "I'm not fat. At least not yet."

"You're happy, aren't you?" Will asked. "Isn't that what counts?"

Jack shook his head. "Happy? No, I don't think so. I miss her, Will, I still miss her every day." The worst part was that he couldn't remember her face, not without seeing—

"I know," Will said, interrupting his thought. "They say time heals all wounds, but they never say how much time it takes."

"Yeah."

"But the art...you love this shit, don't you?"

"I used to," Jack admitted. "But now I'm just content to do it. I mean think about it, it's a dead end. You and Raymond are the only ones I've taught so far that take the shit seriously, but even you two aren't going to do it as a day job."

"Only because I don't think I can. I'd love to do this." Jack started to speak, but Will cut him off. "You don't know how good you have it. One day though, when..." he hesitated, swallowing. "When enough time passes, you will appreciate it."

"Maybe, and maybe people will one day take what we do seriously, but I have doubts on both counts."

"Are you done feeling sorry for yourself?" Will said with a grin.

"No," Jack said. "Pass me the bottle."

A man in ill fitting clothing shambled into the parking lot's far side headed in their direction. He saw them and paused, then turned towards a nearby bush and stopped in front of it.

Will sat up. "Is he doing what I think he's doing?"

"Taking a piss?" Jack said, squinting to see better under the faint orange glow of the low pressure sodium street lights.

"He was headed this way," Will said. "He only stopped when he saw us." He jumped to his feet and turned to glare at the spot where he had been sitting. "Do you think…"

Jack frowned and slowly climbed to his feet, lacking Will's youthful exuberance.

"Yeah," he said, resigned. "Yeah I bet he does."

"Fuck," Will cursed, swiping at the back of his shirt. Jack, more practical, leaned down and took a whiff.

"I can't smell anything," he said, and sat back down.

Will stopped swiping, bent to sniff, shrugged, and followed suit.

"We are a couple of sorry sons of bitches, aren't we?" he asked.

"Yeah," Jack agreed. "We sure are. But at least we have twenty thousand dollars. I plan on sharing it with you. Fifty fifty."

Will shook his head. "Damn, you suck with money. No, you can't share it with me, you need it for the school. I won't take more than five." He grinned sheepishly.

Jack laughed. "Fine, five it is. What will you buy?"

"A new sword. Or two."

"And *I* suck with money?"

"Touché."

They shared a chuckle, then Jack said, "What do you want to do for the rest of the night?"

Will shrugged. "I dunno. I think I saw that new chick upstairs practicing with a couple of her friends. Maybe I'll go hit on her."

"Sounds good." Jack allowed students access to the school at all hours, except when he was sleeping or travelling. Many had room to practice at home, but the school had a lot of equipment most of them couldn't afford.

"Come on old man," Will said, getting to his feet and offering Jack a hand. "Come watch me work."

* * *

Bright light pierced the uncovered windows and lanced into his eyelids, beckoning him to abandon the peaceful respite of deep sleep. He cursed under his breath and reached for a pillow to put over his head, but it refused to move. He tugged harder, but it still didn't yield. Opening his eyes, he turned to investigate and saw the back of a head: long blond hair, thin strands fading to light brown near the root.

It all came to him in a flash, and he felt his cheeks burning.

Leyna turned around, blinked a few times, then saw him and smiled.

"Good morning," she said.

He stared at her, his eyebrows raised like those of a helpless puppy, afraid to move. "Hi," was all he could manage to say. What had he done?

She giggled, and shoved him playfully. "You weren't this shy last night." Her breath was pungent and sharp, but not at all unpleasant.

"I, um…" Dammit. He had been joking about dating his students. It wasn't proper at the best of times, but hopping into bed with them on their first day? Damn Jack Daniel's to hell. Will was right, he was a terrible drinker.

"Do you want to back out of our agreement?" she asked, running a hand through his hair. His nervousness seemed to amuse her. Her smile glinted in the sun, bright metal braces catching its rays for an instant before a cloud swallowed enough to extinguish the glow. She smelled flowery, like scented soap or shampoo, and as she placed her leg over his thigh he felt himself stirring despite his self condemnation. Her skin was warm and soft against his, her flesh firm yet yielding.

"Our agreement?" he asked, reaching out to stroke her back under the sheet. It was hard to be this close to her and not feel aroused.

"You don't remember? You must have been really wasted. We were going to pretend this never happened. I really want to be a student here, and I wouldn't want this to get between us."

"Oh," he said, both relieved and somewhat disappointed. "Yeah, I guess." Now that she said it, it came back to him. The laughing, the drinking, the flirting. "I'm sorry about this, I shouldn't have." He was not the sort of man who enjoyed casual affairs, and the fact that she was a student made it a lot worse.

She shook her head. "Um, *I* seduced *you*, remember?" She leaned over and kissed him, immediately sticking her tongue into his mouth with no preamble. Clumsy, inexperienced, but delightfully erotic.

"I guess it would be for the best," he said, his disappointment edging out. She had no interest in him personally, only what he represented. A conquest—the teacher, the master. This was, according to Will, the main reason he wanted to be a college professor. Jack couldn't blame him—well, he could, and should, but then he would be a hypocrite in deeds if not ideals.

"We don't have to start right now," she said, and pulled the blanket off, revealing small round breasts, a slender waist and curvy hips. Whatever cloud had obscured the rising sun was gone now, leaving her pale skin to glow gold in the warm light. She moved her legs just enough to show the edge of a trimmed patch of hair. Jack shuddered, his desire growing. "In fact," she continued. "Maybe we can remember…sometimes." She kissed him, and he was helpless.

They made love again, after which she dressed and kissed him goodbye. "As a lover," she explained. "As a student, it's 'see you later, my handsome master.'" She smiled, pecked him on the cheek and left.

He smacked himself on the forehead a few times, then got dressed and set some water to boil in the electric tea pot. He barely remembered the girl's name, and yet now that she was gone he felt alone. More alone than usual. It had been almost two years since Alison's death, and that was both an eternity and an instant.

"Alison," he whispered, and despite a cry of warning from the part of his mind that was still capable of reason, he reached into a kitchen cabinet and pulled out a framed photograph, setting it down on the counter. Deep auburn hair, bright blue eyes, a smile that seemed alive even printed in dye sublimation on plastic coated tree pulp. Alison had stayed with him. Alison had loved him. She never played games, never made him wonder how often he should call her, or how much time was okay to spend with her before she felt smothered. Every night she would come home and sit with him, talk about her day and his failing dreams. Every night, but for that one.

"I almost died today," she would sometimes say. "I totally fell asleep at the wheel."

"Buy some munchies," he had suggested. "That's what I do on long drives."

"Do you want me to get fat?" she teased.

"I want you to live."

She had bought munchies, but on that day she must have run out. It was probably one of her usual lapses, just a fraction of a second, but enough to send the car veering into the opposite lane of traffic where a tractor trailer lay in wait, one of a legion of monstrous predators that prowled the congested streets of New York City. Her purse must have been flung from the car, because they had wanted him to identify the body. He had looked under the sheet. Looked at the thing that his beautiful Alison had become. A husk of tortured flesh, torn apart and mangled.

He stared at the picture, but he could no longer see her. Instead he saw that thing.

The tea pot clicked off, but he didn't reach for it. Instead, he put the picture back into the cabinet and moved aside a box of cereal to reveal another bottle of Black Label. It was going to be one of those days.

The phone rang before he got the bottle open. He considered not answering, but it could be a prospective student asking about class times. He could handle that, just a simple question or two. He picked it up.

"Kingston Academy of Arms," he said.

"Is this Jack Fischer?" a man's voice said in an official tone. Boredom mixed with elitist amusement.

"Yes," he said, wanting nothing more than to end the call and down the entire bottle. What had he been thinking, looking at that photo?

"This is Special Agent Hick, Federal Bureau of Investigation. I'd like to speak with you, if now is a good time?"

Jack instantly tensed. "No," he said tersely. "It's not. What is this about?"

"We'd like for you to come down to our headquarters in Manhattan, Mr. Fischer. You're not in any trouble, don't worry, in fact we could use your help, and perhaps we will be able to compensate you. Financially, of course."

"My help?" Jack said, feeling the bottom drop out of his gut. He looked in the direction of his desk downstairs, where fifteen of the twenty thousand lay locked in a drawer.

"If you will just get a pen," the agent said. "I'll give you an address. Are you available tomorrow?"

Tomorrow? Tomorrow was no good. Tomorrow meant he would spend the entire day torturing himself, trying to play out scenarios in his mind, trying to figure out how much trouble he was in. He looked at the wall clock: 9:00AM.

"I'm busy tomorrow," he said. "How about today? I can be there in a couple of hours."

The agent hesitated. "Uh…yeah, okay, that will be fine. But let's make it one in the afternoon, okay?"

"Sure. Give me the address."

"26 Federal Plaza," he said. "Do you need directions?"

"Suite number?" Jack asked.

"Just give the people at the front desk your name. They'll sign you in and tell you where you need to go. Thank you, Mr. Fischer, I look forward to speaking with you."

"Yeah, thanks," Jack said, and hung up. He called Will right away.

"Jack," Will said, his voice tinny through Jack's cheap cordless phone. "You animal. That chick was all over you. Tell me you nailed her."

"I need you to cover all my classes today," Jack said.

"Sure," Will said lightly. "You give me some money and now you own me."

"I'm serious."

"What's going on?" he asked, sounding concerned.

"I'm not sure, but I'll let you know when I get back."
"Is this about…" He left the question hanging.
"I don't know," Jack lied. He knew very well.

Chapter 7

If you examine the parry, you will find it to be a form of fear, because if you were not afraid of harm, you would not see the need to defend. This type of defense can therefore be dubbed obedience, even servitude, all the more when it is performed out of a sense of necessity, because he who does not wish to be wounded sees himself compelled to parry.
- Salvatore Fabris Lo Schermo, overo Scienza d'Arme – 1606.

Her rapier pointed at her opponent, she advanced into misura larga, wide measure, one step away from a fatal thrust. Mark had let her find his sword, to position hers in a mechanical advantage, so that he could not thrust successfully without repositioning. His line of attack closed, he was in obedience, responding to her initiative. She was surprised that he had allowed this, but it was Mark, so he was definitely up to something.

He stood still, as a poor fencer would, letting her maintain advantage. She would have pressed, but her hand had started to feel numb a few minutes before and was decidedly worse now. Of all the lousy timings.

He stepped back, and like an unthinking fool, she followed. Only his step wasn't real, it was a motion of the body designed to fool her, and in the tempo of her foolish advance he performed a cavazione, an exchange, moving his sword under and around hers, and thrust. She tried to parry but he had the mechanical advantage and her grip failed her. Her rapier clattered on the hardwood floor as she felt Mark's sword push into her breast, right over her heart.

He took a step back, pulled off his mask, and looked down at her weapon, confused.

She bent over to pick it up and took a guard, ignoring his concern. He shrugged, put his mask back on, and faced her once more.

She repeated her advance, and he once again did nothing and allowed her to find his sword. This time she did not wait for him to feint retreat but stepped into misura stretta, close measure. He used another cavazione in the tempo of her advance, but she ignored it and thrust. He twitched, aborting his attack, and she scored on the bib of his fencing mask, right over his throat.

He cursed, stepped back and pulled off his mask yet again.

"Dammit, Freddie, what the hell is wrong with you?" He was breathing heavily and his forehead was shiny with sweat. He was working her very hard, and it was clear that he himself wasn't used to this level of exertion. "If I hadn't stopped my thrust, we'd both be dead."

"But you did," she said. "And I'm not."

"So you're going to count on suicidal bullshit to win?"

She slumped. "No. I'm sorry, I don't know what came over me." He was right. She had allowed her anger and frustration to control her.

"And what's wrong with your hand? Did you hurt it? If you can't hold a sword, there's no way you can fight in that..." He couldn't finish. His loathing of the very idea of the tournament was quite apparent, making her wonder why he was working so hard to help her. Not to mention how he knew about it in the first place.

"It'll heal," she lied. "But it's bothering me now. Let's call it a day, okay?"

He narrowed his eyes at her, but nodded reluctantly. "Will it be better by tomorrow?"

"I think so."

She packed her gear bag and left without another word. Mark retreated to his office, still with no apparent interest in conversation. A small blessing, but one that was very much appreciated. There were a lot of old wounds between them, mostly on his end, and no good could come of bringing them up. She had left him because he had failed her as a teacher, focusing more on scholarly pursuits than physical skill and trying to force her in the same direction, but he was still a great fencer and she needed him.

She decided to stop by her school to dump her gear before going home. A few of her students' cars were in the parking lot, including Roger's. He was taking over many of her classes, and though he did not yet know it, he would soon take over the school as well. Any teacher would be fortunate to have a student like

Roger, but she was doubly so, because of her recent negligence.

"Maestro," Roger said as soon as she walked in. He had lost weight, or at least fat. His chest looked broader, shoulders and arms more powerful. He had also let his hair grow and the reddish locks floated around his head in a wavy mess.

Her first impulse was to chastise him—there were only two Maestros of the rapier in the world, though how they got the title was beyond her. There were no living lineages of any European sword art older than classical fencing. Still, their titles came from the International Historical Fencing Federation, which gave them a lot of clout. She'd always wondered about the IHFF—their headquarters was a beautifully restored castle in Bavaria. The thing had to cost millions, but if every serious historical fencer in the world pitched in a buck it probably wouldn't pay a month's mortgage on that place. But these were the concerns of another life, and she lacked the energy for them.

"Hello Roger," she said, managing a brief smile. "How are things?" There were seven other students in attendance, a good showing for an afternoon class, at least in rapier. The rapier was her passion, but the much larger sport fencing classes were the school's bread and butter.

"Good," he said. "But, I, uh, I need to talk to you. Privately."

She frowned. "Can it wait?" She wasn't in the mood to talk to anyone, not even Roger.

"Not really."

"Fine, let's go in the office." It was more of a glorified closet: there was barely room for a small desk and two tiny chairs. Roger shut the door behind him.

"If you don't tell me what's going on with you," he said without even giving her a chance to sit down. "I am going to let the others go ahead with the intervention."

"What intervention?"

"They think you've started using drugs, or something like that. They would skewer me if they knew I was telling you."

She frowned. "I'm fine, Roger. Tell the others to leave me the hell alone."

"Come on, Frederica." He rarely used her full name. "We care about you. *I* care about you. Tell me what the hell is going on.

Don't leave me in the dark like this, it isn't fair. I've been busting my ass these last few months." He held up his hands, seeing her about to snap at him. "I don't mind, I really don't. But I need to know *why*. Please."

She sighed, and sat down. What was the use? If she couldn't tell Roger, who could she tell?

"I need you to come see a lawyer with me next Thursday," she said.

"What?"

"I'm signing over the school and the lease to you. If you want it. If not, I'm shutting it down."

"Holy shit, Freddie, what's wrong?" He walked up to her chair, barely squeezing between the edge of the desk and the wall, and crouched in front of her, on one knee, as though he were proposing. "Tell me."

She shrugged. "I have MS. Multiple Sclerosis. Carl left me, and took his insurance with him. I can't afford the medication."

He stared at her, blinking slowly. "How…how long have you known?"

"Less than a year."

"And you never said anything? So that time you fell down, it wasn't your back?"

She shook her head. "It wasn't."

"And when you dropped your sword?"

She nodded, holding back tears.

"Holy shit, Freddie, this sucks."

She nodded again, this time unable to resist the impulse to cry. "It sucks," she echoed. He put his arms around her and held her while she wept.

"What about Obamacare? Doesn't that change anything?"

"The plans I can afford don't cover the meds I need. They want me on something cheaper that doesn't work for me."

"We'll all pitch in," he said. "I have some money. We'll get you your medication. I mean how much can it cost?"

"Fifty thousand a year," she said.

"Jesus fucking Christ." He let her go, got to his feet and began pacing in the small space. "It's a crime to charge that much. A god damned fucking crime. People should hang for it."

"There's nothing you can do, Roger," she said. "Except take over the school. But don't do it for me, do it only if you want to. I wouldn't want to burden you with something like this."

"But where are you going?"

"Away," she said. "There's a small chance for me, and I'm going to take it."

"You can't tell me more?"

She shook her head.

"But I'm not ready."

"You are," she said. "You're more than ready."

"If you say so," he said with obvious reluctance. "But know that I'll sign it back over to you anytime. All you have to do is come back. You've been the best teacher I've ever had, and the others feel the same way. This will always be your school."

"Thank you, Roger, that means so much to me. Don't tell the others I'm leaving, okay? Not yet. I'll tell them when I'm ready."

"Of course."

He left her alone, and she cleaned herself up and left through the back door. When she was back in her apartment, she sat down in front of her computer and went on Facebook, one of her few forms of escape. She wished the damned tournament would come already so she could get it over with. The hours between her fencing sessions with Mark were almost unbearable.

Chapter 8

Four openings know,
Aim so you hit knowingly,
in all driving
without confusion for how he acts.
- Liechtenauer's Verses, Von Danzig Fechtbuch – 1452

The drive had been nothing more than a two hour opportunity for him to wrap himself up into a tense bundle of stressed nerves. He half expected to be arrested as soon as he announced himself at the front desk, but they just handed him a visitor ID card and gave him a floor and office number.

"Do you validate?" he asked one of the men behind the desk. It was more of a complaint than a question.

The guard stared at him blankly for a moment before answering. "Excuse me?"

"Do you validate," Jack repeated. "As in parking. There was no street parking and it cost me almost fifty bucks to park in one of the lots."

"That's something you'll have to discuss with the agents," the man said with obvious disapproval.

"I will." Jack proceeded to the elevator where he was joined by at least ten other people. They were probably coming back from lunch, as were the hordes of pedestrians that swarmed the streets of the city just outside the building. Jack honestly could not remember how he had lived in this overcrowded Abaddon. His palms were sweaty and his heart beat hard enough for him to notice it. He shook his head, trying to clear it. He needed to get a grip before he said something stupid to one of the people he had come to see.

Barely squeezing out onto his floor before the doors closed, he set off in search of the office number. Men and women in dull suits and glazed over expressions passed by without seeming to notice him. When he found what he was looking for, a plain faux wood door bearing Hick's name plate, he knocked.

"Come in," said a familiar voice. There were three men in the office, which was surprisingly small and sparse.

"Mr. Fischer?" one of the men said, holding out his hand. "I'm Special Agent Hick." He didn't look anything like Jack had imagined. A proud roman nose and friendly eyes made to seem smaller than they were by thinly framed oval glasses. He was bald, but only partially due to nature. Thick stubble darkened the better part of his scalp, leaving only a receding hairline and a small spot on the very top of his head bare. If Jack saw him walking down a random street, he would assume he was a school teacher or maybe a space physicist.

"Hi," Jack said, shaking his hand tentatively. He raised his brows at the others.

"This is Bernard Cognot of the French DRCI," Hick introduced the taller of the two. He was lanky, with unkempt hair and small shifty eyes. Jack shook his proffered hand and then turned to the shorter man.

"Donald Easton," the man said. "United Kingdom, SOCA."

"Soca?" Jack asked. He didn't know what DRCI was either, but it fit the mold of government acronyms and was therefore uninteresting. The only "soca" he had ever heard of was a West Indian club in Queens called Soca Paradise. A girl he dated in college used to make him go there.

"Serious Organized Crime Agency," Easton explained. "We are a bit like your FBI here." His accent was thick but pleasant, with lots of soft consonants and a prevalence of "sh" sounds.

Jack smiled, despite his mood. "Seriously? You guys just called it 'serious organized crime agency'? Is there a 'trivial organized crime agency' also?" Humor was his way of coping with difficult situations, though he recognized that it was a bad idea to toy with these people.

"Quite serious, Mr. Fisher," Easton said, his smile replaced by a slight grimace. "As is the reason we brought you here."

"Please," Hick said, indicating an empty chair. "Have a seat."

Jack frowned, but did as he was asked. It was a cheap fabric covered chair with no armrests. The entire office, chair included, was disappointing in its plainness. There was no American flag on an ornate brass pole, no giant flat screen displaying satellite footage, no wall plaques with depictions of J. Edgar Hoover in bas-relief. Instead there were chalky white walls with black scuff marks at chair level, cheap furniture in bland colors, a whiteboard with indecipherable scribbles and family photos haphazardly arranged on a desk with stacks of paper, sticky notes and crumpled sandwich wrappers.

It could have been a middle manager's window office at any of the dozen or so companies Jack had worked for before starting his school, and being there was a painful reminder of the wasted years of his life. So much time, sitting behind just such a desk, staring at walls just like these. Meetings, emails, forced politeness, hours upon hours in front of a machine, hammering away at keys for a paycheck just large enough to keep him coming back for more. The only thing that had kept him going was Alison.

"So what's this all about?" Jack asked, looking from agent to agent. "You mentioned something about needing my help? "

"Just a moment," Hick said. "We're waiting for one more. He'll be here shortly."

The door swung open not a second after Hick finished speaking and a short man who reminded Jack of a balding Jeremy Irons rushed in, his skin glowing with perspiration.

"My apologies," he said in a light accent Jack immediately recognized as German. "I was held up." He offered his hand. "Mr. Fischer? I'm Jan, Jan Heim, Bundeskriminalamt." He noticed Jack's raised eyebrows and added, "German federal police." Jack rose to shake his hand, then returned to his seat.

"Alright then," Hick said, taking charge. "Mr. Fischer, I think you must have some idea of what this is about."

Jack pressed his lips together and narrowed his eyes. "No, I don't."

"Mr. Fischer," Easton said, shaking his head. "Don't be coy, please. This is about your invitation."

"Oh," Jack said, locking eyes with Easton. "That. Obviously a prank. I threw it away. Why would you want to see me about that?" Cops generally wanted to arrest suspects and put them through the system, not help people or solve crimes. The less he told them, the less they could use against him. He had done nothing wrong that he knew of, but with this government one could never be certain.

"It is not a prank," Cognot, the Frenchman, said. His accent was almost non-existent. "It is, unfortunately, quite real. That is why we are all here."

"Okay," Jack said, turning to look at Hick. "So it's real, great. Obviously I have nothing to do with it. I'm not going to accept the invitation, so if that's what you're worried about, I can go now, right?" He had of course known that the invitation was not a joke, not when it was accompanied by that much money, but this confirmation chilled him. Somewhere out there, people just like him would be fighting to the death. He knew what a sword could do to a human body, and the knowledge terrified him. It was perhaps an ironic reaction for someone in his trade, but swords were some of the most efficient and brutal killing devices ever created by man. Guns punched holes in flesh, sometimes neat, sometimes sloppy, and could be used at great distances. Swords tore people apart, turned them into slabs of meat, face to face.

"As I said, Mr. Fischer," Hick said. "We need your help."

"My help? For what? I don't know anything."

"Aren't we getting ahead of ourselves?" Heim asked. "Perhaps some background information?"

"Indeed," Easton agreed. "We're part of a multi-agency, multinational task force, Mr. Fischer. Each of us is the liaison for our respective agencies and governments."

"A taskforce that deals with underground sword fighting clubs?" Jack asked skeptically. Until yesterday, he didn't even know such things existed outside of bad jokes and low budget movies. Now there was an international taskforce? "So instead of finding missing kids and serial killers, you guys are going after volunteers who choose to kill each other?" He hesitated. "They are volunteers, right?"

"It's not the bureau's highest priority," Hick admitted. "But it's not something we can just ignore. People are dying, and to answer your question, yes, they may be volunteers at first, but we have no way of knowing exactly what happens once they're inside. You're the expert, Mr. Fischer, you tell me. Do you think most of your colleagues would be able to go through with it after seeing someone die that way?"

"My colleagues?"

"People in your community, other instructors, et cetera."

"Oh." Jack considered it. "To be honest, no. I don't think they would. I know I wouldn't. But that can't be why you called me here. So what do you want from me?" He decided to stop being cheeky. This was turning serious. "If there's something I know that can help, I'll be glad to tell you. If they recruit from our community, I might also be able to help you track them down online. I know pretty much everyone, both here in the US and abroad. We're a small, tightly knit community, even though some of us don't really like each other."

Heim nodded and smiled, pleased. "We appreciate that, Mr. Fischer. We will indeed have need of your very specialized knowledge. But that is not why we called you here."

"Oh?"

"Let me explain," Hick cut in. "We've known about them for several years, and we've been picking up their pieces. Dead bodies, missing persons. The only way to unravel this organization would be to get an agent on the inside, but that's proven impossible. They work by invitation only, and they only invite well known experts. It would take us five or ten years to get an agent in a position in your community where it would even be possible for him to be considered, let alone invited."

"I can help with that," Jack said. "I can train him, get him established. If they've already invited me, they'd probably be interested in my students. I can even pretend he's been a student for several years, introduce him on Facebook, that sort of thing."

The four agents exchanged glances and raised eyebrows. "That is an interesting proposition," Easton said. "We had not considered that approach."

"Then what did you have in mind?" Jack asked.

"We were hoping for something a bit more immediate," Hick explained. "We were hoping to recruit you, Mr. Fischer."

"Recruit me? For what?"

"To be our man on the inside," Easton said. "To bring down the…we've coined the name 'Talhoffer Society' for the organization. After the fifteenth century fencing master."

Jack narrowed his eyes at Easton. "I know who Talhoffer is."

He was actually surprised that *they* knew who Talhoffer was, or that they would make the connection between him and a bunch of thugs hacking each other apart for sport. It was quite a leap.

"Yes, of course," Easton said quickly. "My apologies."

Then it hit him. "Hold up now," Jack said, leaning forward in his chair. "You want me to go fight to the death and risk my life so you people can make some arrests? Have you lost your minds? What the hell could possibly make me want to do that?"

"Other than helping your fellow fencers?" Hick asked.

"Like I said, a lot of us hate each other." Jack leaned back in his chair and folded his arms across his chest. Alison had called this position "stubborning up."

"You would not be in any danger," Heim said quickly. "We would provide you with a micro transmitter that will give us your location. All you would have to do is go there, witness people being killed, and activate the transmitter. It sends out a very powerful signal for a few minutes, enough to let us pinpoint your location anywhere in the world, even inside buildings and, to a certain extent, underground. As soon as we get the signal, a tactical team will be dispatched, by air, to secure the location and extract you, and no one will ever know that you had anything to do with it. You don't have to fight, and I doubt you would be there long."

Something the German had said rubbed Jack the wrong way. "Witness people being killed?"

Hick frowned. "Unfortunately that would be the only way to bring the people involved to trial. Even if we knew where it was going on, if we tried to make an arrest before anyone was killed then all they would have to do is deny everything. There are many such gatherings among your community every year where live weapons are present but no one is harmed. It would be impossible to make the charges stick unless we had a body and a witness, hopefully more than one. Um...more than one witness I mean. And it has to be someone being killed, not just hurt, that is very important, and sadly unavoidable."

"So you would need me to testify then?" Jack asked. "You just said no one would know I was involved."

"Not necessarily," Easton said. "Any of the other 'volunteers' could give testimony to save themselves from prosecution, though it would fall upon you to do so if the others fell through."

"We could still guarantee your anonymity," Hick said quickly. "We have several nations' worth of laws to work with. Your testimony could be done in closed chambers."

"No thank you," Jack said. "I think I'll go back to my life now. I see no reason to get involved in this." He didn't believe a word they said. They would tell him anything he wanted to hear to get him to do what they wanted, and after he was killed by some bloodthirsty maniac with an oversized meat cleaver, they would just say "oh well" and file him away with the other dead fools.

"You would turn you back on your fellow martial artists?" Heim said. "Just leave them to their fate?"

Jack thought of all the bullshit that went on in the community. "Yes I would, if they're stupid enough to go along with it. Then there's also the fact that no one that I know of has disappeared under mysterious circumstances as long as I've been in the community, so I think you're overstating the impact this has on us."

"Your country needs you," Easton said. "You would be doing a great service." Trust a Brit to bring up nationalism.

"My country," Jack said. "Sends young men and women to die overseas to make old rich men richer. No thank you."

"You're very cynical," Hick said. "I can understand that in this day and age. Maybe this will appeal to you more. The prize for just showing up is one hundred thousand dollars. We were able to locate offshore accounts for some of the deceased. Some had significantly more, even millions. We could arrange for you to keep whatever money you receive, tax free."

Jack thought about it. A hundred thousand dollars. That could buy a lot of chicken wings and beer. Of course he would have to be alive to enjoy them. "No."

"We know about the money," Cognot said. "The money that you received with the invitation." Jack didn't much care for any of these men, but if he had to pick his least favorite, it would be the Frenchman. The superior way in which he looked at him made Jack angry.

"What money? There was no money."

"Mr. Fischer…" Easton began. Jack stared at him, unable to

suppress the beginnings of a grin.

"Like I said, there was no money." He wondered how they could possibly have known the contents of the envelope. Come to think of it, how had they found out about the invitation so quickly? Were they monitoring the website? If so, good. They would have other people to approach, which might just let him off the hook.

"We can have a warrant to search your home in a matter of hours," Easton said. "And of course that money would be confiscated as evidence. If you've spent any of it—"

This made Jack even angrier. How typical—he had exercised his right as a citizen to refuse to cooperate, and instead of recognizing his right they were trying to coerce him with threats. Bastards.

"Do you think I'm an idiot?" Jack asked. "You think this is one of those TV shows where you can tell me what you know and I'll confess? I don't care what you know, Mr. Easton, you can't prove there was any money in that envelope. You'd better have the warrant and your agents at my doorstep before I can make a phone call, otherwise all you'll find is pocket lint. Now if you will excuse me." He stood up and made to leave.

"Hold on a second," Hick said, putting up his hand to stop him. "We've completely bungled this. Agents Easton and Cognot have no authority to ask for a warrant in this country, Mr. Fischer, and I have absolutely no intention of doing so." Hick momentarily glared at the other two. "They are guests of the FBI and they acted hastily and improperly. Please, forgive them, and please consider helping us. People are dying."

Jack hated to admit it, but Hick had mollified him. "I don't know."

"I guarantee you," Hick continued. "That you will receive one hundred thousand dollars upon entering the tournament, but I'll do you one better. The bureau will match that amount, and deposit it to an account of your choosing the moment you agree to help us. Right now, even. And we'll pay the taxes for you."

Jack stopped. "That's...that's something to think about." Two hundred thousand dollars? And all he had to do was show up and press a button? "I'll think about it, you have my word." He was horribly tempted, almost enough to agree on the spot, but there was something about these men, about what they were telling him, that just didn't seem right.

Hick nodded. "That's all I ask." He stood aside and motioned to the door. "You are free to go, of course, but please take this." He handed Jack a business card. "Call me when you decide, either way."

"I will," Jack said, and left Hick's office after a cursory farewell nod to the others. As soon as he was out of the building, he felt like a caged animal suddenly set free. He considered calling Kanemori for a late lunch, but decided against it. He was desperate to get to his car and get the hell out of New York City.

Chapter 9

I say to you truthfully,
no man protects himself without danger.
- Liechtenauer's Verses, Von Danzig Fechtbuch – 1452

All of the street parking by the school was taken, leaving Jack little choice but to use the lot. That meant he either had to walk around the building the long way or jump over the little stone wall and hope his feet didn't kick over one of the bushes planted there. He chose the wall, and the bushes survived intact.

Fiddling with his keys, he saw a tall white box through the glass door, about a foot and a half wide. The UPS guy had the same keys Jack gave his students and usually left packages inside when there was no one to sign for them.

"That son of a bitch," Jack said. There was no mistaking an Albion box. Will must have paid off something on layaway and had it shipped overnight.

Shaking his head and smiling, he let the door close behind him, took the box and started up the stairs, trying to force himself not to open it and peek inside. Albion made the best production longswords in the world. Very expensive, but worth every penny. Jack had five of them, and loved every one. Quality reproductions had only recently come on the scene, at least from Jack's perspective. Before that there were only cheap wall hangers and crowbar-like stage fighting swords.

It probably wouldn't bother Will if he just took a peek. Maybe it was a sword Jack himself didn't already own. Will would let him handle it, of course, but the temptation to open the box then and there was very strong. When it came to swords, Jack was an oversized child.

A woman screamed. It came from upstairs.

Jack stopped. Straining to hear, he wondered if he had been mistaken.

"You have five seconds, bitch," a man's muffled voice shouted. Feeling confused and uneasy, Jack slowly edged up the stairs until he could just look around the corner. He saw a young man and woman, huddling together near the training sword rack. They didn't see him, their eyes were fixed on something out of Jack's field of view. The girl looked familiar, but it was hard to recognize her. Her face was red and contorted with fear, glistening from tears that rolled down her cheeks. The boy was one of the new students, the ones who had joined at the same time as—

"Please," the girl cried. "I don't know when he'll be back." At the same time as Leyna. There was no mistaking her now.

Jack instantly set the box down and reached for his pistol, but his hand found only empty space.

"Shit," he swore under his breath. New York City did not honor the state's pistol permits, and so he had left his gun in the safe. Upstairs.

"She's telling the truth, man," the boy said, his voice shaky and high pitched. "We're new."

"Was I talkin' to you, faggot?" The unseen man's voice was also familiar. Very familiar.

Jack braced himself against the wall and stuck his head around the corner, just enough to see. A man in disheveled clothing stood in the middle of the training floor, one arm thrust forward, terminating in a large stainless steel revolver that was pointed straight at Leyna. Through unkempt hair and thick stubble, Jack immediately recognized Terrance.

"One," Terrance said. "You better tell me bitch, or I'll shoot the fag and fuck you till you die." His speech was slurred, his eyes bloodshot. He was drunk, or maybe high.

Jack retracted his head and reached for his cell phone, but immediately put it back and took out his folding knife instead. There was no time to call the cops.

"Two." What the hell was Terrance doing? Why would he do this? But there was no time to think. People's lives were in danger.

He was about to push himself off from the wall and charge him when he remembered the big white box on the floor.

The Albion box, the one with the sword inside.

Without wasting another second, he bent down and cut open the packing tape holding it together, but he had to move slowly lest he make too much noise. He didn't have enough time.

"Please," Leyna cried. "I have some money. Take it. Take my watch. My ring."

"I have a watch too," the boy said. "And cash!" Mostly likely tuition money.

"I don't give a shit about your fucking watch," Terrance roared.

The box opened smoothly, revealing a beautiful longsword suspended in dark gray packing foam. This model was called the "Crecy," after a famous 14th century battle of the Hundred Years War. It had a wide cutting blade terminating in a wicked point and an oval grip wrapped in black leather, just long enough to hold with two hands.

Jack pulled it from the foam gently and froze, realizing what he was intending. Terrance had a gun, but...what did he think he was going to do? Strike him with the sword? A human being? This was no tatami mat.

"I want Fischer," Terrance shouted. "No one humiliates me like that. No one. Fuck you. Three, bitch. Four. Now you both gonna die."

Humiliate him? Jack hesitated. He hadn't humiliated Terrance at all. He had given him a book and promoted him to the advanced class. What the hell was he talking about?

"Five."

Jack stood up and turned the corner. Terrance noticed him right away.

The man stared at him, wide eyed. Leyna screamed. Jack realized he had a fraction of a second. He closed the distance between him and Terrance in quick, sure steps. The man brought his gun to bear. Jack was almost on him. Terrance cringed, seeing the three foot long blade looming over his head. His trigger finger moved, the cylinder began to rotate. He pushed the gun out and away from him in his left hand.

There was a terrible concussive blast followed by the splintering of wood. It should have been painful, but his ears felt nothing. Left hand? Wasn't Terrance right handed?

All too soon Jack was in range, his strike poised. For the briefest of moments his mind recoiled from what he was doing, he paused for but a fraction of a second. That was enough. Terrance reoriented the gun for another shot and pointed it at Jack's head. This time he was aiming. Something had changed in Terrance's eyes.

Crooked on nimbly, throw the point on the hands.

Jack's sword arced before him like a windshield wiper, moving left as Jack sprung right. The revolver thundered once more, this time accompanied by broken glass. The crooked stroke passed over Terrance's left arm, and *through* it. *Thunk.* A slight vibration made it to Jack's hands as the blade passed through bone.

Time slowed. Jack stopped, hands held at chest height, sword point down and forward at an angle to his left, watching the man's left hand and forearm slide free of his body and slowly accelerate towards the ground, still gripping the revolver. They hit the floor with a long, muted crack and fell apart, gun and appendage sliding in different directions. Blood was starting to well from the stump, thick and red.

Leyna's scream grew louder, Jack's ears started to hurt, and Terrance just stood there, staring at the empty space just below his elbow where his forearm had been. He started to scream, then fell down, shortened limb flailing.

Jack couldn't move, he only stared at the floor where Terrance's severed hand was still moving.

* * *

"You're going to take the sword?" Will asked the police officer. "That's mine, and I just paid a thousand dollars for it."

"We have to take it," the cop explained. "But if the DA doesn't file charges, you'll get it back. And I doubt he will, not for this. Call in about a couple of weeks, it'll probably be resolved by then."

"Thanks," Will said. "I'll do that."

Jack sat on one of the benches, shivering, covered in a blanket. He didn't remember who had fetched it for him, or where it had come from. Somewhere in the background, he heard Leyna talking to someone he assumed was a cop. She was sobbing and her voice was weak. But she was alive, as was her friend.

An ambulance had come with the police and taken away

Terrance and his severed arm. Several dark red puddles on the training floor were all that was left of him. Jack had heard one of the paramedics mention something about reattaching it.

"Mr. Fischer?" a woman's voice called to him. He looked up and saw a short brunette in a dark summer jacket, maybe late twenties or early thirties. A gold badge was visible on her belt. "I'm Detective Summers. Can I ask you a few more questions?"

"Sure," Jack said, looking back down at the ground. He wasn't sure how he felt about what he'd done: he was confused and tired and just wanted to sleep.

"The gunman, you knew him right? I know the other officer asked you this already, but please bear with me."

He nodded. "Terrance Calloway. He was a student here. Still is...well, no, I guess not anymore."

"Do you have any idea why he would do this? One of the other witnesses said something about how he was humiliated?"

Jack shook his head. "He did say that, but I don't know what he could mean. I did beat him pretty badly when he wouldn't listen...I mean at fencing, not like *beat him* beat him...but that was almost a month ago. He's been back to class many times since then and he's acted perfectly normal. The other day I even promoted him to the advanced class. I don't get it."

She looked down at a notepad she was holding. "The officers that questioned you said you didn't call the police. Is that right?"

He nodded. "One of the students must have called them after."

"Can I ask why not?" Her tone was not accusing, but he knew better.

"By the time I got upstairs and saw what was going on, he was giving them five seconds before he shot them. There wasn't any time."

"I understand," she said. "We ran a check on you…you have a pistol permit, unrestricted carry. You didn't have your weapon on you?"

He looked up at her. "No, I was coming back from the city. That's an odd question, isn't it? Would you rather I shot him?"

She shook her head. "No, not at all. I much prefer the way you disarmed him—" She froze and brought her hand up to her mouth. "Oh my god, I didn't mean…"

"It's okay," he said. A slip like that might eventually be considered funny, but not today.

"It's just that the way the papers are going to see this, you know, a man who teaches sword fighting injures an intruder with a sword…"

"An intruder," Jack said sternly. "Who was about to shoot one of my students and rape and kill another. An intruder who shot at me."

"Yes, of course," she said quickly. "I doubt any charges will be filed."

"Are you certain?" he asked, his anger suddenly replaced by unease. "The DA…isn't it his job to try to put people in jail?"

"I can't be sure," she said. "Not completely. But you have multiple witnesses who can corroborate your version of events, and New York state law doesn't require you to retreat in your own residence or place of business. You were not only protecting yourself but two others, and the rape thing, that helps. Plus you technically didn't even use deadly force."

"Thank you, detective."

"That's about it then," she said. "You can clean the blood, or call this number." She handed him a business card. "They're not expensive, and they do a very thorough job. If you want a carpenter to fix the holes…" She motioned to the damage done by the two bullets, one of which had shattered Jack's office window. "I can recommend someone." She lowered her voice and leaned closer. "I'm not supposed to, but my brother in law, he's in the business and does really good work." She handed Jack another card.

"Thanks," he said, and put both cards in his pocket. The police started to clear out, and the camera flashes from outside intensified. Some reporters had asked to come inside, but Jack told the cops to get rid of them. Hopefully none of them would camp outside the school.

After everyone else was gone, Will walked up to him. "You okay?"

Jack nodded. "Peachy. Sorry about your sword."

"No way," Will said. "Don't be an idiot. What's important is that you're okay, and you're a fucking hero, man. You saved those kids, and your new girlfriend. I bet she'll be real grateful."

Jack smiled, despite everything. Classic Will. "She's not my girlfriend. She wants to pretend it never happened so she can take classes. That's the deal we made. Only now, I doubt she'll ever come back."

"She will," Will said. "I'll bet anything. She knows what you did for her, man. We all do."

"We'll see." Jack was still shaking, and he kept feeling the blade pass through Terrance's arm, as though that sensation was forever branded into the nerve receptors in his hands.

"You want me to hang with you?" Will asked. "Or do you wanna rest? I'll take your classes tomorrow, and the day after, and as long as you need me to."

"You're a good friend," Jack said. "Tomorrow would be great, but that's it."

Will patted him on the back and let himself out. Jack went upstairs and sat on his couch, holding his head in his hands. He had turned down an invitation to fight men with swords, only to hack one apart in his own home. It would be a long night.

Chapter 10

In all Winding,
Hew, stab, slice, learn to find.
- Liechtenauer's Verses, Von Danzig Fechtbuch – 1452

"There are four primary guards," Jack said, facing the largest assembly of students he had ever seen in his school. "Vom Tag, Ochs, Pflug and Alber. We won't get into how to use them just yet, but I'll show you how to hold them." It felt good to teach again: it had been almost a month since he tackled a full class by himself. The days following the incident were very difficult. He'd been all over the news for more than a week. The local papers ran garish headlines like, "Sword Fighting Teacher Goes Medieval on Gun Toting Intruder." And that was among the better ones.

"Vom Tag means from the roof or from the day, depending on who you ask, and can be held either just over your shoulder or like this." He raised his hilt over his head, sword angled back slightly, prepared to strike. "It is used to launch powerful strikes." For the first two weeks he couldn't go anywhere without people pointing, whispering and giving him all manner of looks. He hadn't dared log onto Facebook or even go online at all for fear of what he might see there.

"Ochs means ox, as in the animal, and is held like so." He lowered his hilt to just above and in front of his shoulder, but turned the sword to point straight ahead like the horns of an ox. "Ochs threatens with the point and protects the high openings." The nights had been even worse. He constantly dreamt of swords, and in his dreams he cut people apart. Strangers, friends, relatives, he was indiscriminate. He woke several times a night, sheets soaked with perspiration, blanket twisted into knots and pillows on the floor. There was never anyone there to comfort him.

He then lowered the hilt until the pommel touched his thigh, point held at throat level, facing up and forward. "This is Pflug, which means plow. Pflug and Ochs are guards, but they are also hangings to be used in the bind."

As he looked the students over, his eyes found Leyna's, and she quickly looked away. Will had been right after all, though it took her two weeks to come back, and she kept her distance when not in class. Whenever she spoke to him, she looked down at the floor, perhaps afraid of him, perhaps hiding from the memory of what had happened, or what had almost happened. Their relationship, such as it had been, was no more. She had seen his true nature and it had repulsed her. He wasn't sure that he didn't feel the same way.

Her return was not the only unexpected development. The attendance rate of his old students went up significantly, and over the course of a few weeks eighteen more joined the school, mostly young men. Jack knew why they had come, but he wasn't about to turn them away. Most would leave soon enough, when the intrigue wore off and the hard work began.

"The last of the primary guards," Jack said, lowering his sword until it was held in front of him, point almost touching the ground. "Is called Alber, which means fool. Can anyone tell me which openings I am protecting with this guard?" A student raised his hand, and Jack motioned for him to speak.

"The legs?" he asked.

"That's a good answer," Jack said. "And partly correct. Alber does protect the legs, but high attacks have greater reach than low attacks, and so low attacks are not advisable in the approach except under special circumstances, like that one handed leg shot I showed some of you last week, the Gayszlen. No, Alber is a guard of provocation. When I stand in it I'm saying, 'come get me, I'm wide open.' But what I want you to think about is why it is called the 'Fool.' Am I a fool for standing in a guard that doesn't protect me, or are you a fool for attacking me while I hold it?"

Most of the students stared at him blankly. Some of the more seasoned ones grinned, having seen all this before.

"That's something we're going to have to explore a bit later," Jack continued. "Now let's try holding some of these guards."

He demonstrated Vom Tag one more time and instructed the students to spread out and try it on their own. As he began to walk around and make minor corrections, Will came out of the office, holding his recovered Albion longsword and a gray oil rag, wiping it lovingly along the blade. When not busy covering Jack's classes, Will had spent his time harassing the police and district attorney's office about his sword. Eventually they gave it back to him, and Jack helped him polish out the surface rust from the gunman's blood. Most of it came clean, but there was a dark patch of steel where the blade had passed through Terrance's arm that Jack could not remove. The oxidation had gotten into the pores of the metal.

"Sorry about the stain," Jack said, his voice low so as not to disturb the class. "I can keep trying if you want."

"Don't worry about it," Will said. "I know you're going to think I'm insensitive or some shit, but I like it. This sword was *used*, and used justly. I want there to be a reminder."

"If you say so," Jack said, turning back to the students. Will put the sword away and went downstairs to check the mail.

"Okay, stop" Jack said. "Switch to Vom Tag on the other side. It's going to be awkward at first, but keep at it, you'll get it." He couldn't be mad at Will, but he was perturbed by his attitude. He was right though, the sword had been used justly. The Japanese would have called this katsujinken, the life giving sword. A terrible crime had been prevented without loss of life, and Jack had read in the Daily Freeman that they had successfully reattached Terrance's forearm without significant loss of mobility. But Jack knew something that Will didn't.

The Krumphau strike that he had used was a last minute improvisation. If he had not hesitated, not given the gunman time to aim his weapon, then that sword would have come down on the man's head with all the power and precision that Jack could manage. The same strike with which he severed triple rolled tatami mats would have struck Terrance's skull. Jack couldn't bring himself to try and imagine what would have happened. At least not while he was awake.

He walked around the class and felt a chill as he passed the window. The summer was almost over, with August drawing to a close and the evening temperature occasionally dropping down into the sixties. Many of his students would soon either reduce their attendance or stop coming altogether, too busy with classes and the jobs they needed to pay for them. That was alright, because now he had many more of them than ever before, and he would likely run in the green for many months to come.

Will returned a few minutes later carrying a manila envelope. Jack put a senior student in charge and excused himself from class.

"More money?" Jack asked with a half smile as he reached for it.

Will shook his head and handed it to him. It was from the law offices of Kenton Murphy, Esquire. Jack felt his stomach tighten. Tearing it open, he read the first page, and with each line he sank deeper into despair. Just like that, the peace that he had begun to rebuild was shattered.

"It's a lawsuit, isn't it?" Will said.

Jack nodded. "He is suing me for five million." The notice of complaint said that the "victim" had lost most of the tactile sensation in the fingers of his left hand and suffered from chronic pain that did not respond to medication. He claimed it hurt too much to work and was suing for lifetime wages. Terrance had been convicted on several felony charges and sent to prison, but his lifetime wages were supposed to be five million dollars?

"That motherfucker," Will said. "He's in jail. How can he sue?"

"Don't know," Jack said. "But apparently that doesn't stop you these days."

"Oh man. What are you going to do?"

What, indeed. "Get a lawyer, I guess. And hope this is a big fucking joke."

* * *

Jack sat in his car outside the school. A light rain teased his windshield wipers, letting through the occasional splat that signaled an imminent downpour. For the first time since Alison's death, he felt as though he would burst into tears. Random tragedies seemed to define the course of his life. First a simple accident, then a poorly timed home invasion. If he had been carrying his pistol, if he had shot the bastard dead, or if he hadn't hesitated, had split his skull and spilled his brains onto the floor…

Squelching his grief, he picked up the phone and dialed the school.

"What did he say?" Will said as soon as he picked up the phone.

"They're not going to settle," Jack said, his voice even, calm. "They want to take it to trial, and Harcourt thinks we don't stand a chance in front of a jury. Not if they see the pictures."

"It's only been a week," Will said. "Give him time, he'll get greedy. Besides, that's bullshit. The guy broke into the school, had two people at gunpoint, almost raped Leyna. Come on. Harcourt is an idiot, you should get a new lawyer."

"I've already paid his retainer. Besides, he doesn't seem like an idiot. He seems like he knows what he's talking about."

"So what will happen? I mean if he wins. You don't have five million dollars."

"Harcourt says they won't award that much, maybe a million, maybe less. There's apparently a formula for calculating wages. Thank god for small favors."

"Um, you don't have a million either."

"I know," Jack said, glad that Will wasn't there to see him shake. "I know. The school insurance won't cover it, neither will homeowner's. I have some equity in the school, they will make me sell that, of course, and my car, and my swords."

"Holy shit, man! Holy shit."

"Will, if I had to…" He had almost made up his mind, but it was still very hard to say. "To go away for a little while, would you cover for me? Could you run the school?"

The phone was silent for several seconds. "Of course I can, I'd be honored. I'd have to change the schedule a bit, but sure. Why? Where do you need to go—wait a second, you're not...I mean..."

"Don't," Jack said, a little more harshly than he intended. "Don't ask me. Just don't. We can talk about it later. I want you to take the rest of the money from the envelope as payment, along with your usual salary. I don't know how long I'll be gone."

"No, I won't take it."

"Dammit Will," he swore. He had no time for generosity. "Just take the fucking money, okay? I need peace of mind right now."

"We'll talk about it later," Will said, and hung up the phone.

This was it. Now or never. If he didn't do it immediately, he would lose his nerve. Jack reached into his pocket, pulled out a business card and dialed the phone number.

"Special Agent Hick."

"Yeah," Jack said. "It's me, Jack Fischer."

"Mr. Fischer," Hick said, feigning surprise. "What can I do for you?" It was clear to Jack that the smug bastard had expected his call.

"I don't suppose you've been keeping tabs on me?"

Hick hesitated. "We have, and if you want to know if we're aware of the incident and the lawsuit, we are."

"Get rid of it, make it go away," Jack said. "Then I'll do it. I'll go to the fucking slaughterhouse, I'll be your spy."

"The FBI has no authority over civil courts, Mr. Fischer."

"Fine," Jack said. "Have a nice day then."

"Wait," Hick said quickly. "I know a good attorney, very, very good. He's expensive, but I can guarantee you he will make this go away. Twenty, thirty grand tops, and it will be like it never happened."

"I don't have that kind of money."

"Say the word, say you'll help us, and give me an account number. Whatever you have in there, it will be one hundred thousand more in two days. I've taken the liberty of getting the paperwork approved while you were considering."

"Just like that?" This was it, the devil's contract. He had slit open his palm and dipped the quill, but he could still turn back.

"Just like that. I don't have to tell you what will happen if you try to fuck us."

"So be it. I agree, I will help you." No turning back.

Chapter 11

Who is strong against you,
Running through therewith mark.
- Liechtenauer's Verses, Von Danzig Fechtbuch – 1452

When Jack thought of underground dueling societies, he pictured abandoned parking garage basements, gray concrete walls, flickering fluorescents, perhaps some dripping water from rusty pipes. From the moment the Mercedes sedan pulled up in front of the school, that image began to unravel.

The driver, a young Swede named Anders, had given him instructions on what to take with him and had even helped him pack. He was to bring two swords, any kind that were covered by the Liechtenauer tradition. Jack owned an assortment of spears, poleaxes, arming swords and other weapons, but his primary interest, and perhaps the true love of his life, was the longsword. Although he was afraid he might not get back what he brought, he wanted to cover his bases in the event he actually did have to fight, so he brought his two favorite swords, both made by Albion.

One was a light and superbly balanced dueling weapon, a precise recreation of an original from a museum in Brescia. The other was a heavy hollow-ground sword of war that was not as agile but could take a lot more punishment. The difference in weight between the two was about a quarter of a pound—the big one topped out somewhere near three and a half—but where swords were concerned even a few ounces could make a drastic difference.

Anders told him that his luggage would always be taken care of and that he didn't have to worry about it. This made things a lot easier, if not less stressful. The two hour drive to Cape Liberty cruise port in Bayonne was nerve wracking and the tiny transmitter Hick had given him was heavy in his pocket. He kept wondering if they would somehow detect the thing and order Anders to turn into a dark alley where he would blow Jack's head off with an exotic Eastern European machine pistol. Fortunately reality failed to meet expectations and the drive was uneventful.

The terminal was filled with crowds of excited families and their luggage. There were two big ships to choose from, and Anders steered him towards the larger of the two before bidding him farewell.

Turning back to look at New Jersey for perhaps the last time—maybe the one good thing that would come of all this—he walked up the gangway and presented his boarding card to the pretty uniformed Asian girl who stood by the card scanner. The ship, or what he had seen of it from the parking area, was immense. There was a lively breeze and a slight chop, but the blue and white behemoth was as still as a mountain in its resting place by the dock.

"Welcome aboard the Constellation," she said with a pleasant accent. "Please look into the camera." He stared at the lens, waiting for a click or a flash, but there was nothing. She returned his card and he put it in his pocket.

"Thanks."

"You will be disembarking in Bermuda?" she asked.

"Um…" Jack hesitated, unsure of what to say. The details of his itinerary had not been discussed with him. "I guess so."

She smiled patiently. "You will be notified when to leave your luggage outside your stateroom door. Please be sure to attach the luggage tags. Those will be given to you as well."

"Thanks, I will." He walked past her and into the ship, where young men and women waited with trays of water, champagne, and assorted fruits and cheeses. Jack had never been on a cruise, but found himself wishing he had come aboard on a genuine vacation instead of a possible one way trip to a violent death.

The ship was a confusing network of opulent lounges, grand promenades and cozy nooks with comfortable reading chairs. He couldn't take it all in, things were happening too fast. With help from the crew, he eventually found his stateroom on the Panorama deck and used his card to open the door.

He stepped into a material embodiment of luxury: a small but lavish suite with wood paneled walls, queen bed, sofa, writing desk and more. A large flat panel television was suspended in a corner next to a wall length mirror, its screen reflecting the glare from the curtained veranda door. Every detail was the essence of perfection: none of the sloppy caulking, cracking plaster or specks of leftover paint that he found in even the best hotel rooms.

Stepping onto the veranda was disappointing, as the only thing to see was yet another last view of New Jersey. He was anxious to see what it was like when the ship was at sea, but for the time being he went back into the room and pulled the curtain shut.

Looking around, taking in the details, he was a bit overwhelmed. A suite like this could easily cost five grand per person, or more, and that was with double occupancy. He and Alison had priced some cruise vacations before deciding to go to Disney World instead, a decision he did not regret. Maybe it was corny, but he loved the place, and Alison had shared his passion for recapturing their childhood. He couldn't remember a better time.

He smiled. Not all memories of his wife were painful.

Deciding to relax on the couch a bit before going to explore, he looked over some of the documents he had been given at check in. According to the itinerary, he had three days and nights on the ship before it docked at King's Wharf, at which point he would be getting off.

A colorful cruise brochure showed extensive exercise facilities, which he planned to make use of. Once he had committed to this insane venture, he had had only a week to prepare before his departure. Even though he wasn't supposed to actually fight in the tournament, he wanted to be ready just in case. Will had helped tremendously, making himself available for full intensity drills and more free fencing than Jack had done in the last year. He had also started running, though endurance was not exactly the most critical aspect of being prepared for a duel.

A real unarmored sword fight, one in which the weapons actually inflicted damage, was unlikely to last more than a few seconds. Far more important was a fighter's ability to deliver a burst of power for a short period of time, over and over again. This was best developed by interval training—short bursts of intense exertion followed by milder exercise. At least that was Jack's theory, and it had served him well in the tournament circuit.

After using the bathroom, he left the suite and explored the ship, walking along the corridors and exterior walkways. He eventually found his way to the bow, where a small group of people stood and waited for the boat to leave the port. He could see the Verrazano bridge off to the right—or rather the starboard. Manhattan's skyscrapers clustered in the distance off the port side, just past the comparatively tiny Statue of Liberty. Everywhere else where there wasn't water lay an endless sea of concrete sprawl that faded into the horizon in almost all directions.

Seeing all the buildings, picturing the sheer mass of humanity that crawled in that maze like mindless worker ants, he experienced a peculiar sense of pride. He was not one of those ants, not bound by the convoluted and unnecessary complexity that this biological mass had inflicted upon itself. He was separate from it, above it. A warrior, on his way to face death.

He shook his head to clear it of unwelcome thoughts. He was *not* going to fight, he was going to stop the fighting, to help the task force bring those responsible to justice. He'd had a taste of what it was like to use a sword on a human being, and it had brought nothing but grief. He had no idea where these juvenile feelings were coming from, but he wanted no part of them.

He stayed on the deck for a while, watching as the thousand foot colossus gracefully maneuvered its way out of the impossibly narrow dock using a multitude of bow and stern thrusters, then turned towards the Verrazano on its way out of Narrows Bay and into the open ocean. A stiff offshore breeze eventually sent him back inside, his t-shirt and jeans inadequate to shield him from the unseasonable cold.

Checking his watch, he hurried to his state room to change for dinner and saw that his luggage had been delivered. Two rifle cases lay on the bed. His rifle cases. He opened each to confirm that his swords were inside, then closed them and stepped away, his whole body shaking.

Weapons of any kind were strictly prohibited on cruise ships. He knew this for a fact. Luggage was carefully screened in the same way it was at airports. You couldn't bring so much as a multi-tool or a Swiss army knife on board. Yet they had brought him his swords. In unlocked rifle cases. If this was not his final destination, there was no need for him to have them. They had sent him a message.

Just who were these people, that they could do this?

Chapter 12

When it clashes above,
Then stand off, that I will praise.
- Liechtenauer's Verses, Von Danzig Fechtbuch – 1452

The Constellation pulled into King's Wharf while Jack was sleeping off a night of drinking and poker in the ship's casino. His luggage had been picked up by the time he got dressed and made ready to leave. As he walked down the pier, he turned back and took a long last look at the ship. He'd had a nice time, despite being lonely and apprehensive, and he would miss it.

He wasn't sure where he was supposed to go, but wasn't particularly worried about it. If these people wanted him to make it, they would take care of it. If not, he would spend a few days in Bermuda, then call Hick and tell him the whole thing was a bust. The lawsuit against him was gone—Hicks's high-powered attorney had somehow made it disappear not two days after Jack hired him—and that was the only thing Jack really cared about.

He doubted Bermuda was his final destination, but if it was, it wouldn't be so bad. The weather was nice. Warm without being hot and not too much humidity. A gentle breeze rolled off the ocean and brought the scent of iodine and salt. Perhaps this whole ordeal would be over soon and he could get on with his life.

He kept walking until he made it to the taxi pickup area where another luxury sedan sat waiting for him, this time a Jaguar. A man holding a card with Jack's name on it waved him down and held the door open while he climbed in the back. So much for going home.

Bermuda reminded Jack of the Caribbean, though a lot less run down. Low, stately colonial buildings in pastel colors, lots of greenery and few pedestrians. The drive was relaxing, but brief. They passed through the "city" of Hamilton, which made Kingston look like a bustling metropolis, and drove the length of the tiny island nation before arriving at yet another cruise port.

"This is St. George's," the driver said in a melodic Caribbean accent. He was a short black man with well defined features.

"Why are we going to another port?" Jack asked.

"You'll be boarding a ship, sir," the driver explained.

Jack perked up. "Another cruise ship? Not that I mind, but when do I finally get to where I'm going?"

The driver turned back and smiled. "I'm very sorry, Mr. Fischer, but I don't have that information." The port was small, much smaller than either Cape Liberty or King's Wharf, and there was only one cruise ship docked there—a rather small and unimpressive boat perhaps half the size of the Constellation. There were several private yachts resting along the docks, though the small cruise ship towered above them all. Size was, as always, relative.

They drove around a small cul-de-sac and stopped in front of a terminal building. There didn't seem to be many other passengers coming or going, which probably meant he wouldn't have to endure another long line like the one he had suffered through in Bayonne.

"No need to check in, Mr. Fischer. Just walk up to the gangway and tell them who you are."

"You mean show them my ID, right?" Jack asked, reaching for his wallet. "I don't have any tickets or anything."

"No need, sir," the driver corrected gently. "Just your name."

"If you say so," Jack said, unconvinced. "Thanks for the ride."

"Godspeed, Mr. Fischer." For some reason, those words made him shiver. He was reminded of a plate from the Hans Talhoffer fechtbuch that was captioned, "Here begins the messer. God please do not forget us." If things didn't go the way Hick said they would…

He entered the terminal as the Jaguar pulled away and saw doors on the other side leading to the dock. Feeling conspicuous, he crossed the building without stopping at any of the check-in desks and went back outside on the other side of the terminal, raising his hand to his eyes to ward off the blinding rays of sunlight that peeked above the ship's funnels.

The ship was a lot more impressive up close. Not a speck of rust could be seen anywhere, not even by the anchor. There was also an elegance to the design, a quality to the details that he hadn't noticed on the bigger ship. There were several men in white uniforms standing by the gangway.

"Good morning, sir," one of them said with a Nordic accent. "What can I do for you?" He was young, with sandy blond hair and a pleasant smile, but there was something underneath the façade that Jack immediately recognized, something predatory. The man was dangerous, a fighter. Probably some kind of professional. The other two that were with him were the same way.

"Um…" he hesitated, not trusting the driver's instructions. "My name is Jack Fischer, I was told—"

"Ah, yes," the man said, smiling warmly. "Welcome, Mr. Fischer, welcome." He walked up to a podium and typed something on the laptop. He looked at the screen, looked at Jack, and his smile broadened. "Welcome to the Invictus. You may board at any time." He reached into a drawer in the podium and pulled out a card, not unlike the combination room key, charge card and ID Jack had used on the Constellation.

"This is your key," he explained. "Your apartment is on deck seven. There is an elevator just inside. We will not be sailing until nine o'clock this evening, so if you wish to take a look around Bermuda, I can call a car for you. Complimentary, of course."

"No thank you," Jack said. "But, um, don't you mean stateroom?"

"Excuse me sir?" the young man asked, confused.

"You said this is the key to my apartment," Jack said.

"Ah, I see. No sir, it is indeed an apartment. The Invictus is not your typical cruise ship. It…" He hesitated. "You'll see when you get on board."

"Okay," Jack said. "I don't need a car then, I'll check out the ship first."

"Very good, sir," the man said, and motioned Jack towards the gangway.

As soon as he stepped aboard, he knew something was different about this ship. There were many small details, but what he latched onto first was the complete lack of carpeting. Just past the gangway, the floor was a richly lacquered teak. Past the entryway he saw lustrous marble. The walls were paneled wood, just like on the Constellation, but where they differed was in the details. These panels were carved with intricate patterns that did not seem to have the repetitive uniformity of machine work.

There was no one there to greet him with champagne and fruit, but he suspected that was because there was no mass boarding in progress. He picked the most likely direction and soon emerged in an open central plaza—and stood there with his mouth hanging open.

The Constellation's grand foyer had been a glittering jewel, all brass and shiny stone and bright lights. This foyer was a masterpiece of refined elegance. Three levels high, lustrous granite floor, fluted marble columns, glass dome ceiling. At its center, the thing that had caught Jack completely off guard, was a fountain.

Four or five years ago he and Alison had gone to St. Petersburg. Her company had sent her on some sort of high stakes errand, but they'd had a few days to explore. One of the places they visited was Peterhof Palace and its grounds. It was filled with some of the most beautiful and elaborate fountains Jack had ever seen. Golden statues, dazzling sprays of water—his mind had balked at trying to assimilate their complexity. This fountain, while not as grand as some of the larger ones he had seen in Russia, easily bested most of the smaller ones. There were eight Greco-Roman statues, either pure gold or something that looked enough like it to fool him, standing in a circle amidst dizzying patterns of arcing water. The base was ringed with black marble inlaid with gold leaf.

It was more than impressive, it was frightening. Though it wasn't clear if they owned the ship or were merely using it to get him somewhere else, these people had tremendous resources—the scope of it was overwhelming. He thought of Hick's office with its chalky walls and scuff marks. He thought of the *smallness* of it. How could something so meager ever contend with such splendor? But then both of them, this grandiose lobby and that tiny dingy office were little more than facades. The power behind each was not as easy to measure.

"Beautiful, isn't it?" a man said from behind him. Jack whirled around, startled. The speaker was a short old man with thin white hair ringing a shiny bald head. He was pleasant looking with a friendly face and an easy smile.

"Yeah," Jack agreed. "This ship is something else. I'm, uh…I just got on board, and—"

"Of course, Mr. Fischer," the man said with a knowing nod. "Please, come with me. I will take you to your quarters."

"Okay." He should have been surprised that the man knew who he was, but he was so overwhelmed by his sudden and strange circumstances that this was just another snowflake in a blizzard.

Jack followed the man to an elevator, which took him to one of the upper decks and into a corridor that looked like the cabin section of the last ship, except that the doors were spaced much too far apart. The no carpet trend continued throughout the ship. The floors were either parquet, marble, granite or varying shades of lacquered hardwood. Eventually they came to a dark mahogany door. The old man reached into his vest pocket—Jack suddenly noticed that he was dressed like an upscale British butler—and produced an ID card. He waved it in the air near a small wall panel and a pleasant metallic chime sounded inside the room. Enough time passed that Jack was about to ask if the card was damaged when the lock suddenly clicked and the door swung open slowly, powered by some hidden solenoid.

"Besides yourself, only the maids, security and I have access to your chambers," the old man explained. "However, if we use our keys, the chime you just heard will sound and you will have ten seconds before the door opens to deny us entry."

"How do I do that?" Jack asked, not really paying attention. It was all way too much for him. He missed his rundown school and small but cozy loft.

"Simply say, 'Deny Entry' in a firm and clear voice."

"Really?" Jack asked, impressed despite his state of mind. "That's a lot of technology for a simple door lock. This is a very fancy cruise ship you've got here."

"The Invictus is primarily a permanent residence ship," the old man explained. "The majority of the apartments are privately owned. Some few accommodations are available for passengers, but they are far less opulent than where you will be staying."

Curious, Jack walked inside and took a look around. It really was an apartment, but it was like no apartment he had ever seen.

The doorway led to a living room decorated in a maritime style with lots of woodwork, mostly cherry, with custom in-wall cabinets and a raised ceiling with hidden lighting. The cabin sole was teak, similar to that in the entryway, but with smaller slats and a richer color. Jack saw a bedroom through a double sliding door that looked like something he had seen in a yacht brochure. The lines of the bedroom's floor and walls were designed to make it look like it was inside the bow of a sailing yacht, with a slight taper to the walls and a floor that inclined towards the head of the king sized bed. A modern kitchen with pale wood cabinets and black granite counters was opposite the bedroom, and a substantial veranda and marble tiled bathroom completed the cross shaped layout.

Jack had never dreamt of accommodations this luxurious.

"I don't understand," he said, starting to feel nervous. "How long is this trip? How long before I get to where I'm supposed to be?" He looked around the apartment as he spoke and noticed a partly open door belonging to what looked like a ceiling height in-wall cabinet. A glint of steel from inside a partly opened cabinet door caught his eye, so he pulled it open.

Inside was a dark wood backing with pegs spaced to accommodate a variety of weapons. The pegs were mostly unused: only two swords hung towards the center of the display. Two finely crafted longswords, one a quick dueling weapon and the other a hollow ground war sword.

His swords.

Suddenly, he knew that what he had suspected since seeing the fountain was true, and he felt light headed. This ship wasn't just another leg of his journey, it was his last stop. This place, this gilded cage, was the home of the tournament that he had been promised he wouldn't have to fight in. The apartment, which had but a moment ago seemed the height of luxury, became a cold tomb in an ocean going mausoleum called Invictus.

Chapter 13

Hear what is bad there.
Fence not above left if you
are right [handed].
If you are left [handed],
With the right you also sorely limp.
- Liechtenauer's Verses, Von Danzig Fechtbuch – 1452

"You are where you're supposed to be, Mr. Fischer," the man said. "This is your final destination. We return to Bermuda in a week and a half. Until then, this is your home."

Jack stared at him for several seconds without speaking. He was still the same little old man with the ready smile, but he had taken on a sinister aspect, as had the apartment.

"My name is Allan," he continued, undaunted. "And I will be your cabin steward for the duration of your voyage. You may call me Allan, or Mr. Teague, or just Teague. Whichever you are most comfortable with."

Jack narrowed his eyes at him. "Do you know why I'm here, Allan?"

The steward suddenly looked uneasy. "In a general sense, yes, but I don't know the specifics. They will tell you everything you need to know during the orientation tomorrow morning."

"So am I a prisoner?" he asked, feeling ballsy. "Was it all a bunch of bullshit about how the tournament is voluntary?" He knew such direct questions were probably not such a good idea, but he couldn't help himself. The same self destructive impulses that had made him fish Alison's photo out of the cupboard were in control.

"No, sir," Allan protested, either appalled or putting on a very good show. "You are a guest here. If you wish to disembark before the ship leaves port, you are free to do so."

"And after it leaves port?" he demanded.

Allan frowned. "Sir, I understand your hesitation. As I have told you, I am not very familiar with the event or its particulars, but I assure you that you are a guest here, and will remain so for the duration of the voyage. I am here to see to your needs, and if you wish to remain in your quarters until we return to port, you may do so."

Jack stared at him, but didn't say anything.

After a few seconds, Allan shook his head and said, "I need to measure you, sir." He reached into his vest pocket and produced a tape measure.

"For a casket?" Jack said acidly. He wasn't sure why he was taking his anger out on the old man, but this pretense annoyed him. In a matter of hours or days they would expect him to shed his blood for the amusement of some rich bastards and their teenage girlfriends.

Allan sighed. "For your formal attire. There will be a reception tonight in the grand ballroom."

"A reception?" Jack asked. "For what?"

"To meet the other attendees, as well as some of your hosts. It is black tie, and you did not bring anything appropriate, so proper attire will be provided for you."

"How much?"

"Everything is complimentary, Mr. Fischer."

"Fine." Jack submitted to the measurements, after which Allan excused himself, but not before telling Jack how to access the ship's services on an in-wall computer. When he was alone, Jack reached into his pocket and pulled out Hick's transmitter, though he kept his hand closed, afraid he was under surveillance. He leaned against a mirror on a nearby wall and tried to calm himself with steady breathing. He desperately wanted to go home. It wasn't right, being here. Not right at all.

"Relax," he said under his breath, so faintly that not even a microphone on his lip would have picked it up. "The cavalry is a button push away."

The mirror showed him a frightened and pathetic face and he felt a sudden need to rationalize and justify his reaction. He was not afraid of death. He had suspected as much since Alison's accident, but his experience with Terrance had confirmed it. He had moved toward the man without hesitation, pausing at the end not out of fear for himself, but because he had not wanted to strike a human being with his sword. He was, however, afraid of this place, of this tournament.

He'd had a dog that was diagnosed with diabetes and did not respond well to insulin treatment. Eventually he succumbed, experiencing kidney failure and other complications. He lay in his bed all day, barely able to stand, unwilling to eat. Alison hated to see the dog suffer and wanted Jack to put him to sleep. Jack, heartbroken, had refused. He understood that the dog would want to die in his own home, with his family. That was important, even and perhaps especially to an animal. He had gotten the dog pain killers instead, and eventually it had passed on, comfortable and happy.

Jack was not afraid to die, but he was afraid to die on the ship, away from everything and everyone he cared about, butchered and left to bleed to death on a cold concrete floor while the world's elite watched, laughed and placed bets.

Afraid he would set the transmitter off by accident, he put it back in his pocket and went to the weapon rack. He took out the dueling sword, pulled it from its scabbard and held the leather covered grip with both hands, admiring the lines of the blade. There was just enough room to take a swing, so he raised the sword to his right shoulder and struck diagonally down, enjoying the telltale whistling of proper edge alignment. Holding the sword calmed him, gave him courage. If they did make him fight, he wouldn't go down easy.

Feeling better, Jack put the sword back and checked out the room service menu. After being frustrated by the dizzying options, he settled on a sandwich and some beer. An attendant brought his food within minutes, and Jack ate out on the veranda while watching small boats going in and out of the harbor. Feeling tired after the meal, he decided to get some rest. He worried that he wouldn't be able to fall asleep, considering where he was, but he was out moments after lying down.

* * *

He woke to a familiar chime and sat up in bed. The mattress was soft and supportive, made from high-end memory foam. It had lulled him into a deep sleep that was not easily shrugged off. Confused, he looked around, not entirely certain of where he was.

He remembered almost in time. "Deny Entry," he said, but it was too late. He heard the lock click, followed by soft footsteps. He got out of bed and went to meet his visitors. Perhaps it was a couple of goons from the tournament, come to take him to his cage in preparation for his slaughter. He reached into his pocket and felt for the transmitter. It was still there.

Allan waited for him in the living room, holding a garment bag and a pair of shoes.

"Your evening wear, sir," he said. "I hope you had a restful sleep."

"Yeah," Jack said, rubbing his eyes. His sense of balance felt off and there was no light coming from the windows. Still confused, he walked to the veranda door, slid it open and looked outside. A cadence of rushing water greeted him just before the rich sea air filled his nostrils. Pale gray and blue clouds covered the sky, set aglow by a full moon. It's light left slivers of gold rippling among the waves. Save for the moon, clouds and sea there was nothing all the way to the horizon. It was one of the most beautiful sights Jack had ever seen.

"The reception starts in one hour," Allan said from behind him. "You do not have to attend, of course, but I highly recommend it. You are suspicious, which is natural, and I think it will do you some good. That is, if I may be so bold as to suggest it, sir."

"I'll go," Jack said without turning around. "Just leave the stuff hanging somewhere."

"Very good, sir. Call for me when you are ready, and I will escort you. You can use the wall terminal or the voice system. Just say, 'Call cabin steward.'"

He left the apartment, leaving Jack alone with the view. What magnificence there was in a world filled with such evil.

Chapter 14

The Parter
is dangerous to the face,
and with its turn,
very dangerous to the breast.
- Liechtenauer's Verses, Von Danzig Fechtbuch – 1452

He felt like a buffoon in the tuxedo, but almost every man he spotted in the halls was wearing one, even the staff. The women—of which there were few—were almost exclusively dressed in dark colored evening dresses, some shimmering, some flat toned. He did spot an Asian woman in a bright lavender dress, but she was the exception. At least in her dress color—more than half of the people he saw were Asian, probably Japanese by the look of them.

The lighting was dimmed throughout the ship, lending an old world charm to this obsolete ritual of dress up and curtsy that he found somewhat endearing. The most difficult part was constantly reminding himself where he was, and why. This was all so civilized, so proper. This ship was the Leper King's gilded mask, and he imagined that if he tried hard enough, he could smell the putrescence under the lilies.

"Jack?" a familiar voice called when he stepped out of the elevator near the plaza with the fountain. A slight mist from its trickling water jets gave the air an earthy taste. Jack looked around and spotted Logan. He was tall and thin with long flowing hair he hadn't bothered to bind behind his head. The big grin he wore as he approached was infectious.

"Logan Holbrook?" Jack didn't know whether to give in to the joy of seeing his friend or to be afraid of what it meant to see him at the tournament.

"I love the way you say my name like it's all one long word," Logan said, opening his arms for an embrace that lifted Jack onto his toes. Holbrook was taller and lighter, and probably stronger. Easy enough for someone in his twenties.

"What the hell are you doing here?" Jack said, grabbing him

by the upper arms. He had never seen Logan in anything but jeans and a t-shirt, but the tuxedo suited him. "Not that I'm not happy to see you."

"I bet it's the same thing you're doing," Logan said, still wearing his grin.

"Shall I take my leave, sir?" Allan asked. "I believe Mr. Holbrook knows the way to the ballroom."

"I do," Logan said.

"Okay," Jack said. "Um…thanks, Teague."

"Very good sir." If he was irritated at being addressed in that manner, he didn't show it.

"So, Jack," Logan said, motioning ahead. "What the hell are *you* doing here? You all but dropped off the face of the earth for the last couple of years." They started walking down the corridor amidst a steadily growing procession of penguins and their painted queens. Some of the faces looked oddly familiar, though Jack didn't see anyone he actually recognized.

"Sorry about that," Jack said, clapping Logan on the back. "I really missed you, Holbrook." Logan was one of the few genuinely good people that Jack knew. He was his best friend in the community, and one of the few people with whom he did not have to hide his feelings behind witty banter. His smile left him as he once again forced himself to remember his circumstances. "But we're either going to keep asking each other what we're doing here for the rest of the night, or we're going to talk."

Logan nodded. "Yeah, we do need to talk. I questioned my own sanity, but seeing you here is messing with my head." He looked at the lapel of Jack's tux. "I see you're a three, just like me."

"A three?" Jack asked, looking down at his own jacket. There were three tiny pips there that he hadn't noticed before, little metal disks glued to the fabric of his lapel. "What the hell does that mean?"

"Beats the shit out of me. I'm a three, so is Ukrainian Boris. But Rob is a two. There are lots of threes and twos, but very few ones."

"Boris the Ukrainian Terminator? He's here? And Rob? Jesus." He was edging towards exhilaration, so many of his friends and colleagues, all on the ship with him. But there was also a dark undertone, something he hadn't quite worked out yet, and was afraid to.

"Yep, they're here. A few others too." He motioned at a man down the hall who was stepping through a pair of elaborate double doors. "There's Todd Marrone, your favorite person."

"I know what he looks like," Jack said. "Though I wish I could forget." He glared after the back of Todd's head, but otherwise ignored him. "How long have you been here?"

"I got here last night," Logan said. "This ship is amazing. There's so much to do."

"Logan," Jack said, a bit more sternly than he had intended. "You know why we're here. Doesn't this disturb you? The way they roll out the red carpet?"

Logan shrugged. "It did, and it should, but I really believe they're honest about the voluntary part. You know they're offering a million dollars a fight, right?"

Jack stared. "A *million*?"

"Yep. And if you win two or three fights, you win your division and get five million on top of that."

"Okay," Jack said. "Impressive, but Jesus Christ, Logan, you have to fucking survive."

Logan nodded, abashed. "Yeah, I know, and honestly, I don't think I'm going to fight."

"Then why did you come?"

"Why did *you*?"

If only he could tell him. He trusted Logan with his life, but what he had to say might get them both killed.

"Touché," Jack said, deciding not to show his hand just yet. "That's why I think we really need to talk." But what would they say? Better to focus on the pips for now. "So what do you think the thingies mean? Maybe we're both three because we're Liechtenauer guys?"

"I don't think so," Logan said. "Ukrainian Boris doesn't just do the medieval stuff, he's into just about everything. And Rob does Liechtenauer only, like us, but he's a two. I've been thinking about it all day, but I can't come up with anything that fits." They passed the double doors and stepped into the Grand

Ballroom. It was a continuation on the theme of refined elegance and reminded Jack of the James Cameron Titanic movie. Elaborately molded white plaster walls, crystal chandeliers, black velvet curtains in evenly spaced alcoves and a ceiling with gold inlays in floral patterns. It was like something out of the French Revolution. He half expected to see a porcelain skinned woman in a seventeenth century dress chased across the parquet floor by a mob of peasants.

"Okay, this is getting on my nerves," Jack said. "Does *anything* on this damned ship suck?" He watched well dressed men and women pass by tables stacked with ornately arranged delicacies while stewards walked the ranks with trays of champagne and appetizers.

Logan laughed. "The engine room is quite bland. It's cool that they let you go there though."

"Son of a bitch," someone said in a heavy Eastern European accent. "It's Jack Fischer." Jack turned just in time see Boris bearing down on him. A bit taller and stockier than Logan, Boris was a bear of a man, but he moved like a stalking leopard. Caught off guard, Jack held out his hand, but Boris brushed past him and grasped him around the back, though unlike Logan he refrained from lifting him off his feet.

"It's good to see you, Jack," Boris said in his usual thick accent.

"You too, Crazy Boris," Jack said. "It's just really weird to see you guys here, you know what I mean?"

Boris nodded. "Yes, Jack, it is." He was a first generation Russian Ukrainian and looked the part, with a big Slavic nose and deeply recessed eyes that glinted with homicidal rage whenever he fenced. "I can't believe you're here. Shit I can't believe I am here." He raised a finger, pointing to Jack's pips. "You're a three too."

"You know what it means?"

"Nope. But I have theory. Threes are cool people. That's why Rob is a two."

Logan laughed. "I'll buy that."

"Speaking of," Jack said, noticing the short curly haired man by a table stacked with seafood. "We should go say hi."

"Nah," Boris said, turning serious. "Leave him alone. He is

freaked out. Maybe tomorrow he'll get over it. He got here today, just like you."

Jack nodded. "I guess I can't blame him. I'm more than a bit freaked out myself."

"Let's go say hi to Todd Marrone instead," Boris said. "Come on, Jack, I think you will like him in person."

Jack was certain he would *not* like Marrone. From dealing with him online, he thought the man was a pompous, belligerent jackass.

"You guys go on," he said. "I'm starving." He actually was hungry, and the seafood table where Rob had been a moment ago looked quite tempting.

"Aw, come on," Boris said. "Give him a chance."

"Later," Jack lied. "If I don't eat soon I'm going to kill one of you and cut off pieces."

"Okay, okay," Boris said, laughing and holding up his hands defensively. "Here that is funnier than usual." And there it was, the thing that was bothering him before. So many friends. What if he had to fight one of them?

They walked off into the gathering crowd as Jack went over to the seafood table. The most interesting thing there was a plate of jumbo shrimp, about three times the size of the biggest shrimp he had ever seen. It would not have surprised him if someone had genetically engineered these living lobster tails specifically for this ship. More pomanders for the nosegays to ward off the smell of death.

"Pockets full of posies," he muttered, and picked out a particularly large example, dipped it into a bowl of cocktail sauce and took a bite. A very delicious pomander.

Noticing someone in his periphery, he turned in time to see a dark haired woman approaching the table. She was tall, slender, elegantly dressed and beautiful—an alien, from a planet where people like him were routinely denied visas. He smiled at her briefly, then stepped away from the shrimp plate to make room.

Instead of walking past him as he expected, she stopped, tilted her head slightly and raised an eyebrow.

"Jack Fischer?" she asked.

He was taken aback. "Um, yeah, I'm he…him…Jack." He

shook his head and smiled. "Let me try again. Yes, I'm Jack Fischer." He was too old to be tongue tied around women, but this one was so far out of his league it was a wonder she could hear him without a satellite dish. Alison had been out of his league as well, but somehow that had worked out anyway.

"Much better," she said, and smiled. She had been beautiful before, but her smile transformed her. She wore a low cut black evening dress, thick strapped and with a flower-like ribbon on her left shoulder, also black. Her dark brown hair was tied up in a simple and tasteful arrangement that left wavy locks dangling on either side of her high cheekbones. Her face could have graced the cover of any fashion magazine, but it was not the boring perfection of a professional. There was the slightest imbalance of features, a nose a tiny bit too long, ears a tad too high. Individually, they were flaws, but on her they coalesced into a transcendent loveliness that any supermodel would commit murder to duplicate, assuming she had any taste. There was also something peculiar about her eyes and her smile, an intriguing contradiction of projected emotion.

"How do you know me?" he asked after too long a pause. She reached for a shrimp and took a bite before answering. Her other hand held a full champagne flute.

"These are very good," she said, then drained her entire glass in one long pull. "Sorry…what did you ask?"

"How did you recognize me? Do we know each other?"

"On Facebook we do," she said, pointing her empty flute like an accusing finger. "Also, I've seen your videos."

"Oh," he said, disappointed. Of course it would have to be the most obvious and least interesting explanation. "What did you think? Of the videos, I mean." Like most instructor types, Jack put out a fair share of HEMA videos, mostly interpretations, cutting demos and snippets of tournament fights.

"Very nice work," she said, reaching for another shrimp. "I'm a bit of a fan, actually." A waiter came by and she took another glass of champagne. "I really shouldn't have another."

"Downed a few, eh?" he said, snatching one himself before the waiter walked off. The young man had been too busy staring at the woman in black to even notice Jack.

"Nope, that was my first. I'm Frederica, by the way." She held out her hand, and he took it, not sure if he should shake it or kiss it. He ended up holding it awkwardly before letting it go.

"Frederica?" he asked, suddenly making the connection. "Frederica Dragoste?"

"One and only," she said, then gulped down her second glass as quickly as the first. "I really have to stop drinking these. I don't exactly have a high tolerance." She looked at him and cocked her head. "You pronounced my name correctly."

"Thank god," he said with a chuckle. "I was afraid to butcher it completely. I just said it how they do in the song."

"God I hate that song. I mean, it's a nice song, but you can guess how many times people bring it up when I tell them my name."

"I'm sorry if—"

She shook her head. "Not at all. You get points for getting it right."

"Thanks. I can't believe I'm finally meeting you, here of all places," he said. "I'm a fan of yours too. You rarely post, but when you do, it's like you cut through all the bullshit and say the most profound things."

"Like agreeing with you?" she asked, and this time her smile almost reached her eyes.

"That never hurts," he admitted with a grin.

A microphone popped several times, and they turned towards the back of the ballroom. A white haired man was preparing to speak, and people were making room around him.

"Ladies and gentlemen," he said. "A most heartfelt welcome to all of you, and a sincere thank you for coming."

"Oh well," she said. "There goes the party. Now the work begins." She turned to look at the speaker.

He should have paid attention to what the old man was saying, even if it was mostly nonsense about centuries old traditions and how it was their honor and privilege to—well, something. He didn't really care. He looked at Frederica's back, at the bumps of her spine on her dusky skin, the shape of her waist and hip as she leaned from one foot to the other, trying to get comfortable in her heels. She was someone he had never met, but had known for many years. He had often imagined what she looked like—she had one of those evasive Facebook profiles with no personal photos—but even on its best day his imagination had fallen well short of reality.

With a shock, he realized that he was interested in her. Not just in her body or her face, but in *her*. There was something about her that had profoundly affected him in a way that hadn't happened since Alison. He drained his champagne glass, put it on the seafood table and walked to the back of the room, near the doors. He stood there awhile, looking around, trying to put her out of his mind. No good could come of this, especially not on this ship.

Eventually, the old man stopped talking, but his droning was replaced by music. Grabbing another glass from a passing waiter, he decided to find his friends and use their company to help clear his head. As his eyes scanned the crowd, he saw Frederica, dancing with a tall and handsome man that looked somewhat familiar, though Jack was certain he had never met him. Another internet personality.

"Well," he muttered to himself. "That's the way the cookie crumbles." At least he still had his jumbo shrimp.

Chapter 15

Thereon you grasp:
All art has length and measure.
- Liechtenauer's Verses, Von Danzig Fechtbuch – 1452

Back at the seafood table, he was glad to see that either the partygoers hadn't made a dent in the shrimp plate or the proprietors of this floating coliseum had replenished it.

He was on his third one when a woman's voice said, "I thought I'd find you here."

He turned and, to his surprise, saw Frederica walking towards him.

"Do you wanna dance?" she asked. "I don't get drunk very often, and I'm actually enjoying myself."

He felt his heart racing. If only he could say yes. "Um, I…" This was the part where he politely refused with some artful excuse, but he couldn't bring himself to do so now. "I can't dance," he admitted. "I don't know how. Never learned."

"*You*?" she asked incredulously. "You can't dance?"

He looked down at the floor, embarrassed. "No, I'm sorry. I really would like to dance with you."

"But you're so beautiful," she said, and his head snapped up to look at her. What had she just said?

She put her hand over her mouth, and her cheeks turned red. "Oh my. That didn't come out right." She giggled. "I told you I shouldn't drink. I meant the way you move, in your videos. It's beautiful. You're graceful, like a cat. I can't believe you don't know how to dance."

"I'm sorry," he said, heady from her compliments. "I really wish I did." Particularly now. He had always been able to get by without it, had even tried to learn on occasion, but he had been told he lacked rhythm.

"Come," she said, holding out her hand. "I'll teach you. It's easy." Her body language told him she would not take no for an answer. His fear of embarrassment was strong, but his desire to be close to her won out.

He took her hand and she led him to the dance floor, pulled him close and put an arm around him. Her perfume was musky, slightly floral. The muscles of his back tensed at her touch.

"Just follow my lead," she said. "This is a slow song, easy to dance to." There was a song? He heard it now, but it was inconsequential. She was the only thing he could focus on.

She started to move, and he stumbled trying to keep pace.

"Your art, it has wrestling," she said. "You know how to sense pressure, right?"

"Yes, when fighting."

"Then fight me," she said. "Feel my pressure. Where I push, you yield, where I yield, you push."

"Like work in the bind," he said, thinking of Liechtenauer's principles. "Work around strength, exploit weakness."

"Exactly."

She moved, and he reacted, and it worked. She yielded, he advanced, she pressed, he withdrew. Within moments they were moving across the dance floor. Not just moving, they were *dancing*. Soon he was able to stop focusing on the movements and just enjoy being close to her. She had called him graceful, but he was a lumbering oaf compared to her. Her body was made for motion—she glided along the floor as though defying the laws of gravity.

As much as he was enjoying it, he was unaccustomed to the strain and grew tired. Not physically, but mentally, from the effort of keeping pace.

"Want to take a break?" she asked, sensing his increasing awkwardness. "You're doing really well, but you have to pace yourself."

"No, not unless you do," he said. "I'm having a great time."

"Me too." Suddenly she stumbled forward, as though she had tripped on something—only she hadn't. He caught her and held her up and she clutched at his arms, her fingers digging into his tux sleeve.

"Are you okay?" he asked. He expected her to recover and stand, but she didn't.

"Shit," she swore, her voice desperate. "Not fucking now."

"What's wrong?" He was suddenly very afraid, though he had no idea what he was afraid of.

"Nothing," she said. The tone of her voice was different now, tense, almost angry. "Hold me for a second, please. Just a second."

"Of course," he said. "As long as it takes." She didn't weigh much, but he was holding up all of her weight with his arms. He pulled her close to ease the strain and held her tightly, making sure no one noticed. "Is it a leg cramp?" Her legs were loose though, not tense as they should be if one of them were cramped.

"Yes," she whispered. "A bad one."

He held for a few more seconds before she pulled back and her legs took her weight. Her eyes were wet.

"Are you okay?"

"Fine," she said without looking at him. "Excuse me." She walked out of the ballroom without so much as a look back. He stood there a moment, watching the doorway where she had just been. Some people were looking at him, no doubt wondering what he had done to upset the lady, but he ignored them.

He walked out after her and took random turn after random turn until he came to an automatic glass door that let him out onto the exterior deck, where he found a convenient railing and looked down at the rushing black ocean below. A warm wind tousled his hair as he lost himself in the motion of the waves, visible only as shadows under the white froth churned up by their passage.

He didn't understand what had happened, what he had done wrong, but it didn't matter. He was mostly mad at himself for letting it get to him. He should be used to it by now.

"I'm not here to have a good time," he said. "I'm here to fight." He stood there, staring down at the water for several seconds before he realized what he'd said. To fight? He was here to stop it, to stop Logan, Boris, Rob and even Frederica. But was he a hero, or a ripe bastard?

"I guess I do deserve it," he said, and turned away, headed for his quarters, where he was certain he could find a well stocked bar.

* * *

Frederica didn't wait for the solenoid and slammed the door

shut behind her, then fell back against it, letting the tears flow. Just a few days left to live, and it couldn't leave her alone. It couldn't let her have just this brief, insignificant period of time to enjoy what was left of her life. But didn't she deserve it, with her idiotic behavior?

"But you're so beautiful," she said in a mocking tone filled with self loathing. She thought she'd been off the meds long enough for alcohol tolerance to return to what it had been, but apparently she would be denied even that. Perhaps it was worse than she thought—had the alcohol brought on the attack? In small amounts, it sometimes helped to soothe some of her minor symptoms, like the trembling and the occasional numbness. But too much could, according to Prabhu, do the opposite.

Too much, too little, it was just all so god damned complicated. She didn't want to deal with it anymore, didn't have the strength. This ship, this tournament, it was supposed to be an escape. She'd been so numb the past few months, walking through her life like a zombie, barely able to pay attention. Now it was different, she felt alive, excited, perhaps because she knew that this was the end, an end that was of her choosing, on her terms, and it was to have nothing to do with her disease or its complications.

She let herself cry a little longer, then swiped at her cheeks with the back of her palms and started for the bathroom, where she would take a nice hot bath, consequences be damned. She hated to waste such precious time on so petty a pleasure, but she had blown it with Fischer.

Thinking of Fischer made her angry again, and she stopped walking, closed her eyes and tried to calm herself. She had been attracted to him since she saw his videos and associated them with the level headedness of his posts. He was sensible, not arrogant, not interested in posturing like many of the others. She liked his posts, and often supported him when their paths crossed. When she saw him, it was only natural for her to connect the intellectual aspect with physical. He was everything she liked in a man—competent, strong, rugged. She didn't care for the slender men with feminine facial features that she typically attracted. This ship was no exception. There were plenty of them, drawn to her like flies to rotting meat. An appropriate metaphor if there ever was one.

She had looked up Fischer on Facebook, but his profile said he was married, which had kept her from trying to contact him, however unlikely that would have been otherwise. Yet there he was, at a live steel tournament. Would a wife possibly allow a husband to go, or had he snuck off on a pretense? In any case, it didn't matter. She'd made a fool of herself in front of him and it was best to just forget him and move on. That jackass Marrone had hit on her several times, and he wasn't bad looking. She couldn't afford to be too picky.

Turning towards the bathroom, she noticed a white box on the dining table. She was still trying to get used to the idea of such a big luxurious cabin on a ship being hers to use, but it was a hell of a way to spend her last few days. Curious, she walked up to the table and examined the box.

It looked like a small shipping carton, though it wasn't sealed or labeled. She pried open the top flaps and took out a white Styrofoam cooler. It reminded her of the type of container her medication was shipped in. She set the cooler down on the table and opened the lid, and froze.

The first thing she saw was a small blue and white box labeled "auto*ject* 2." Below it was a packet of 30 Copaxone syringes. A month's supply.

She took a step back and stared at the contents of the cooler. They *knew*. And not only did they know, they hadn't kicked her out of the tournament, but had actually provided her with her medication. Her mind raced to try to explain it. Did they want her at her fighting best, so that she would amuse them with a clean death? Then why give her so many more than she needed? But then, she was thinking like a bottom feeder. These people could order a thousand syringes as easily and with as little thought as they could order one.

Whatever the reason, they had given her what she needed, and she would not waste it. Her spirits somewhat lifted, she removed the auto injector from the box and prepared to load it. She could have found a spot in easy reach—using the syringe without the injector reduced the size and discomfort of the welt—but at that moment what she needed most was the ritual. Loading and prepping the injector, waiting for the two red lines that indicated the medicine was spent, removing the syringe. There was comfort in familiarity, even when that familiarity brought despair. Sometimes one familiar pain could ease another.

After her injection, she went ahead with her bath, hoping the water would soothe the burning from the shot. As she lay there, enjoying the warmth and ignoring the numbness in her feet, she couldn't help but think of Fischer. A part of her wanted to see him fight, wanted to see him cut down his opponents, his longsword glinting in the sunlight like it sometimes did in his videos, a modern day knight in black athletic wear, cutting through legions of those who would harm the object of his affections. A macabre thought, made more so by the sexual desire it inspired, but she decided not to resist it. Life was, after all, short.

Chapter 16

Hew crooked to the flat,
The masters you will weaken.
- Liechtenauer's Verses, Von Danzig Fechtbuch – 1452

Jack found a seat next to Rob, who looked up at him, smiled briefly and turned to stare at the floor. The group occupied the first few rows of the ship's theater. Refreshment tables were set up in front of the stage, and Jack spied Marrone there talking to Frederica. She was wearing blue jeans and a cream colored short sleeve top. Her hair was down and covered all but the front of her slender neck. Jack had no intention of fighting in the tournament, but if he did, he wanted to fight Marrone.

"Hey Rob," he said, taking his seat. "You looked upset last night. What's up?" Rob was a little shorter and plumper than Jack, and by far the most timid martial artist he'd ever met, at least on the surface. That shyness disappeared quickly when Rob picked up a weapon.

"Nothing, nothing, I was just thinking." That was Rob, not even a hello, as none was necessary the way he saw it. His refreshing lack of adherence to obsolete rituals kept him on the fringes of most of their community's social circles, but Jack liked him just fine.

"About?" Nothing like someone else's problems to get his mind off his own.

Rob shrugged. "Stuff." He looked up. "I'm scared, Jack. I'm thinking coming here was a mistake. Please don't say anything to anyone, okay?"

"I won't, and don't worry, I'm scared too. I'm sure everything will be fine. If you don't want to fight, don't." It was easy to be sure with the transmitter.

Rob smiled briefly. "Thanks, Jack."

The white haired man who had made the speech Jack ignored the night before was standing on the stage, talking to a taller man with thinning gray hair. The taller man adjusted his collar, presumably turning on a microphone, and approached the head of the stage.

"Ladies and gentlemen," he said in a refined British accent. "If you would kindly take your seats, we can get started."

Jack watched Frederica, who followed Marrone down the aisle. She noticed Jack looking at her, then turned down his aisle and approached him. He watched her get closer, his heart racing. When she was near the empty seat to his left, she crouched next to him.

"Hi," she said, smiling briefly. "I just wanted to say I'm sorry about last night."

Jack shook his head. "No, please, you have nothing to be sorry about. I get leg cramps too, pretty nasty ones, and they last longer than yours did. You must be training pretty hard."

She cocked her head slightly. "Um, yeah, I have been."

"Are you sitting with anyone?" he asked. "This seat isn't taken, as far as I know."

She looked at the chair, then sat down. "Thanks."

He smiled at her, enjoying the excitement of the moment, consequences be damned. Perhaps he had misread the events of the night before, and that was an intriguing notion, though he warned himself not to make too much of it.

"Thank you," the gray haired man continued. "I'd like to welcome each of you aboard the Invictus and to our tournament of arms. My name is Reginald Hastings, and I am the event coordinator." He was a distinguished looking gentleman, someone who belonged in a position of authority. Late fifties, perhaps early sixties, stern of face with crisp features, bright blue eyes and a perpetual half frown. He wore an expertly tailored suit with an understated tie and gold cufflinks, not the sort of clothing Jack would have expected on a criminal. Then again, these people were very upscale criminals. A fancy suit was nothing compared to a high end cruise ship.

"You are all about to receive a package," Hastings continued, motioning to some attendants who were walking up and down the aisles, handing out small boxes. "These packages contain a confidentiality agreement, which, despite what you may think, can and will be enforced legally. Also in the package is information that you will need to access numbered accounts that have been created for each of you. These accounts are guaranteed to be fully anonymous, in spite of recent regulations and treaties. An amount of one hundred thousand Euros has been deposited into each of the accounts as a token of our appreciation for your attendance."

"Holy crap," Jack muttered. "That's like..." He tried to remember the latest conversion rate. Hick had told him it would be dollars.

"It's just a little over a hundred thousand US," Frederica said. "The Euro isn't doing too well lately. Still, a lot of money just for showing up." She had a strange look on her face, as though the amount disturbed her.

"This money is yours regardless of whether you choose to participate in the tournament," Hastings continued. "Your package contains information on how to access the money online, which will allow you to transfer funds in whatever portions you desire to a bank account of your choosing. In addition to this, should you choose to participate in the tournament, you will be awarded one million Euros for each contest of arms, and an additional five million if you win your division."

"My god," Jack said. "Logan was right." He turned to Frederica, but she was staring at Hastings and didn't comment.

"I know you must have many questions, and I will not waste time before answering the most pressing. First, the tournament is indeed fought with sharp steel weapons. This is highly illegal, even in international waters between willing participants. We have made the assumption that each of you was aware of this before coming here and that you would not take issue with it. If that assumption was not correct, or if you have changed your mind, please let us know immediately. You will be confined to your quarters for the remainder of the voyage, though you may keep the hundred thousand Euros regardless." He looked around, waiting for someone to say something.

Jack looked at Rob, who shrugged, then at Frederica, who was still lost in thought. A man came by and handed each of them a folder. Jack's folder was addressed to him by name and contained what looked like a standard non-disclosure agreement—something that seemed absurd and out of place—and the promised information regarding the numbered account.

"Good," Hastings said. "We will cover the rules extensively in a moment, but I will give you a brief overview now. While the tournament is fought with deadly weapons, it is not a fight to the death." This got Jack's attention. How could a live steel sword fight not be to the death?

"The tournament is fought until the first strike, though combatants can choose to ignore incidental wounds. After each strike that draws blood, you will retreat to your starting positions and wait for your opponent's decision. Fatalities do, and have, occurred in the tournament, at a rate of about one in ten participants. Fight stopping injuries are far more common, at about a four in five rate. The degree of severity of such injuries does, however, vary greatly. They can be as minor as some loss of mobility in a non essential extremity, such as a finger, or as major as full body paralysis.

"It is important that you understand that any attempt to deliberately kill or injure your opponent will be frowned upon, though we recognize that for many of your arts, the infliction of such injuries will be ingrained in your training. We do ask that you exercise whatever level of control you can manage, so that if you thrust, try not to thrust into the face or heart, and if you cut, avoid cutting to the head."

"Jesus," Jack muttered, suddenly very nervous. The transmitter was in his pocket—he was too afraid to leave it in his quarters lest someone find it. He felt like taking it out and pushing the button there and then. Something about the matter-of-fact way Hastings was stating the conditions of the tournament mortified him. Cold blooded murder in dark pits was the stuff of Hollywood, hard to take seriously. But this calculated caution, this was too real for his liking.

"Cold feet?" Frederica asked him. He turned to look at her, to see if she was joking, but she was looking straight ahead, her expression hard to read.

"You could say that," he admitted. "You don't?"

She shook her head. "It's in the cards."

He was about to ask what she meant, but Hastings resumed his speech. This time, Jack didn't want to miss a word.

"These men and women," Hastings said, pointing to the front row. "Are some of the finest surgeons and physicians in Europe. Please, stand up." Several people, Jack counted ten in all, stood and faced the rest of them. Most looked older than Jack, some older than Hastings. "They will be prepped and ready to go in two state-of-the-art operating rooms that you will get to see later today. No expense has been spared, and consequently this ship has some of the finest trauma facilities on the planet. Should you sustain injuries in the tournament, and most of you will to one degree or another, there is no place in the world where you could find better treatment. Your total transition time from being wounded to being in the Operating Room will be less than three minutes, and there will be a trauma team at the tournament site to guarantee immediate stabilization, when possible."

Jack looked at Frederica again—it was hard not to. She was looking at Hastings, like before, but now there was a noticeable frown on her face. Something the old man said bothered her. He wished that they were anywhere else, perhaps at an ordinary tournament. He really should have gone to more events in the last couple of years. Perhaps he could have met her at one of them.

"To conclude the overview," Hastings said. "There will be no mixing of time periods in the tournament. You will be pitted against those who practice arts contemporary to your own, limited also to the general geographic location. For many years, this has been exclusively a Japanese event, but in recent years they have graciously opened the way for participation by European martial artists. Doubtless many of you have noticed at last night's reception that the Japanese represent the vast majority of attendees. To forestall any questions about the matter, there will be no contests between Eastern and Western stylists, even in overlapping time periods. Although we do have several exhibition matches scheduled, and may set up more depending on the outcome of the Western portion of this tournament. This is the second such tournament that has included historical European swordsmanship, and I am personally very gratified to see our collective heritage so well represented here. Both myself and the other hosts are immensely proud of the work that you are doing. You are the finest historical fencers from around the world, the best of the best. Each of you has been carefully selected based on your views, your work and your accomplishments."

"I wonder how they learn about us," Jack said to Frederica. "Do you think they go on Facebook?" He was confused, talking in an attempt to find equilibrium. Hastings's words had affected him deeply, much more so than he was prepared to handle. He made jokes about being a sword bum as though that were some sort of honorific, but he knew the truth. The arts that he dedicated his life to were a joke to most, a curiosity to the rest. Very few took them anywhere near as seriously as he did. To be treated this way, told that there were people who were proud of what he was doing, filled him with something he rarely experienced—pride. Not pride at winning a bout, or doing something well, those he had in abundance. This was a more profound feeling. He was, for perhaps the first time in his life, genuinely proud of who he was and what he had accomplished.

"Yeah, probably," she said. "Though it wouldn't shock me if they had spies in our schools. Their resources are incredible."

"We will now cover the rules in greater detail," Hastings said. "And then go on a tour of the training and medical facilities. Please take a moment before we leave this theater to read over and sign your confidentiality agreements. They will be collected at the door."

"Doesn't that scare you?" he asked. "They're giving us a ton of money, they have this ship. Where do they get it all?"

"They probably do high stakes gambling," she said. "People pay a lot of money to watch thugs beat each other to death with fists, imagine what they'd pay for this."

"I guess." What bothered him almost as much as the sudden reality of the tournament was how nonchalantly Frederica was handling it. He recalled from the night before that she'd had a single pip on one of the shoulder straps of her evening dress. He had noticed it but hadn't thought about it until now. He wondered if there was some connection between her attitude and the number of pips she wore. She was the only "one" he had seen thus far.

As Hastings talked, Jack paid careful attention to the rules, which were both surprisingly nonexistent and strict at the same time. There was a lot of protocol to observe, but once the bout began there were basically no rules except to avoid deliberate and unnecessary injury. A lot of what Hastings said applied to different arts and was lost on Jack, who tuned him out and occupied himself with his own concerns.

"Some of you are wondering about the pips," Hastings said, and Jack snapped back to attention. "These are for logistical purposes. You have been divided into categories based on your dietary, medical or other requirements. It would assist the staff if you wore the pips as often as possible, though you may of course choose not to do so."

"Bummer," Jack said. "I was hoping for something more sinister."

"Were you?" she asked, sparing him an amused glance.

"I guess not," he admitted. "But certainly more interesting than dietary or medical needs."

"You're assuming he just told us the truth," she said.

"There is that."

Hastings had them assemble and exit the theater while uniformed attendants collected their signed confidentiality agreements.

"If you will follow me," he said once everyone was gathered in the hallway, then led them down the stairs to one of the lower levels. The first stop on the tour was a training area with a lot of empty floor space, racks of training weapons and several pells—both fixed and free hanging wooden posts used to practice striking and distance control. It was a very impressive and well stocked facility. It would be a joy to practice there, if only he were practicing for something other than murder.

They passed the Japanese practice area, similarly equipped except in place of pells there was a massive stack of tatami mats in one corner. Jack had never seen so many. There were hundreds or maybe even thousands of them.

"Excuse me," Jack said. "Mr. Hastings?"

"Yes?" the man asked, coming closer to Jack. "What can I do for you?"

"Would it be possible to get some of those tatami mats? I need them for my practice."

Hastings smiled. "Of course, Mr. Fischer. We anticipated your need and allocated one hundred mats for your personal use, though if you need more it can easily be arranged. You may come to this training facility and use them whenever you wish."

A hundred tatami mats. Jack was genuinely excited and hoped he got to cut them all before he had to activate that transmitter. They were being so generous to him, he almost felt guilty for wanting to bring this to an end. Almost.

Hastings saw his smile and nodded appreciatively. "The protocol here can be a bit more formal than most are used to, but you shouldn't have any problems." He turned to the others. "There are some for each of you as well, should you wish to use them. If you're not familiar with Japanese culture, however, I'd ask that you ask one of the staff to fetch them for you."

"Tatami chopping," someone muttered with obvious disdain. Jack didn't bother to turn to see who it was, though he had a pretty good idea. He had more important things to think about.

They proceeded on the tour and stopped by the operating rooms, which looked like something out of a fancy television medical drama. Monitors, racks of equipment, giant overhead lights, glass walled observation rooms. Not the shabby stuff he was used to seeing in emergency rooms, but really impressive high tech equipment.

"These facilities," Hastings said. "Were constructed to tend to the emergency medical needs of the ship's residents, who tend to be very old, and very wealthy. As such, they are top of the line, and every effort will be made to both spare your lives and repair any damage that you may suffer, both cosmetic and functional. Two of the physicians you met earlier, Doctors Finley and Winslow, are among the United Kingdom's top plastic surgeons. The rest are of varying specialties, including a neurosurgeon, vascular and cardiothoracic surgeons and, of course, anesthesiologists."

"This is freaking me out, man," Rob whispered to Jack. "That's a lot of god damned surgeons."

"This is supposed to calm us down," Jack said. "Let us know we're in good hands."

"Could be fucking stage props for all I know," Rob said.

"You think so?"

"No. But what I do think is that we're going to get cut to shit and these hacks are going to try to stitch us back together, and that is *not* comforting, Jack. Not in the fucking least."

"Yeah. I know what you mean." It seemed that looking at these facilities was having the opposite effect of what Hastings intended. Or was it?

"This concludes the orientation," Hastings said, and Jack couldn't help but smile. He'd been right, this was a wakeup call. Leaving them near the operating rooms, that was definitely deliberate. His smile faded as he asked himself why they would do that. What could they gain from scaring people off?

"If you have any questions or concerns," Hastings continued. "Please come see me in my office at any time. Any of the staff will be able to tell you where it is. You have the rest of today and most of tomorrow to train and prepare, and also that much time to decide if you will participate. Unless you tell me otherwise, we shall proceed on the assumption that you will do so. Your first fights will be announced on the morning of the opening day. Now, if you will excuse me, I will take my leave. Please enjoy the rest of the day, and feel free to use any of the ship's facilities."

Hastings disappeared down the hall, leaving most of them staring at the operating tables.

"I'll catch you later," Rob said, and turned and walked briskly away before Jack could say anything. Marrone walked up to fill the space where he had been. He was a bit taller than Jack and a bit stockier, but not at all fat. His skin was deeply tanned, made to look even darker by his long black hair.

"Hey Freddie," he said. "Ready to go?"

"I guess so," Frederica said, smiled faintly, then turned to Jack. "Todd invited me to play tennis. It was nice to see you again, Jack." She turned and started to walk away, and Jack started to let her. But something about today was different. Perhaps it was what Hastings had said about him, perhaps it was seeing the operating rooms and realizing what they represented. Or perhaps because he was tired of giving up before trying.

"Hold on a sec," Jack said, catching up with her. Marrone narrowed his eyes at him.

"What's up?" she asked.

"Can I have a word with you?" He turned to Marrone. "It will just take a sec." He didn't normally do things like this, especially since she was leaving with someone else, but she had sat next to him, not Marrone, and that had to mean something. She had also asked him to dance the night before. Jack wasn't usually smart about women, but he wasn't blind either.

"Sure," she said. "Todd, give us a minute?"

"Sure thing," Marrone said, pursing his lips, and went to lean against a nearby wall, glaring at Jack.

"What is it?" she asked. He tried to read her expression, but she was well practiced in the wearing of masks.

He took a deep breath. "I, uh, I don't suppose you want to get together later today? Maybe have lunch? Or dinner? We could talk about, you know, sword stuff…"

She raised an eyebrow. "Are you asking me out on a date? In the middle of all this?"

"Yeah," he said, shaking his head. "I'm sorry, I guess it's a bad idea." His face burned, but at least he had tried.

"Okay."

"I'll let you go now."

"No," she said. "I mean okay as in yes. How about we start with lunch and see where it takes us?"

He started to say something, but all he could manage was to move his mouth. He had done something impulsive, foolish, and it had paid off.

"Is lunch okay?" she asked. "We could have dinner instead if you have plans."

"No, no, lunch would be great. How will I find you?"

"Just meet me in front of that big restaurant in the back of the ship. Can we make it a late lunch? One o'clock? I have something to do after tennis."

"Of course."

He watched her walk off, watched Marrone's ridiculous victory grin as they left together, and all he could think about was what he would do for all that unbearable eternity before one o'clock.

Chapter 17

...there is no actual advantage between two fencers who are both stationary in their guard: since they are waiting for the very same thing, an opportunity can equally arise for either. Likewise, both face the same dangers while waiting.
- Salvatore Fabris Lo Schermo, overo Scienza d'Arme – 1606.

She hadn't wanted to play tennis with Marrone, the man was a pompous jackass. He posted online as though he were an enlightened spirit sharing wisdom with the unwashed masses. He prattled on about the dangers of the sportification of the arts but didn't seem to understand how to train martially. She had known all this about his online personality, but had foolishly allowed herself to consider the possibility that he was different in the real world.

After their game, the idiot had brazenly invited her up to his cabin, as though seeing him running around in short shorts had gotten her all hot and bothered. She tolerated it all with a smile and a polite refusal, because she had other things to think about, and because she had been wrong about Fischer. It seemed she hadn't blown it after all. She was a little disappointed that he had asked her out so directly, the man was married and she expected more from her knights, both of the shining armor and black athletic wear variety. However, considering the situation, and the alternative, she could overlook a minor character flaw.

She arrived at the door the attendant had described. She raised her fist to knock, and found she couldn't do it. She was afraid, terrified even. Not of the implications of her decision, but of opening up to someone else. But she would have to do just that to get what she wanted.

She almost turned around, walked away, but she didn't dare. She would never be able to have peace if she did not ask for what she wanted, and whatever fleeting joy she would find in Fischer's company would be overshadowed by the darkness of her indecision.

Frederica could not control her disease, could not control the world that had denied her the treatment she needed, but she could control her fate, and her actions. She knocked.

"Please come in."

She opened the door, walked in, and closed it behind her. Hastings looked up from his desk and smiled. He stood up, and offered his hand.

"Miss Dragoste," he said. "A pleasure. How may I be of assistance?" He was intensely handsome in a patriarchal way: a slender face and broad chin with a mouth made for the sort of smile that reached all the way up to his blue eyes and soft, wrinkled brow.

She shook the offered hand, then clenched her fist to gain the strength she needed.

"I'm here to make arrangements…medical arrangements."

Hastings nodded. "Please, have a seat."

She lowered herself into one of the comfortable leather chairs.

"Good," he said. "Now what can I do for you? We are aware of your needs, though if there is anything we have overlooked, we are prepared to rectify the situation immediately."

"No," she said. "Nothing like that. And thank you so much for the medicine. This is about…" She stopped, finding it hard to go on. Hastings waited patiently. "It's about the surgeons, and the operating rooms."

"Yes?"

"I don't want them."

Hastings frowned. "Pardon me?"

She bit her lower lip, then said, "If I am…injured to such an extent that I would die without medical attention, then I want you to let me die."

"I don't understand. Didn't you come here to…"

How did they know so much about her? It didn't matter, not anymore.

"To get the money I needed for my medicine, yes. At first."

He nodded, understanding. "But something has changed."

"Yes. Something has changed." Long before she had arrived on the ship, she'd realized how tired she was of living in fear, of wondering when her next attack was going to come. Tired of painful daily injections, of having her sword fall out of a numb hand, of people like Mark looking at her with pity. Of collapsing into someone's arms because her legs suddenly stopped working. But things were different now.

Before coming to the tournament, she had never had a chance to really *live*, not since her diagnosis. On the ship she wasn't Frederica the diseased freak, she was a fighter, there to test herself in combat to the death, and to play at life and love in the days in between. This was the life that she had dreamt of since she was a child, and it was the thought of leaving this life to return to the other that she could not bear.

"I will honor your wishes," he said.

"You're not going to ask me why?" She couldn't believe he was just giving her what she wanted so easily. Her eyes filled with tears, threatening to let loose.

"I must admit it pains me greatly. Not only are you a striking and intelligent woman with a bright future, but you are an artist of incalculable worth. It would be a terrible shame to lose you. I must admit I find myself hoping that you win every match." He hesitated. "You're not going to deliberately—"

"No," she said quickly. "Not at all. I'll give it everything I've got." That she would win every bout had not occurred to her, but she was not overly worried about it. She would deal with that if and when it happened.

"I am glad to hear it. I am not supposed to have favorites, Miss Dragoste, but I will be rooting for you."

"Thank you," she said, and got to her feet. "Now if you will excuse me, Mr. Hastings, I have a lunch date."

Hastings smiled, and she recognized that smile, having seen it in the mirror many times before. He was genuinely sad, and it moved her.

* * *

"So, your name," Jack said. "It's Romanian, right?" They had found a quiet table for two by the back next to the massive window in the main dining room. The seas were calm, and beautiful blue waves churned up behind the ship as it sped along towards its destination, wherever that was.

"Yeah," she said with a half frown. "My father, obviously. He was an American though, like fifth generation or something." She forced a smile and looked away for a second. He could see there was a difficult memory there.

"What about your mother?"

"Brazilian," she said, nibbling on a string bean she had impaled with her fork. "My dad lived there for work." Her teeth were bright and even, but not perfect. She had slightly protruding canine incisors, upper and lower, that were spaced a bit apart from their neighbors. They gave her a predatory aspect that Jack found very appropriate.

"Were you born there?"

"Yeah, in São Paulo. We moved to the States when I was eight."

"Was it nice?"

"São Paulo? It was a shit hole."

Jack chuckled. "That nice, huh? What was it like? To live there I mean." He picked up what was left of his smoked brisket sandwich and swallowed it almost without chewing. Whoever these people had cooking for them had to be a world class chef. The brisket was masterful—smoky, moist and tender.

"We didn't have a lot of money," she said. "So we were sort of on the edge, just poor enough to see it, but too well off to live it. I got into a lot of fights. I never knew when to keep my mouth shut."

"I bet you kicked a lot of ass," he said, trying to lighten the mood.

She shrugged. "No. I got beat up a lot, more so after we moved back to the States. American kids are meaner for some reason. My father, he was always away on business, and the other kids made fun of me, said I had no father. I knew it wasn't true, but it still hurt, and then one day it *was* true."

"I'm sorry, that must have been hard."

She shrugged. "I don't remember that much of it." She hesitated for a moment, and he could tell she was doing exactly what she claimed she couldn't. "Let's talk about something else."

"Sure. There's actually something I've been thinking about. It's been bothering me since the orientation."

"What is it?"

"Hastings said this was the second tournament with HEMA people, right?"

"Yes, he did."

"So…" Jack said. "Who was in the first?"

"Good point," she said. "But there are people who knew about it. When I got the invitation, I knew what it was, or at least I suspected."

"Really? How? I had no idea."

"There was actually a post about it on Sword Forum, back when it was still relevant." She furrowed her brows, trying to remember. "The symbol, the East/West mixed thingie, that was actually in the post before the mods took it down and banned everyone involved."

"Maybe it was a small gesture, to test the waters."

"Maybe."

"So what did the post say?"

"Not a lot, just that the person posting had been to a live steel tournament and survived, and wanted to share his story. It didn't get very far before people started to accuse him of bullshitting, and then of course it all hit the fan. The moderators got to it less than an hour after it was posted. One of them called it 'malicious drivel.'"

"Those guys are such drama queens. So that's how you knew?"

She nodded. "That and a few other tidbits online. But when the money showed up…"

"Yeah, that scared the shit out of me."

"Oh?" she said, one corner of her mouth curling in a crooked smile. "The mighty Jack Fischer? Scared?"

He laughed. "Who said I was mighty?"

"Aren't you?"

He turned serious. "I guess we'll see." No, he corrected himself, there would be nothing to see, because he would not be fighting. Why did he constantly have to be reminded of that?

"Well," she said, finishing the last of her salmon. "That was delicious. I had a lot of fun, Jack, thank you."

He tensed, hoping this wouldn't be the end, but knowing that it probably was. "Do you have any plans for the rest of the day?"

"Not really." Once again, her expression became unreadable.

"Do you want to do something else? Maybe take a look around the ship. Unless you're planning to train…"

She smiled and shook her head. "Jack, Jack, Jack. How about we go to your cabin?"

Caught off guard, he didn't know what to say. His mouth moved, and he had to exert his will to force coherent sound out of it. "My cabin?"

"So we can keep talking," she said. "I'm tired of being around all these people." Most of the tables in the spacious restaurant were empty, but he understood her point.

"Oh, sure, yeah," he said quickly. "That would be great."

The walk to his apartment was short, as it was situated towards the back of the ship, just two levels up. He swiped his card and followed her inside.

"Very nice," she said, looking around. "I like the nautical motif. Mine is more English country house."

"It's not like it's really mine," he said. "We're here for less than two weeks."

"The rest of my life," she said softly.

"Huh?"

"Nothing," she said, smiling brightly. "There's something I have to know, Mr. Jack Fischer."

"Shoot," he said. "Anything."

"How did you ever get your wife to let you come here? No offense, but she's either crazy or gullible as hell. Twenty days away from the love nest?"

Jack flinched, looking away.

"Oh don't worry," she said. "I don't mind. That you're married I mean." He couldn't blame her, she didn't know, but it still hurt. She was a stranger, talking this way about Alison, it should have bothered him, but aside from stirring up memories, it didn't.

"My wife…she died. Two years ago."

Frederica stared at him a moment, her face darkening. She looked the way she had the night before, after she collapsed in his arms.

She turned away and let out a short angry breath. "I'm so

sorry, Jack. I didn't mean to…"

"No, don't apologize, you didn't know."

"Oh god, I'm such a bitch," she said, then shook her head and started for the door. "I really should go. I'm so sorry."

He watched her leaving. Such loss from the parting, and she but a stranger. It would be so easy, to just say nothing. But what could he say?

"Please don't go."

She stopped, her hand on the knob.

"I don't want you to go," he said. "You didn't say anything wrong."

"Why do you want me to stay?" she said without turning around.

It was his turn to look away. Why indeed? What would he do with her if she stayed? What could he offer?

"I just do."

She turned from the door and walked towards him. She didn't stop until she was so close that he reached out and held her around the waist.

"It wouldn't be fair to you if I stay," she said. "I started this thinking only of myself, but I can't do that anymore. I would only hurt you in the end."

"Then hurt me," he said, feeling bold, and fatalistic. Understanding, reason— these were unwelcome strangers. What he felt, whatever it was, would not be swayed.

"You don't deserve it."

"You don't know me."

"I want to."

He leaned forward, afraid she would pull away, but she didn't. She kissed him, briefly but fiercely. He was lost in it, forgetting everything else, and when she pulled away, it was as though he were gasping for air. The feel of her body pressed against his, the warmth of her skin, the soft texture of her clothing—the sensations were surreal and exhilarating.

She stepped back, and he reluctantly let her go.

"So, um," he said. "What do you want to do now?"

She smiled and swiped at her eyes, which were glistening in the sunlight pouring through the veranda curtain. "There is something I really want to do, but we don't have to if you don't want to."

"What is it?"

"Let's go cut some tatami. I want to try it with my rapier and I don't want to pass up the opportunity to get pointers from the very best."

He felt his face flush at her compliment. "Sounds like a plan."

Chapter 18

This has been composed and created by Johannes Liechtenauer, the one High Master in the Art, may God be gracious to him, so that princes and lords and knights and soldiers shall know and learn that which pertains to the Art. Therefore he has allowed the Epitome to be written with secret and suspicious words, so that not every man shall undertake and understand them. And he has done that so the Epitome's Art will little concern the reckless Fencing-Masters, so that from the same Masters his Art is not openly presented or shall become common.
- Anonymous Introduction, Von Danzig Fechtbuch – 1452

She enjoyed watching Jack interact with the Japanese. There was a lot of formality and subtle gestures. She knew that people bowed upon entering a training hall, but she hadn't realized that they were bowing to something—the kamidana, a little Shinto shrine suspended on the back wall. Most Historical European Marital Arts practitioners scoffed at such rituals, but she saw value in them. The men in the room—and there were only men—were serious, determined and focused. It wasn't easy to switch gears, walking from an evening on the town into a place where one trained in the arts of death. The rituals helped. She could use more of them herself, to prepare for what was coming.

Jack smacked the mat down on the sharpened peg, then took hold of it to see if it was firmly fixed. When it didn't wobble, he nodded in satisfaction and went to get his sword.

"You wanna take this one?" he asked. "Ladies first and all that?"

"No," she said. "I'll get the next one. Show me what you've got." She noticed several of the Japanese watching him. They were mostly curious, but there was one who didn't look happy. He was a strange looking man—the top of his head was shaved bald and the rest of his long hair was arranged in an intricate top knot, like something from a tapestry in a sushi restaurant. He had introduced himself as Junichi and seemed to be dominant—the others deferred to him in subtle ways. Jack hadn't picked up on it, but as a woman in a predominantly male activity, she had learned to be sensitive to masculine body language.

Jack took a few steps back, raised his sword to his right shoulder and started walking towards the mat like a prowling panther. When he reached misura larga his sword lashed out faster than her eye could follow and painted a diagonal line along the textured olive surface of the target. Before the severed top segment could fall, his sword circled and came up again, cleaving the foot long chunk as it began to slide off the remaining mat. The sword came around again for a horizontal cut with the hands held high, loping off another small chunk off the top of what remained standing. She looked immediately at the Japanese that were watching. They seemed satisfied, and even Junichi appeared less grumpy. She had seen them cutting as they entered, and they tended to be faster and smoother than Jack was, but then their swords were more suited for this purpose and test cutting was more firmly integrated into their art. Jack was among the best at this in the European arts, but those arts were far behind the Japanese in this respect.

"That was beautiful," she said as he turned to her. He looked almost like a puppy, needing approval. She found the incongruity between his innocent affection and the deadly ability he had demonstrated endearing.

"Thanks," he said, smiling. "Your turn." He removed what was left of his mat, tossing it into a common pile of discarded pieces, then fetched another and mounted it for her. She went to her sword case, took her rapier, and took a guard facing the mat.

"That's a beautiful sword," he said. "Who makes it? I love the leafy engravings in the…what do you call those?"

"Arms, rings, ports," she said. "We don't really classify them individually though, it's part of the complex hilt. It's made by Arms and Armor, I'm sure you've heard of them."

"Yeah, they make some of our blunt trainers."

"I'm not going to be able to sever this, you know." She glanced towards the spectators. "I don't want them to think I suck." Her hands, her legs, her feet, they were all cooperating. She wasn't sure if the medication had taken effect so soon, or if it was her relief at being on it again, but she felt completely normal, and it was exhilarating.

"The goal is not just to sever a mat," he said. "The goal is to be able to use your sword in a way that is true to your art on a target that reveals the flaws in your technique. Everyone here will understand this." She nodded, pleased by his answer. Like Marrone, he was almost exactly the man he appeared to be online, which in his case was a very good thing. Meeting him had been a stroke of fortune, but it was also potentially problematic. She would enjoy the time she had with him, but there was a danger of enjoying it too much. What if the last few days of her life included watching him die?

"Got any pointers?"

"Is your sword sharp?" he said with a smile.

She nodded. "You can shave with the first few inches."

"Excellent. I wouldn't try to sever the entire mat, that blade is too light and slender...try to take some chunks off the top. Your aim will have to be perfect."

She nodded, then advanced towards the mat, point on line, then deliberately moved it well to the side, as though she had just performed a wide parry. Cuts were not the optimal form of attack with a rapier, and were generally only used when the point would take too long to bring to bear. Facing the mat, about to cut, she found her heart beating a lot faster than she expected. It was a simple exercise, just slice into a rolled straw mat, but it summoned the same sort of reaction newer students had when engaging in free fencing, and perhaps the kind of reaction she herself would experience when faced with the real thing. That alone made it a worthwhile exercise.

She flicked her wrist, using her legs to put her entire body behind the cut, and felt her blade bite into the top of the mat. A small section, about two thirds the diameter of the whole, flew neatly off the top. She felt an immediate and profound satisfaction.

"Outstanding," Jack said, grinning widely. She cut again, and lopped off a slightly larger section, then another. She then took a step back and lunged, impaling the mat neatly through the center. She did it three more times, retreating, thrusting, retreating, thrusting. When she was done, she turned to Jack and saw him watching her strangely.

"What is it?" she asked. "Am I not supposed to thrust at it?" Had she committed some sort of cultural faux pas? She looked for warning signs in the faces of the onlookers, but they were watching her with expressions of approval, at least as far as she could tell.

"No, nothing like that," he said. "It's just…you're really dangerous with that thing. I guess I didn't really think about that until now."

"Are you worried you'll have to fight me?" she asked with a grin, though of course they had been assured there would be no anachronistic match ups.

He shook his head. "No, I could never…" He stopped suddenly, turning to look at the entrance. A young Japanese man had just entered, escorted by Hastings and the white haired gentleman from the reception. The Japanese had all turned to him and were bowing deeply. She looked back at Jack, and his face was white, eyes wide and mouth open.

"What is it?" she asked.

"Son of a bitch," Jack muttered. "That motherfucking son of a bitch."

* * *

Some of the men turned to glare at Jack, but Kanemori only smiled guiltily and said, "I'm going to have to speak to Mr. Fischer alone."

"Of course," Hastings said, and he and the white haired man left the training area and disappeared down the hall.

"Son of a bitch," Jack repeated, shaking his head. He turned to Frederica. "Will you excuse me for a moment?" He was afraid this would end their day, but he had to shake the truth out of that lying sack of shit Kanemori. He couldn't believe yet another of his friends was actually on the ship. So many people he knew, at an event he would not have thought to attend in his wildest dreams.

"Sure, I'll stay here and play with mats." She gave him a reassuring smile and touched his arm. "You go do what you have to do."

"Thank you." He followed Kanemori out into the hall and closed the door to the training room. All sounds from inside immediately dropped to a murmur. This would have done for a private venue, but Kanemori led the way to an empty room down the hall. It was plain, with white walls and a gray accordion partition stretched across one end. There was no furniture except for two folding tables stacked along the back wall.

"Jack..." Kanemori began.

"You knew," Jack said, pointing an accusing finger. "When I showed you that invitation, you knew exactly what it was. You lying son of a bitch."

Kanemori nodded. "I knew."

"Why did you lie to me?" The words were coming out of his mouth, but they felt like a prerecorded message. The shock of seeing Kanemori was seriously messing with his equilibrium. If Will walked into the room holding a bottle of single malt, Jack's head would probably explode.

"The decision to come, or not, had to be yours," Kanemori explained. "And honestly, I wasn't sure if I wanted you here."

"You don't think I'm good enough?" Jack was experiencing a maelstrom of emotions, from surprise to anger to joy at seeing yet another friend, despite the circumstances. He hadn't meant to ask the question, but now that it had come out, he felt very self conscious. What if it was true?

"No, you're good enough," Kanemori said. "But nothing is certain. I don't want anything to happen to you. You're a good friend, Jack." Once again, Jack forced himself to remember why he was there, or at least why people would think he was there. To fight, and maybe to die.

"Okay, forget about that for a second," Jack said. "What the hell are *you* doing here? You have so much going for you, and you have Aiko. How could you risk dying on her?"

"I'm not here to fight, Jack. Not this time." He grinned. "It's really pissing off Junichi, too. That fucker wants a crack at me, real bad. I kinda want a shot at him too. Is that nuts?

Jack frowned. "What do you mean, *this* time?"

"Do you remember me telling you I won the last two championships in Japan?"

"Yeah…"

"Well they weren't exactly in Japan."

Jack took a step back, feeling faint. "You…you won two of these tournaments?"

"Yes."

"Is that...is that where you got your money? I mean the Jag, moving out of the karate place?"

"Yes."

"You...you killed people?"

"One of the men I fought ended up dying, yes," Kanemori said grimly. "It's not an easy thing to live with, but I believe in what they're doing here, and I can't fully regret it. He knew what the risks were, as you must."

"I don't…" Jack said, shaking his head. "I don't know what to think. You…I had no idea." Without thinking, he reached into his pocket and grasped the transmitter, finding the activation button by feel. "How could you?"

"That's an odd question to ask, Jack, considering you're here to do the same thing."

He tried to think of a way to respond without giving away his purpose. "I'm not going to fight. I only came because I was curious, and stupid. I'm not killing anyone, and I don't see how you could have. It's fucking murder, man. You could go to jail." He *would* go to jail, once Jack did his duty. He had to figure out a way to get Kanemori, Frederica and his other friends off the ship before the feds swooped in.

"You're not going to fight?" Kanemori asked, seeming surprised. "How could you turn away from this?"

Jack couldn't believe what he was hearing. "How can I turn away from cold blooded slaughter? Are you mad?"

Kanemori took a deep breath, and nodded. "You don't get it yet, but you will."

"*I* don't get it? *I*?"

"What is it you do for a living, Jack? What is your life dedicated to?"

"Martial arts," Jack said acidly. "Which last time I checked were about preserving life, not taking it."

"Really? So when you cut a tatami mat in half, you're

practicing for surgery?"

Jack glared at him, angry. "You damn well know what I mean."

"No, Jack, I don't. Bushido, chivalry, it's all bullshit that romantic writers used to paint over the blood and gore of the reality. You know as well as I do that people in the past used these arts to hack each other to bits."

"So what? That was then, this is now. There is no need for that sort of crap anymore."

"So you think you can just cut a mat, swing a sword, and call yourself a swordsman? You're basing your life on something you don't have the balls to actually do, Jack. And before all this you had the luxury of pretending that was the only option you had. Well you can't pretend anymore. These people have given you the opportunity for your life to be about something real, something important, and they did it in the safest and most hospitable way possible. And now you know the truth, that there are people out there, people just like you, who put their asses on the line. Their lives, their dedications, they mean something, Jack. They're not just playing. If you walk away from this, that's all you'll ever be doing, like a little boy fighting with wooden swords, and you'll know it."

"Horseshit," Jack said. "People in 15th century Europe didn't murder each other just to say they did. They fought for something, and it wasn't to train…they had free play for that, just as we do. Fencing masters weren't even allowed to duel in some parts of Europe, did you know that? You yourself are living proof you don't have to kill to know what you're doing."

"How's that?"

"You never fought before you fought, jackass, then you did, and you won. It was your training that made that happen. Or maybe you forgot everything you learned, maybe you were too busy quenching your taste for blood." His anger was building, taking control. He had to get a hold of himself before he said something that he could never take back.

Kanemori narrowed his eyes at him. "We're both on edge, saying things we don't mean."

Jack nodded. "We are." Thank god at least one of them had the sense to call it quits.

"You don't yet understand the nature of this tournament, but you will, and when you do, I hope you make the right decision. I have to go now, get ready. I'm the grand marshal...one of the judges, though there's not usually much to judge. I have to help with preparations."

Jack nodded without looking at him, then heard him walk away. He made his way back to the Japanese training room. Frederica was gone, as was her rapier. That was just great. One of his closest friends was a lying murdering bastard and the first woman he was genuinely interested in since his wife died had run off on him. Could life be any better? He missed Will. He wanted a real friend to get drunk with and complain to.

He picked up his sword, wiped it down with an oil rag and put it back in its case. He was just about to leave and find an open bar when a man walked up to him.

"Sumimasen," he said. "Jacku-san." He held up a note on a folded piece of paper and handed it to Jack.

"Arigato gozaimasu," Jack said.

"Kini-shinaide," he said informally, then returned to his training.

Jack looked at the note. It was from Frederica. She apologized for not waiting and asked that he meet her in her cabin in an hour. The note included her room number. Jack smiled, despite his mood, and felt his spirits lifting. He returned to his apartment, where he cleaned and put away his sword, then got the shower ready while he rummaged through his luggage to find something nice to wear. It was silly, to feel this way, to act this way, but he couldn't help himself. There were sword fighting tournaments to the death, and then there were the important things in life.

Chapter 19

Art regulates nature, and with safe escort guides us according to the infallible truth, and by the ordinance of its precepts to the true science of defense.
- Ridolfo Capoferro,
Great Simulacrum of the Art and Use of Fencing – 1610

Jack couldn't wait any longer and knocked on her door. He had three minutes to go before the hour was up, but that would have to do. He heard the familiar chime and the door swung open.

The apartment was shaped similarly to his own, but it was brighter, its walls adorned with cream colored wallpaper and moldings. His eyes were drawn past the white couch and loveseat to a pair of decorative wooden columns.

"Jack," Frederica said, stepping out of the bedroom. She was wearing a knee length summer dress, white with green flowers. "Glad you could make it."

"Wild horses," he said.

She cocked her head a moment, then got the reference and smiled. "Come, have a seat, I'll get you a drink." She motioned towards the couch and turned to the bar. "What will you have?"

Jack closed the door behind him and settled onto the soft cushions. "Water, or maybe seltzer."

She stopped and grinned at him. "Come on Jack, don't be difficult. I'm trying to get you drunk."

"Oh." He loved her straightforwardness. "In that case, watcha got? I love champagne, but it's not a holiday, so…"

"Champagne it is," she said. "We could die tomorrow, so every day that we don't is a holiday." She took a bottle and popped the cork, then handed it to him.

He looked at the bottle, then at her. "No glass?"

"Are you a man, or a dandy like Marrone?"

Jack laughed. "Bottle it is." He took a swig as she sat down next to him. The champagne was really good, light and fruity and not at all bitter. Frederica reached for the bottle and swallowed several mouthfuls.

"There," she said. "That should give me courage."

"Didn't you say you had no tolerance?"

"None whatsoever," she said, leaning towards him. "I'll be helpless against your charms in a moment. Feel free to try and seduce me."

"You don't have to tell me twice," he said, and kissed her. She responded with sudden intensity, pushing forward so hard that he fell back onto the couch. Her hair fell around his face, the scent of strawberries mixing with her heady perfume. She started unbuttoning his shirt, and he realized that this was it, they were going to make love. He expected to have a problem with that—he was sober, and she wasn't Alison—but it felt familiar, it felt right. She was one of his kind, living in his world, sharing his passions. Beyond her strength and confidence was an uncertainty, a sense of vulnerability. He wasn't sure why, but he felt as though she needed him as much as he needed her, and that mattered. Instead of stopping himself, he reached behind her and tugged at one of her shoulder straps.

"Not here," she said, and pushed off as she got to her feet. "Come." She took his hand and led him to the bedroom, where she doused the lights and closed the door, then pulled him towards the bed. Light from the curtained window bathed the room in a faint violet glow.

She slipped out of her dress as he pulled off his shirt. They looked into each other's eyes as what was left of their clothes began to fall away, and when they were done, he took her in his arms, pressing her close. His body surprised him with its urgency, and its potency. Her touch felt familiar, comfortable.

They fell onto the bed and he found himself enthralled by her body, unable to stop touching it, stroking it, tasting it. They made love for hours, and each time he was spent he held her, touched her, kissed her, until he was ready once again. They were warriors, making the most of life on the eve of battle, their senses sharpened to a shaving edge by the threat of impending death. Tomorrow they would fight, kill or die, and all he could think about was surviving to return to this place, to hold her in his arms again.

* * *

Frederica woke first, and searched for her watch. The curtains were closed, but a pale light forced its way through the dense weave. It was six in the morning, a good time to get up. She looked at Jack, lying on this back, his arm over his face and she smiled, reaching out to stroke his chest hair. She felt her eyes tear up as she thought about how well she had chosen for her last lover. He had been so gentle, so passionate. He knew his way around a woman's body, but he hadn't been following some rote routine, she had sensed the depth of his attraction. Not only that, but when she faltered, such as the time on the dance floor, he had held her up, literally and otherwise. If this were not the end, she would have wanted—

No sense thinking about it. This was the end, and it would be a great end, whether it was today, tomorrow or a few days from now. He stirred, and she pulled back her hand. If he woke now, she would have to send him away, and she didn't want that.

Carefully lifting herself off the bed so as not to disturb him, she tiptoed into the kitchen and fetched a syringe from the refrigerator, then snuck into the bathroom and locked the door behind her. She didn't have very many obvious fatty sub-dermal deposits on her body, and what few she did have were not within easy reach, forcing her to use the auto injector. It jammed the medicine into her body, leaving a painful, burning welt that hurt for hours. She chose a site on the back of her left arm, loaded the injector, took a deep breath and pressed the plastic tube to her skin. She winced as she felt the medicine course into her body like liquid fire.

Hiding the evidence of her crime, she tidied up the bathroom and went back to bed, where Fischer was stirring.

"Morning," she said, ignoring the burning on the back of her arm. Seeing him smile at her almost made her forget the pain. He was so handsome, not in the feminine way she abhorred, but hard, rough around the edges. He had a strong chin peppered with rough stubble, a full face with deep, kind eyes under a sharp brow that flowed angularly to a proud nose. His body was strong, well muscled but not chiseled. He wasn't overly hairy, but he did not shave or wax. He was exactly how she liked a man, and he made her feel safe when he held her, like a powerful bear snuggling a tiny cub while hapless wolves looked on from the dark woods. A strange emotion to seek in his arms, but the scars of childhood never really healed.

"Morning," he said, and she leaned down to kiss him.

"I was going to make breakfast," she said. "But then I remembered where we are. Have you seen the room service menu?"

She was about to go to the wall terminal to order their breakfast when she saw two cream colored envelopes that had been shoved under the door.

Curious, she picked them up and started to open them when she noticed that only one had her name on it, the other was addressed to Jack. Neither was sealed. How the hell had they known he was in her cabin? But then, these people knew everything else about them, so why not? She opened hers first.

Dear Ms. Dragoste,

Your first contest of arms will be held at 7:00PM this evening, on the Herbert S. Shusker tournament field located on Deck 1, amidships. Your opponent will be Kevin Casey, head instructor of the Massachusetts Academy of Fencing. Weapons are to be rapier alone. The opening ceremonies for tonight's events begin at 5:00PM, in the reception area just outside the tournament field.

Sincerely,

Reginald Oswald Hastings

Below the signature, scribbled in blue pen, was a handwritten note: *Godspeed!*

Her heart pounding, she took out Jack's note. She knew she shouldn't, but she couldn't help herself. She tensed guiltily as the paper left the envelope, but the rushing of water from the bathroom calmed her.

His note was almost identical to hers, except that his fight was at 8:30PM, and his opponent was—

She looked away, almost crumpling the paper before remembering it wasn't hers. Marrone. His opponent was Todd

Marrone.

Marrone was many things, but a bad swordsman wasn't one of them. He was a natural, gifted athlete, and despite several flaws in his ideas and interpretations—at least as far as she was concerned—he was one of the best tournament fighters in the world. Jack himself was no slouch, having placed in many national tournaments even though he was considerably older than most competitors and believed that training to win competitions was a compromise of the art. Some of the emerging ranking systems had even placed him in the top five American tournament fighters before he stopped competing two years before—and of course she now understood why he had all but dropped out of the community. But Marrone had placed multiple times in Europe, where the general caliber of fighting was superior, and had absolutely dominated the American tournament scene during Jack's absence.

It was strange that she would be fighting for her life only twelve short hours from now, but her only concern was for the man in her shower.

Chapter 20

If you readily frighten,
you should never learn fencing.
- Liechtenauer's Verses, Von Danzig Fechtbuch – 1452

Jack stared at the paper, reading it over and over again, looking for some hidden message that would tell him that it was all a big joke.

"Are you okay?" Frederica asked. "You look pale."

"Yeah," he said, crumpling the paper. He looked for a waste basket, found one, and tossed it inside. "It's just really strange to finally be faced with it, you know?" Strange was an understatement. His heart was racing, his hands shaking. He clutched at the towel around his waist, afraid that he would shake so much it would fall off. Frederica had opened her veranda door to let in a steady stream of fresh air, but now the room felt cold, and he was trembling.

"Are you going to fight?" she asked. He looked at her, trying to read her, but all he saw was uncertainty.

"Would you be disappointed if I didn't?" he asked, and instantly regretted it. That was a lot of responsibility and pressure to lay on her. It wasn't fair, nor was it appropriate.

"I wouldn't want to be," she said, giving him an honest answer to the most difficult question he had ever asked anyone. "I would be happy that you were safe."

He pulled a chair out from under her dining table and sat down, adjusting the towel.

"Meeting you," he said. "It changed things. Everything is more complicated now." Another blunder. He was taking their tryst very seriously, probably more seriously than she was. Alison had been old fashioned, but many women, like Leyna, regarded sex almost as casually as some men did.

"I'm sorry," she said, and he saw her tense slightly.

"Sorry? I wouldn't trade having met you for anything." And he kept right on going, unable to stop himself.

"That's kind of you to say, Jack."

"No," he said, shaking his head. "It isn't. It would be kind if it weren't true."

She smiled and put a hand on his shoulder, but her eyes were far away.

"So," Jack said. "Um, do you need to train? Get ready? I mean…shit, I didn't even ask you if you're going to fight."

"Why didn't you?" she asked.

He shrugged. "It's weird, but for some reason, I know you will."

"You're right. And no, I don't need to train. I trained my butt off before coming here. But you probably do, so…"

He stood up and looked at the pile of his clothes on the bedroom floor. The last thing he wanted to do was leave, but he knew a dismissal when he heard one.

"I don't have to train," he said. "But, if you have things to do…"

She laughed. "I don't want you to go, Jack. So if you don't want to, don't."

He felt suddenly lighter. "Are you sure?"

"Yes. I want you to stay." She really was too good to be true.

"That's good, because I really, really don't want to go."

She walked up to him and kissed him. "What ever shall we do, though?"

"I can think of a few things."

"Oh?"

He led her to the bedroom, where they made love again. This time, the light from the open curtain and doorway bathed them with its pale glow, and his eyes swam over every inch of her body. He noticed a welt on the back of her arm that hadn't been there before, and wondered if he had caused it. After they were done, they dressed and ordered room service.

"Jack," she said as they finished eating. "I want you to go train."

He frowned, confused. "I thought you said…"

"I know. And I meant it. But if something happened to you because I kept you here, I would never forgive myself."

"I guess," he said, uncertain. He wasn't going to fight, he

didn't need to train. But he couldn't exactly tell her that.

"It's one in the afternoon. The event starts at five. That only gives you a few hours."

"Okay," he said grudgingly. "I guess I'd better. When can I see you again?"

"At the event." She led him to the door. "And after my fight, if I live, I'm going to walk right up to you and give you a big sloppy kiss in front of everyone."

"I'm going to hold you to that," he said. She kissed him goodbye, and he walked out of her apartment into an empty and suddenly dreary hallway.

* * *

"Do you think maybe we should do some fencing?" Logan asked. "They actually have feders." He pointed to a rack of training longswords. "I didn't bring mine." The training room was huge, and there weren't many people in it.

"Nice feders, too," Jack said, impressed. They were expensive and he had never seen so many in one place before. "But no, I don't think so. We need our strength, and someone might get hurt."

"Still sore about the finger?" Logan asked, his smile a mix of guilt and amusement.

Jack held up his right hand, showcasing the deformed digit. "No, not sore, but I have enough fingers I can't fully straighten."

"Good point. Some drills then?"

"Yeah," Jack said. "Might as well." They walked over to the rack and took out a pair of training swords. Another rack nearby held an assortment of fencing masks.

They practiced for an hour before Boris showed up with Rob, and they joined in, making the training session more varied and productive. They were excellent fencers, and it felt good to train with them, though the situation lent a special kind of urgency to their exchanges. After another hour, Jack wanted to take a break, and the others joined him. They sat in a half circle, leaning on two stacks of wrestling mats in a corner.

"So," Logan said. "I saw you dancing with Frederica." He poked Jack in the shoulder.

"Yeah," Jack said, suddenly very conscious of where he really wanted to be.

"I'm sorry it didn't work out for you."

Jack raised an eyebrow. "Eh?"

Logan looked confused. "I saw her hanging out with Marrone."

"Yeah, well," Jack said, grinning slightly.

"You dog," Boris said. "Tell me you didn't. I mean, it's Frederica. She's so fucking hot."

Jack just smiled and shook his head. "You'll get nothing out of me." He wasn't usually tight lipped about such things, especially with good friends, but he didn't want to do anything that would betray her confidence.

"Be that way," Boris said. "Let's talk about something else before I beat the truth out of you."

"I'm still stuck on the pips," Logan said. "We're all threes, except you, Rob. What's different about you?"

"Do you have a medical condition?" Jack asked, remembering what Hastings had said.

"Not unless you count halitosis," Rob said with a grin.

"He also said dietary," Logan suggested. "But you're not a vegetarian, you get barbeque with us whenever we get together."

"Guys," Rob said. "If I had something that fit what Hastings said, I'd tell you. I'm clueless."

"So it's a lie," Jack said. "Hastings flat out lied. It can't be dietary or medical."

"Looks that way," Logan said, and flicked his head to get his long hair off of his shoulder. It was a nervous habit Jack had picked up on a long time ago. "Though he did also say 'other.'"

There was a period of silence, then Boris said, "So, um, guys, who's actually fighting?"

They looked at each other, uncertain, and Jack realized with a chill that he couldn't honestly answer the question.

"I'm not," Rob said. "No way. My first fight is supposed to be tomorrow, but I'm not going to do it."

"Then why are you training?" Logan asked.

Rob frowned. "I don't know."

Jack tried to laugh, but it came out like a nervous giggle. "I don't either."

"So you aren't fighting?" Boris asked him.

"I have no idea," Jack admitted. "I shouldn't, it's crazy. I'm here to—" He stopped himself. He had been about to blurt it out. "To watch, to learn."

"That's why I came too," Rob said quickly. He ran a hand through his curly hair, another nervous habit. Boris's was to rub his head, but Jack hadn't caught him doing that yet.

"I'm going to fight," Logan said suddenly, then nodded, as though to reassure himself.

"Really?" Boris asked. "Are you sure?"

Logan shrugged. "How can I walk away from this? Liechtenauer is what I do, it's my whole life. I left college to do it full time, I don't have anything else."

"Logan," Boris said. "You could die."

"I know," Logan said. "And I didn't come here to fight. I came here to…well, like Jack said. To watch, to learn. But now that I'm here, I can't just walk away. If I do, I'll spend the rest of my life wondering what could have been."

"If you don't walk away," Boris said. "You might not have a rest of your life."

"I know," he said. "And I'm willing to take that chance. I trust my skills and my heart. Time to find out if that trust is deserved."

Jack looked away, his mind in turmoil. A part of him wanted to blurt out, "Me too." But he didn't dare. He had tried to avoid thinking about the transmitter, about his responsibility to the feds.

"We're all crazy just for being here," Boris said. "And God help me, I'm thinking about fighting."

"I'm gonna go," Jack said. "I need to think."

"Yeah," Boris said. "Me too."

They said their farewells, and Jack started wandering the ship, eventually finding himself on an empty aft deck, looking over the rails at the churning water below. He could feel the power of the ship's engines, but they were silent, and all he heard from below was the rushing of the wake. The sun was high in the sky, and a quick glance at his watch told him it was four in the afternoon. Only one hour before the opening ceremonies.

He tried to think, to make a decision, but it was impossible. It was too big, too important. Logan and Kanemori were right, this wasn't something he could just walk away from, not without some serious thought. It was crazy to think that way, to even consider being a part of this blood sport, but the organizers had taken such precautions, treated them all so well, it was hard to see anything sinister in them. Kanemori's past involvement had cured him of most of his suspicions. His friend had fought and won, twice, and returned yet again, which meant Hastings had been sincere in everything he said. How could he betray his friend? And Frederica, how could he be responsible for her arrest and conviction? Or Logan's?

He pictured her, handcuffed, led away down the gangplank to a waiting school of strobe lighted piranhas. She turned in his direction, her head bowed in shame, and met his eyes with a look of betrayal that would kill him as surely as the sharpest sword.

He took the transmitter out of his pocket and, before thinking it through, tossed it overboard, where it disappeared beneath the roiling waves. Whatever happened, it would not be because he betrayed her trust.

Chapter 21

...before all things you shall rightly undertake
and understand these two things –
which are the Before and the After, and
thereafter the Weak and Strong of the sword and the word
Meanwhile, wherefrom comes the entire foundation
of the whole art of fencing.
- Anonymous commentaries on the longsword,
Von Danzig Fechtbuch – 1452

Jack practically sleepwalked through the opening ceremonies. His mind was somewhere else entirely. Hastings made a speech about the continuation of ancient traditions, there was food and drinks and soft music. Most people wore tuxes or fancy dresses, while Jack and some of the other fighters wore modern versions of period clothing. Teague, his cabin steward, had brought him the suit while he was wandering the ship just half an hour before, but he'd had enough time to play with it before putting it on.

It was an impressive garment, two layers of hand spun linen and one of soft wool, giving the same resistance to cuts and slices as 15th century attire. The top resembled a fencing jacket such as the kind Jack wore when competing in tournaments. The pants cut off just below the knee and rested on top of thick tube socks. The suit had modern features like velcro fasteners, an elastic waistband and zippers. It was easy to get in and out of, and wasn't in the least bit restrictive of his movements. It was entirely black, once again like Jack's tournament gear, showing that the hosts respected the community's fashion trends. His three pips—whatever the hell they meant—were permanently attached near the collar.

Others wore similar attire and some were dressed in approximations of later period clothing with waisted coats. There were also the far more numerous Japanese with their hakamas and stately kimonos bearing assorted mon on their chests.

He looked for Frederica, but didn't see her. He was growing increasingly agitated but didn't dare indulge in his craving for the champagne flutes carried on trays by numerous attendants.

After a while the crowd was ushered to the tournament field in a cavernous chamber in the bowels of the ship. It was, ironically, set up similarly to a Medieval Times stadium, though much smaller and without the ridiculous color schemes. There were tables arrayed around an oval field, each successive row slightly more elevated than the last. The tables were covered in white cloth and set with bottles of wine or champagne. A series of lights hanging from the high ceiling brought a sense of daylight to the field itself, though the light was intensely focused and waned quickly past the combat area to the point where the spectators experienced a twilight ambiance. The ceiling above the lights was shrouded in darkness, but Jack could barely make out duct work and pipes.

The field itself was covered in hard packed dirt, completely even. It was about thirty meters long and fifteen wide. Plenty of space. He stared at it as he walked to his table, searching the ground for signs of blood. This is where it would all happen, this neat little patch of dirt with its bright lights. Men would die on that field—and women. He shuddered and wondered how he could just sit still and watch someone try to kill Frederica.

As soon as he noticed them, Jack's attention was immediately drawn to the doctors. Four of them, in surgical scrubs, stood near a pair of fancy wheeled stretchers. The fluttering in his chest that he had felt for most of the evening intensified, his hands began to sweat and he took a deep breath to try and calm himself. Seeing them brought the reality into sharp focus. They were there to clean up the mess.

Attendants escorted him to a table, where he was joined by Logan, Boris and Rob. It seemed that nothing escaped their hosts, however trivial. Logan wore a costume similar to Jack's, but with a dark blue jacket. The other two wore tuxes.

"Jack," Rob said, reaching out to grab his arm. "I'm scared."

"I am too," he admitted.

"It's not too late to change your minds."

"It is for me," Logan said.

They said nothing more as people began to fill the tables. The fighters seemed to be concentrated in the lower levels, closer to the field, while the upper rows were being filled by old men with hard faces. Most were Japanese, but there were many Europeans. Some had dates, and these with few exceptions were young and beautiful. These men were the money behind all of this, the ones that would sit and watch while others spilled blood for their amusement. Jack wondered what it would be like to face a few of them on the dirt field. He wondered how long they would last before soiling themselves.

Hastings and three older Japanese men in dark kimonos sat at a table on the lowest level, closest to the field. Jack saw Kanemori and two other young Japanese men making their way there as well, joining Hastings and the others. Kanemori wore a black silk kimono adorned with his school mon and a light gray striped hakama. He saw Jack, smiled and waved, and Jack, no longer angry, waved back.

He really wanted a drink. This entire event was just too bizarre.

When everyone was seated, Hastings stood up and said, "The tournament of arms will now begin." He turned to the Japanese man seated next to him and said, "Saito-sama, if you will."

The man stood up and gave a speech in Japanese. The only thing Jack understood were a couple of mentions of Kanemori's name, each accompanied by a slight bow in the young man's direction. Each time he was thus addressed, Kanemori got to his feet, bowed deeply and said a very formal thank you.

When Saito was done talking, he sat down, and immediately a troupe of Japanese drummers that Jack hadn't noticed before started pounding on large double ended taiko drums. The music was powerful, forceful even, and unnerving. The volume intensified as the rhythm reached a peak, then abruptly it died off. Two Japanese men entered the field from opposite sides. Each wore a katana tucked through his obi. They stopped, turned to the audience and bowed. Then they bowed to the table with Kanemori, Hastings and Saito, then faced each other and bowed once more.

Jack's heart was beating so violently he could hear and feel the blood pulsing in his ears, drowning out ambient sounds. Or perhaps the murmurs of the spectators had died down, it was impossible to tell.

"Jesus," Boris whispered. Jack looked down on the table at his friend's knuckles, which were bone white. He glanced over at Logan, but his face was blank, unreadable.

The two combatants drew their swords in a slow and ritualistic fashion. The one to Jack's left, in a black kimono and hakama, raised the sword over his head. The other, with a gray kimono and white hakama, stood with the sword pointing down and behind him. These guards had names, even German longsword equivalents, but Jack couldn't think in those terms at the moment. Those men were about to use their swords on each other.

The man in black, sword held high, yelled fiercely and took two quick steps forward, while the other did not budge. A strong memory suddenly surfaced, and Jack was reminded of the Kurosawa film *Seven Samurai* where the samurai Kyuzo dueled with an unnamed swordsman and won. Kyuzo had stood in the exact guard held by the swordsman on the right, while the aggressive ruffian postured and pressed his attack just like the man in black.

The man on the left lowered his sword to Chudan, analogous to the German guard Longpoint, and started to advance. So much for movie duels.

Jack's table was right against the roped wooden posts that enclosed the field. He was within a few yards of where they would likely meet. He cringed away, afraid, anticipating the devastating strike of the katana.

The swordsman on the left kept advancing until he reached the middle of the field, then he stopped, and lowered his sword to the Japanese equivalent of Alber, the Fool, and waited. A few tense seconds passed, then the one on the right started to edge forward without changing his guard, his sword still pointed behind him. He stopped when he was two or three full steps from his opponent in black, his stance low, the hem of his white hakama dark from being dragged through the dirt.

The tension was so strong that Jack could barely sit still. His hands itched to do something, to hold a sword of his own. He picked up a champagne flute and held the stem tightly, his hands shaking.

The man in black suddenly leapt forward with a frightening

yell that startled Jack enough so that he almost jumped in his seat. His sword was a blur of motion that went up then came down and clashed into the blade of his gray and white opponent. Instantly the man in black was moving back, trying to void as the other cut low to his leg. There was a sound, the black hakama parted, and at almost the same time the black swordsman's katana dropped into the shoulder of the man in gray. It could have just as easily been his head.

The man in gray was on the ground in seconds, eyes wild, darting back and forth. The one in black was shaking. He dropped his sword and stepped back, limping. A pool of dark red spread out beneath him. The doctors bolted forward, two in front and two pushing the stretchers.

The swordsman in black bent down, holding himself up on one leg, and parted the torn hakama. He turned white and quickly stood up, putting a hand over his mouth. It wasn't enough. He bent over again and vomited on the dirt by his feet, his bile mixing with the blood.

Jack looked back towards the man on the ground, but he was already on the stretcher. His shoulder, which was close enough to see, was a gaping wound just deep enough to sever the muscle and snap the collarbone. The katana could have done more, so much more, but the man in black had held back. There was a big dark stain on the ground where he had lain. Two of the doctors wheeled the occupied stretcher away while the others ran up to the victor, but they held back.

"Shousya!" someone shouted. Jack turned and saw that it was Saito. "Himura-san. Kimi no yuuki-aru tatakai ni kansya simasu."

The man in black bowed deeply, an impressive feat in his condition, then stumbled. The doctors caught him and put him on the second stretcher. One started to cut the hakama from the wound while the other pushed the stretcher off the field and through the large double doors.

"Akiyama san no yuuki nimo keii-wo hyo-simasyou," Saito continued. "Futari tomo, yoku tatakatta. Yuukan ni tatakatta." The men in the upper rows applauded. It was a somber sound, devoid of cheering or other noises that would have made Jack angry. He was staring at the pools of blood left by both fighters, his heartbeat slowing to an almost normal rhythm.

"Jesus," Rob muttered. "Jesus."

"Fuck me," Boris said.

Jack kept looking at the blood as men entered the field and started to scrape off the layer of contaminated dirt. He was scared, unnerved, like a man who had wandered off the road and was lost in an alien wilderness. He desperately wanted grounding, something familiar, but there was an even stronger emotion fighting its way to the surface. It was not a thing he would have ever expected to feel.

Envy.

Whatever happened to those men now, they had faced something profound and had overcome it. For the rest of their lives, they would always have that. Their art, for both victor and vanquished, would take on a whole new meaning. Jack wanted that as much as he feared it.

After the blood and vomit had been cleaned, Hastings got to his feet.

"Ladies and gentlemen," he said. "It is my honor and privilege to announce our next contest of arms. Entering from the black gate…" Jack looked and noticed that a gap in the roped posts to his left was flanked by two black posts. Red posts marked the entry on the opposite side. "…is Mr. Kevin Casey, owner and principal instructor of the Massachusetts Academy of Fencing. Mr. Casey has a long and distinguished list of victories in competitions across the United States and Europe, and is a leading researcher whose translation and interpretation of the works of Nicoletto Giganti are considered among the finest of their kind. Entering from the red gate is Miss Frederica Dragoste…"

Jack heard a crack, and realized the stem of the flute he was holding had broken in two.

"…owner and principal instructor of the Gaithersburg School of Fencing. Miss Dragoste's interpretations of Fabris and Capoferro are remarkably insightful and have led to great gains in the understanding of rapier fencing, as did her views on general fencing theory. Her victories in competitions across the United States are numerous and distinguished. God have mercy on them both."

The drums beat again, rising abruptly and cutting off, just as before. Two new doctors came through the double doors, accompanied by two of the four from the previous watch. Jack didn't know their faces, but he saw the blood on their clothes.

Frederica entered from the right, dressed in a tight fitting black costume that approximated the shape and materials of the clothing of her period. Her hair was tied behind her head in a tight bun, and she held a rapier, the same one she had used to cut the tatami mat. She was beautiful, and Jack could barely stand to look at her. He wanted desperately to rush onto the field and carry her away.

Casey entered from the left, wearing a dark blue outfit of the same general cut as Frederica's. He too carried a rapier. A sharp rapier, one that he would use to try to kill her.

Jack started to stand up, but felt a hand on his shoulder. He whirled around, angry, and saw Kanemori standing over him.

"It's her choice," his friend said. "She could walk off the field right now, if she wanted to. You have to respect her decision."

Jack sat back down, and nodded. "Thank you." He understood. God help him, but he finally understood.

Kanemori patted his shoulder, leaned down and whispered. "Good luck today. I'll be rooting for you. Remember…win first, then strike." His friend returned to his table, and Jack looked at Frederica, who noticed him and met his gaze. She smiled, winked and made a kissing motion with her lips. She looked completely calm, and Jack had never been more scared in his life.

Chapter 22

Contra tempo is when at the very same time that the adversary wants to strike me, I encounter him using less time and distance. And you must know that while in measure, your adversary's every motion and every pause will constitute a tempo.
- Ridolfo Capoferro, Great Simulacrum of the Art and Use of Fencing – 1610

Frederica looked at the spectators, hoping she would find Jack as Casey entered from the other side. The bright light made it hard to see outside the field. Under the lamps it was high noon, but the effect died abruptly past the barrier, like a focused flashlight in the darkness. It was hard to make out the people in the first couple of rows and almost impossible to see any detail beyond. She felt lost, alone, with a growing need to find him. None of the faces she could see looked familiar.

She gave up for a moment and turned to Casey, who was staring at her, eyes unfaltering even when she returned his gaze. He saluted her with his rapier, and she returned the gesture, surprised by her sudden fear. She had thought herself beyond such things. It made sense, though. She did not want to die just yet.

She looked around again and spotted Jack in the front row to her left, seated next to his Liechtenauer buddies. He was about to get out of his seat, but Kanemori, the young Japanese man from the training room, put a hand on his shoulder from behind. They exchanged words, and Kanemori walked away. Jack turned to her and their eyes met.

She knew what he had been about to do—come to her rescue. She felt a warmth in her chest, radiating slowly outward, and she no longer felt alone. He was with her, her knight. She smiled at him and blew him a kiss, though without the obvious hand gesture. She didn't want to embarrass him.

Casey took his guard and began to approach. The suddenness of it startled her. This was it, no more preamble, no more time to prepare. She should have trained harder. The sword felt alien to her, not the extension of her body she was accustomed to. Then again, she had never fenced with the real thing before.

She took her guard, bending her upper body forward, knees bent, waist tucked back, her sword pointed forward at eye level. Once in position, things started to fall into place. It felt natural again, normal even. The fact that it was real didn't seem to matter anymore.

Casey approached to just past misura larga and stopped, moving his sword slightly to try to find hers. She adjusted her position subtly to prevent it, but he made a quick gesture and his blade touched hers with a barely audible "clink." He had gained the mechanical advantage, but he was a bit too far away to use it. He had made a mistake, and she suddenly realized that he was afraid. More afraid than she was. As if to emphasize her discovery, a bead of perspiration rolled down his forehead. Just as it touched his eye, she moved.

Her sword struck his hard, knocking it aside, and with her point far off line, she lunged forward and cut down. She could have hit his face but she aimed for his right arm instead, and scored. The point of her rapier sliced open his sleeve and bit into the flesh beneath.

Casey jumped back, his eyes filled with panic, and looked down at his arm, where a crimson stain was slowly spreading across the white of his undershirt, exposed by the parted sleeve of his dark blue costume. Score one for Jack's practice. Without it she wouldn't have had the confidence to attempt a cut.

As she had been instructed, she withdrew. Seeing her move back, he did as well. Hastings got to his feet.

"Mr. Casey," he said, his voice cutting through the silence like a ship's horn in a dense fog. "Do you want to continue?"

Casey hesitated, looked at his arm again, flexed his fingers, and nodded. "Yes."

"Shit," Frederica muttered under her breath. She was hoping it was over, but it seemed she would have to beat him twice. She was shaking, her hands were sweaty and her grip on her sword was precarious, or at least it felt that way. The strangest part was that this now felt perfectly normal to her, despite the fact that she had just used her sword to draw blood for the first time in her life.

"Continue," Hastings said, and returned to his seat.

Once again, Casey took his guard and advanced. She saw anger in his eyes. She had outplayed him, and with what would normally have been considered poor strategy to boot. He apparently didn't like that. But angry people made mistakes.

She let him find her sword again, and saw that she was right. His movements were too big, too aggressive. Once he had the advantage, he lunged right away, pushing her point offline as he did so. Frederica stepped sharply to her right, twisting her body until she was both stepping and leaning over backwards, out of the way of his thrust. Her sword slipped over his as she moved. His thrust missed, but her counter did not. She felt almost nothing as her blade entered Casey's right shoulder. It kept right on going, and she with it, until the hilt struck his shirt and the sword stopped. Her face was close to his, and she smelled his acrid breath. His eyes were wide, the whites glowing under the bright lamps.

She moved back, freeing her sword, and Casey dropped to his knees, his left hand clamped over his wound.

The doctors were on the field in seconds, but they hesitated.

"The victor," Hastings said from behind her. "Is Miss Frederica Dragoste. Let us also honor Mr. Kevin Casey for his sacrifice. Both fought well, bravely and with honor." There was thunderous applause, or perhaps it just seemed so after the silence. The doctors loaded Casey onto a stretcher, but before they started pushing him away, she walked up to him and extended her hand.

"Well fought, sir," she said, and waited. Her victory, the entire experience, was exhilarating. She had never felt anything like it in her life. Her heart beat faster than it had before the fight, and a sense of profound and primal elation took hold of her. Everything was forgotten, her disease, her arrangement—well, almost everything. She had a promise to keep.

Casey didn't hesitate. He took her hand firmly. "Well fought." The applause intensified.

As they wheeled him away, she turned to Jack. He looked so relieved that it made her smile. She walked towards him and he got to his feet. Stepping over the ropes, she lay her sword on his table, walked around and into his arms, and kissed him. A few people from the lower tables whistled. The poor man's face turned red.

Logan and the others scooted aside to make room, and someone brought an extra chair. She sat down next to Jack, pretending not to notice the growing red stain under the tip of her sword where it lay on the white table cloth.

"I was so afraid," he said.

"Me too. But then I saw you there, and it…helped." She was afraid she'd said too much, but he didn't seem to notice.

"You were amazing. I mean I knew you had to be good, but this…wow."

"Thanks," she said, her elation growing.

"Are you sure you want to be here?" he asked. "After what you just went through?"

She smiled. "I'm going to break down later. Right now I need to be strong. You're almost next, remember? I'm going to be right here with you."

She saw his lips tighten and his eyes mist over as they danced across her face. He squeezed her hand. "Thank you."

She kissed him again, then turned to the tournament field, where attendants were cleaning up Casey's blood. She shivered, reacting not to the sight itself, but how normal it suddenly seemed to her.

"That was a beautiful inquartata," Boris said. "Nicely done."

"Thank you," Frederica said.

"Mr. Holbrook," someone said from behind them. Jack turned and saw one of the attendants. "It's time for your briefing."

"Oh shit," Logan said. "This is it, guys."

"Don't do it," Rob said. "Come on, man, this is crazy." He turned to Boris. "Stop him."

"I don't know," Boris said. "I'm supposed to fight tomorrow...I think I will, too."

"You're all crazy," Rob said, then looked away, his brows knotted in anger or resignation.

"Good luck, Logan," Jack said, shaking his friend's hand. "And Godspeed." She remembered the scribbled note on her fight card and turned to look at Hastings. He was smiling at her. She smiled back and nodded.

"Thanks, man," Logan said.

"Yeah man," Boris said, his voice tense. "Godspeed." The way he pronounced the word, it sounded like "Godspit."

Logan nodded, swallowed nervously and followed the attendant down the aisle.

"Fuck!" Boris said. "He's going to be down there soon." No one else said anything.

After a few minutes, a Japanese man got up and prepared to speak.

"That's Saito-sama," Jack said. "I think he's the head honcho."

"Sama?" she asked, puzzled. "I thought it was san?"

"San is like mister," he explained. "Sama is more formal. It used to mean lord, like how a samurai would address his liege. Now it's used when addressing someone more important than you are."

"Ah."

Saito began to speak, but she understood none of it. She had always liked the sound of Japanese though, it was guttural and firm.

"...Kanazawa Junichi..."

She perked up. Unless she had misheard, Saito had announced the alpha dog from the training room. This should be interesting.

"Junichi," Jack said. "He's the one everyone is expecting to win. I don't know if you remember, but we met him in the training room. He was the one with the samurai haircut, the one all the others sucked up to."

She turned to him, seeing him with renewed appreciation. She thought he hadn't noticed, but she was the one who'd been missing something.

The drums started again and Junichi entered from the right, wearing stark white flowing robes with gold crests on each side of his chest. A man in blue and gray entered from the opposite side. They performed a series of bows, the drums died, and they drew their swords.

"He has some balls wearing white," Jack said. She turned to ask why, but he was already explaining. "Dark colors hide blood, white shows it. He's saying, 'You're not going to touch me.'"

"How do you know all this?"

"I used to do Japanese sword. I studied under Kanemori."

Junichi approached with his sword held out in front of him, the blue and gray one raised his blade over his head, but brought it down to match Junichi's as he got closer. They stopped just out of misura larga, waiting, their points almost touching. Jack squeezed her hand under the table and she felt him shudder, his skin hot and damp. Fighting a rapier was one thing, but a katana or longsword—she was terrified for him. She knew that in period a thrust was generally more feared than a cut, as it was impossible to clean the wound and the sufferer usually died of infection, but with today's medicine a thrust from a slender sword that didn't get the heart or brain was little more than a minor inconvenience. Casey would probably be up and about in a matter of days. But a cut from one of these savage weapons would be devastating. To have one's flesh parted, bones split—it was horrifying.

The swordsman in blue and gray began to twitch his sword, moving his point under Junichi's, then back again. Junichi flinched in response, seemingly falling for it. The man in blue attacked suddenly, striking at Junichi's forearm, but the white clad alpha countered in a blur of motion. She heard a clang as blades clashed. The blue and gray man's sword slid along Junichi's katana and was deflected by its curvature. Before she knew what had happened, Frederica saw the blood stained point of Junichi's sword emerge from his opponent's back.

With a scream that made her flinch, Junichi kicked the other man in the stomach, pulled his sword out and struck him right on the head. Frederica cringed away from what would surely be a skull splitting blow, but Junichi's sword stopped short. The man in blue stumbled back, a torrent of blood turning his face into a crimson mask.

Junichi, sword held out before him, stepped away slowly. She looked into his eyes and saw unmistakable satisfaction, perhaps even elation. He reveled in his victory.

Saito stood and announced the victor while the man in blue, blinded by his own blood, stumbled into the arms of the waiting doctors and was wheeled off the tournament field. The room erupted with applause. Japanese men in the back rows got to their feet and clapped vigorously.

"Shit, that fucking guy is fast!" Jack said. "Did you see how he faked that flinch? He was in control the whole time. And the way he stopped his cut…so precise."

"Yes," she said. "He was so calm, too." It was curious how similar what she had just seen was to some aspects of rapier work.

"I could take him," Boris said, but he was smiling. "Their swords are too short. We have ten inches on them."

"Just be glad you don't have to find out," Jack said. "They—" He was interrupted by an attendant that had come up behind their table.

"Mr. Fischer," the man said. "It's time to get ready. Mr. Hastings will brief you."

Jack's mouth tightened. "Okay." He looked at Frederica and nodded. "Wish me luck."

"Can I talk to you?" she said, suddenly on the verge of panic. She kept seeing Junichi's sword coming down on his opponent's head. She could almost feel his muscles tense as he brought the blade to a premature halt. Such control under such strenuous circumstances—Junichi was a master. Marrone was good, but he was no Junichi.

"Do I have a couple of minutes?" Jack asked the attendant.

"Of course. I'll be waiting for you by the exit." The man excused himself and walked back the way he had come. Frederica led Jack to the back of the chamber, behind the last platform. It wasn't exactly private, but it would do.

"What is it?" he asked.

"Jack, don't fight," she said, hating herself for having to struggle to get the words out. "I don't want you to get hurt."

"I may not," he said.

"What do you mean?" She had *just* asked him not to, and a part of her was disappointed. What was wrong with her? She actually wanted him to fight. It was difficult to admit, but it was impossible to deny.

"I think I know why they're doing this, but I want to be sure. I'm going to ask him, Hastings. But, Freddie, if it's what I think it is, what I think you believe also, then I will fight. I have to fight, and I think you know that."

"I do." Her disappointment faded, replaced with a steadily growing respect. He would not turn back because of fear. If he turned back at all, it would be a matter of principle. She could not blame him, his body was not being ravaged by disease, he had no reason to throw away his life unless it meant something.

"Come back to me in one piece," she said. "I'll be here waiting." Such strong words for someone she had just met, but she meant it all and more.

He took her in his arms and kissed her, then held her tightly for too short a time before walking away. She wondered if she would have to watch him die.

Chapter 23

Learn eight windings with steps,
And test the driving, no more than soft or hard
- Liechtenauer's Verses, Von Danzig Fechtbuch – 1452

"I'm glad you have decided to participate, Mr. Fischer," Hastings said from the comfort of his padded leather chair. "Please, have a seat, and I'll give you the information you need. It is primarily about not causing unnecessary harm if you can help it."

Jack sat down and folded his arms before his chest. "I haven't decided anything." Behind Hastings's head hung three antique longswords in glass display cases. They looked familiar—Jack recognized at least one from a book by Ewart Oakeshott.

"Oh? I don't understand, you—"

"I want answers. The truth." He was nervous, perhaps even frightened. He didn't know who Hastings really was. Was he a servant of the hidden masters, or a master himself? Was it wise to push him?

Hastings sighed. "The truth is not something that everyone is ready for, but I give you my word that if I do answer your questions, I will speak only truthfully. I do not guarantee, however, that I will be able to answer everything."

"Fair enough," Jack said. The truth or nothing, that would have to do. "I want to know why."

"Why?"

"Why you people are doing this? You, your employers, fellow members, whatever. Do they get off on watching people fight? Do they place bets?"

Hastings frowned, then leaned back in his chair. "I can't blame you for thinking so, not under the circumstances, but you're wrong. Some of the members, they do place wagers, and that is their primary reason for being here. I won't deny that." Jack could sense his disapproval, but was it an act? "The core of our membership, however, are not interested in bets, or watching you harm each other. That is why we take all possible precautions to insure no one is killed or maimed if it can be avoided."

"Then why? For crying out loud, the money you're promising us, there are so many of us here. What…thirty, forty, including the Japanese?"

"Thirty eight."

"A couple million for each? That's a lot of money. And that doesn't include all the other stuff, the ship, getting us here, the doctors. This must cost a fortune."

"It's not inexpensive," Hastings admitted. "For some. For others, it is a small price to pay."

"A small price to pay for what?"

"What do you think?" Hastings asked. "Why do you think we do it?"

"You're asking me?" Was this his idea of being truthful? "I have no idea why you do it."

"Oh, I think you do. Or you wouldn't be considering fighting. Of all the Western fencers here, you alone understand what this means to the Japanese, and that makes you uniquely qualified to understand what it means to us."

Jack nodded, realizing that he would indeed hear the answer he was expecting. He shivered, realizing the implications.

"Just tell me," he said. "In simple terms. I just want to be sure I understand before I risk my life."

Hastings nodded. "For some of us, our culture, our heritage, these things are very important. Those with the resources to do so have always contributed to the arts, to furthering our understanding of where we come from, who we are. When we started to interact with the Japanese in business and then socially, some of us realized that there was an aspect of their culture that they had in abundance, but that we lacked almost entirely. Unlike the Japanese, we did not preserve our earliest fighting arts, instead, ever pragmatic, we allowed them to fade into obscurity while focusing on better and trendier ways of killing."

"Why is that so important?" Jack asked.

"The foundation of Europe's wealth and power was laid down during the Renaissance. The men and women who built that power had qualities that we today lack. Did you know that in city states in the Holy Roman Empire and other parts of Europe, the murder rate was comparable to that of many modern cities, but it was the upper echelons of society that were the most likely to encounter violence? Disputes between merchants, guilds and so on could often escalate into sword fights in bars or even in the streets, and very often did. Most of the fights were not in earnest, striking with the flat, no thrusts, but they could and often did escalate into life and death struggles. Legally, in some of those cities, you could get into more trouble for hitting someone with a beer mug than for drawing your sword and fighting.

"Had I been alive in the fifteenth or sixteenth century, I would have worn a sword and known how to use it, and it would have been almost inevitable that I would have had to do so. Today violence is almost solely relegated to the poor, the ghettos, the seedier parts of society. How strange that it was so different. How much of ourselves have we lost?

"Today, men and women of power can set the course of nations, save or kill thousands, even millions. But to face another man with a bladed weapon that can rend flesh and cleave bone, few if any today would be strong enough to do so. Anyone can fire a gun, but to use a sword…that takes something most people do not have. And if the men and women who control society are so fundamentally different from those who built it, then are we not doomed to unmake what we have inherited? That thought keeps many of us awake at night."

"But any thug can fight in this way."

"A thug, yes, because he is a base creature, without forethought or a particularly high degree of self awareness. But to a man of distinction, of conscience, a man such as yourself, such as the organizers of this tournament, it is something significant, an aspect of martial culture that we have allowed to slip away."

"So you're trying to bring it back?"

"Indeed."

"Is that it?"

"It is not. I know that you understand the importance of the martial arts to the Japanese, but do you truly understand the sense of pride that the sponsors of this event have in their fighters and what they represent? These men believe that they are continuing the traditions of their samurai ancestors on a new battlefield, but one cannot continue something he does not understand. The ancient arts are a direct link to the past, and the men and women who face death with swords in hand are vital to those who hold such views."

"Why? It's not like they themselves are doing it."

"Oh, but they are," Hastings said. "Those who win here, and even those who don't, they have all faced death, and their arts are rewarded by their experience. These people, they go on to teach the arts in a way that those without such experience cannot, and then their patrons learn the arts from them. This helps them to understand the struggle between human beings in its purest form. To men of power, this is a priceless resource that is worth any investment. Only those without power struggle to grasp this."

"And you want the same thing? To help you get ahead in business?" That was disappointing, but understandable.

"Not simply that, no, and I think you know that and are playing devil's advocate. Europe has a very rich martial culture going back thousands of years. We have lost most of it, but thanks to the work of people like you, we're starting to get it back. I know you're aware that in the public's eye, you are a fringe element, not taken seriously."

"Keenly," Jack said with some bitterness.

"That is one of the things we hope to change. You are familiar with the IHFF? The International Historical Fencing Federation?"

"Yeah," Jack said. "They're the guys with the castle. They claim to have the authority to give the rank of master, even to arts that have been lost for—" He stopped, suddenly realizing what Hastings was getting at. "That's…that's you guys, isn't it?"

Hastings nodded.

"Holy shit! You're giving master ranks to people who win your tournaments."

"Indeed," Hastings said.

"But you can't tell people. No one will take it seriously."

"That is not so. I mentioned this is the second such tournament. The first was small, a test run. We've tried before, several times, without success. Only recently has the reconstruction of our arts come far enough to produce fighters on par with the Japanese. This is the first event with full participation by European stylists, and after this tournament we are going to make a big push in the community. We cannot and will not directly reveal the nature of our methods but as I'm sure you're aware, when extraordinary financial resources are brought to bear, few obstacles are insurmountable. This is going to be an exciting time for you Mr. Fischer, but much more so if you agree to participate."

"But the cost in lives," Jack protested. "People are dying, and for what? For art? For money?"

"Life is important," Hastings agreed. "But that is a choice that every man, and woman, must make for themselves. Modern society is obsessed with the preservation of all human life, regardless of the consequences or even the desire of that life to be preserved. We do not share in this obsession. We force no one onto the tournament field. Once you are here, it is entirely up to you whether it is worth it. We will respect your decision."

Jack closed his eyes. He had heard the answer he'd been afraid of. The choice had been made.

"I'm ready. Tell me what I need to know." This was it. No turning back now.

* * *

The taiko drums beat in tandem with his heart, the rhythm intensifying, pounding louder and louder as he held his sword in trembling, uncertain hands. He stood behind the red gate, the one from which Frederica had entered. Hastings had talked him up during his introduction, saying something about his insightful interpretations and dedication to martial purity, and then mentioned his success in tournaments and how he was one of the pioneers of cutting practice in the European arts. Then he'd introduced Marrone, and Jack had stopped paying attention.

The most frightening part was that he was alone, in more than a literal sense. Like most of his colleagues, he had had no teacher in the Western arts. Kanemori was a mentor, but he could not help him directly. He would live or die based on his own theories, his own understanding and the curriculum that had emerged as a consequence. What if he were wrong?

The drums suddenly stopped, and Jack started forward. He was so scared he couldn't think straight, could hardly control his feet enough to walk. The ground rolled gently under his feet, the motion of the ship barely perceptible until that moment of hyperawareness. His palms were damp with sweat, and he absentmindedly wiped them on his jacket as he passed the sword from one shaking hand to the other. He was grateful that the longsword was a two handed weapon, or else he might not have been able to hold on to it.

He saw Todd Marrone as soon as he stepped into the light. He looked to his left, to the table at which he had sat with his friends. Frederica was there, too far away for him to read her expression. He waved to her, like an idiot. There were more graceful things he could have done, as she had, but it was too late. She got to her feet and blew him another kiss, this time with the hand gesture. He made as though he caught it and, before he realized what he was doing, placed his hand over his heart instead of his lips.

Not bothering with a salute, Marrone raised his sword to his shoulder in Vom Tag and started forward. Just like that. He was advancing slowly, but Jack was quickly running out of tournament field. He wanted to call time out, to say he wasn't ready, but instead he raised his sword to his own shoulder and prepared to meet Marrone's advance.

"I have eyes like a falcon," Jack said under his breath, quoting Paulus Kal, the paunchy medieval fencing master. "So that I will not be fooled."

Marrone slowed his advance even more, then lowered his sword and allowed the point to drift offline, inviting him in. Jack remembered watching Marrone's tournament videos and remembered his use of this tactic. Marrone liked to lure his opponents into foolish attacks. He was a master of distance and timing, a very clean fencer who rarely suffered double hits.

"I have a heart like a lion, so that I will strive forward."

Marrone inched closer and started to twitch his sword, up and down, hoping to throw Jack off. As far away as he was, these movements changed nothing, and so Jack ignored them.

"I have feet like a hind, so that I spring towards and away."

Marrone leapt forward and cut. Jack sprang back, avoiding the strike, but Marrone withdrew before he could counter. He was very fast on his feet, faster than Jack. They exchanged a few token feints, each measuring the other. He was really good. Jack wasn't sure he could match him. He remembered that Marrone often admonished others for failure to use techniques from the sources in their fencing. Could he trick Todd into performing a textbook counter?

Jack raised his sword over his head in high Vom Tag, and sure enough, Marrone struck a Zwerchhau, the strike that was supposed to break the guard. Jack was ready, he stepped back, voiding, and Marrone's cut missed. Jack smashed his sword down into Todd's exposed hands, but the taller man managed to pull his hilt back and Jack's sword was caught on the cross. Marrone retreated hastily, his initiative broken, but Jack pressed ahead aggressively. He felt a primitive elation as he herded his enemy. He reveled in the control, the power. This was *his* fight.

Wanting to avoid the possibility of an accidental double hit in the frantic melee, Jack withdrew his attack and took a few steps back, bringing his sword into Longpoint.

Marrone was a distance player, and he saw Longpoint as an opportunity to snipe a hand. He brought the sword to his right shoulder and started to edge forward slowly. Jack read his intention. He had seen Marrone attack this way before, and he did not seem to realize that Longpoint placed the left hand father than the right, as it was lower on the two handed hilt. Striking the left hand would therefore put Jack's point dangerously close to Marrone's face. Would he make that mistake again?

Sure enough, he swung, quick as lightning, for the left hand, the only one he could reach from his right shoulder, stepping slightly offline to avoid the point. Jack almost missed it, but he turned his body and brought his hilt up in time to catch the strike and reorient his weapon. Marrone's sword caught on Jack's cross guard as Jack thrust. A slight extension of the point and the blade sank home, right into Todd's throat. Instead of the blunted tip of a trainer flexing against the reinforced bib of a fencing mask, his sword's awl-like point entered Marrone's neck with the sickening sensation of a knife sliding into a fibrous steak. He felt the tip brush against something hard.

Marrone dropped his sword and stumbled back, freeing Jack's blade. Blood poured from his neck like a ghastly water fountain. His eyes rolled in his head, showing the whites, and he fell to his knees.

"Oh my god, Todd!" Jack cried, rushing forward to help him, momentarily forgetting where he was and what had just happened. He was knocked aside by the doctors who pounced on Marrone like a pack of starving dogs.

Jack felt faint and his feet faltered. He almost fell, but managed to save himself. The doctors were screaming at each other, two of them were on top of Marrone while another pushed the stretcher. The third had a blood pack and was replacing the stretcher's IV bottle. The sword was heavy in Jack's hands, so heavy that he allowed its point to press into the ground, taking some of the weight.

"Will he…" Jack started, barely able to force the words. "Will he be okay?"

"Probably," one of the doctors said without looking up. "Just step back, sir, let us do our job."

Jack backed away as they positioned Todd on the stretcher. There was so much blood.

He felt a hand on his shoulder and turned around. It was Frederica. She reached for him, and he sank into her arms, letting the scent of her hair and the touch of her embrace drown out everything else. Only the feel of his longsword's leather grip, slick in his right hand, remained in focus.

Chapter 24

An art, because it is an assembly of perpetually true and well-ordained precepts, is advantageous to civil discourse.
- Ridolfo Capoferro, Great Simulacrum of the Art and Use of Fencing – 1610

They glided down the hall on feet so light they barely seemed to touch the floor.

"Tell me about Logan's fight," Jack said. He had been in a dark mood until he'd gone to see Marrone and saw that he was going to be okay, but now he was giddy, and she didn't blame him. She felt exactly the same way.

"He was great," she said, walking backwards as she held his hand. She stumbled and almost fell but he caught her and kissed her, and they both laughed.

"What did he do? Who did he fight?"

"I don't know him, Tim somebody, from Florida."

"Oh, that guy. I've heard of him. Don't know much about him. Tell me what happened."

"What's that thing when you bind on his sword and cut behind the blade?"

"Duplieren? Shit. Is Tim okay? That targets the head."

"Yes, Logan hit just hard enough to bite into the skull and they called it quits."

"Those doctors must be seriously overworked," he said.

"Yeah," she agreed. "Partly because of us." She giggled, and she knew it was wrong, but she didn't care. She was flying.

"Oh, you're bad," Jack said, waggling a finger. "You're practically evil."

"Let's be bad together," she said with what she hoped was a suggestive smile. She opened her door with her keycard and pulled him inside.

"I dunno…" he said. "I can be really, really bad."

"Show me."

She pulled him to her and they kissed with a passion she had never experienced. Jack had a lot to do with it, but it was mostly the exhilaration they both shared. They knocked over a lamp near the door, breaking it.

"Oh crap," she said. "That was a nice lamp."

"Fuck the lamp," he said. "We're both millionaires, remember?"

"Yeah, I guess we are." But what was money to her? Remembering that and its implications dampened her enthusiasm and she pushed him away.

"What's wrong?"

"Nothing," she lied, faking a smile. "Let's have some wine first." She hoped that would quell the gloom, at least long enough for her to get back in the mood.

"Sounds good."

"Red or white?"

He laughed. "White. I mean I like red, but, you know…"

She was confused for a second, but then realized what he was talking about and smiled.

"Good point. White it is." She went to the bar and found two bottles of Negro Brut and gave him one.

"I love how you do that," he said. "Just hand me a bottle."

"We all have our peculiarities."

He started to fumble with the cork. "Champagne? I thought you wanted wine."

She laughed, genuinely. "You're such a dark age savage. It's sparkling wine."

"Wine snob," he accused. "If it sparkles, it's champagne."

She screamed as his cork exploded and flew into the ceiling, then she fell onto the couch next to him and laughed. It seemed the wine wasn't necessary for her to be happy, but it would do for insurance. Her cork popped out with a lot less drama.

"Here's to us," he said, clinking his bottle against hers. "Medieval killers."

"Renaissance," she objected. "You're medieval." She was grateful to whatever powers of the universe had brought them together. Her last few days would be wonderful, but that had its own kind of sadness. They both drank deeply.

"Let me change out of this ridiculous costume," she said.

"Don't go anywhere."

"Wouldn't dream of it."

She went into the bedroom and flipped through her drawers until she found a frilly slip, then thought better of it and returned to the living room.

"We're both disgusting," she said. "Cold sweat, hot sweat, I think I sweated every kind of sweat there is today."

"Yeah, me too. What do you have in mind? Do you want me to give you some time to shower? Come back later?" He sounded disappointed, but that hadn't stopped him from offering.

"We could do that," she said. "Or you could get in the shower with me." It was amazing how comfortable she felt with him, this almost stranger she barely knew, and yet knew so well. Not for the first time, she wondered what could have been.

She took his hand and led him to the opulent bathroom, and they slowly and carefully removed each other's clothing while the hot water fogged the mirrors and stroked her increasingly bare skin with its comforting vapors. Every sensation was enhanced by her brush with death and its dealing. Every kiss, every touch was like the first. She ran her hands along his arms, slowly and methodically kneading the rope-like muscles. Should she feel guilt for finding him so intoxicating now that his martial prowess had been proven? Or was she finally shedding the corruption of over-civilization, returning to her basest human predilections? It didn't matter. It was what it was.

She stepped into the shower and pulled him in with her. As the water flowed over them, filling her with warmth, she took him in her arms and inside her, letting the heat, the wine and the exhilaration of their mutual experience carry her away. He held her tight, face pressed to her neck, his breath a light caress. She felt herself floating, almost losing consciousness as the pleasure spread slowly and powerfully throughout her body. It was like a dream, a state of altered consciousness.

When they finished, climaxing together, she washed him, and he washed her, and they made their way to the bedroom, where they made love, again and again, until it was too much for her and she finally gave in to the blackness and faded away.

* * *

It was bright when she woke, well past noon. She felt for Jack, but her bed was empty. For a moment she was lost, anxious, until she heard the water running in the bathroom.

Letting out a deep contented breath, she turned to get out of bed. Her legs stayed behind. She tried again. Nothing. She could feel them, barely, but they were weak, unresponsive.

"No," she begged, fighting a rising panic. "Not now. Please."

She stopped, concentrated, trying to force herself to feel more than her body was telling her was there. Despite knowing better, she cursed herself for not getting up early to take her shot. She knew it didn't work like that, that not taking it had nothing to do with her regression, but it didn't matter. If Jack hadn't been there, she would have taken it, and then—

No. She would not let herself blame him. She tried again, willing her legs to move, and they did, but not enough. She felt something warm spreading under her buttocks. At first she was confused, but then she realized what was happening. She was mortified.

She had wet the bed, lost bladder control from the numbness and the strain. Jack was in the other room. He would come back any second now, and find her like this, a grown woman, unable to move, lying in her own urine. The sense of despair that overcame her was a thing of animate darkness, a pit deep and black, filled with the crushing weight of inequity.

It was over. The fantasy she had built around herself had crumbled in a mere moment, a single exercise of her disease's malignant will. She couldn't live with such shame, couldn't let him see her like this. But what could she do? She couldn't move. There was no way to tell how long the regression would last. Seconds, minutes, hours.

She hated herself, disgusted by her delusions. She had fancied herself a warrior, thought that stabbing a man in the shoulder with a pointed stick made her special. What a fool she was. She was what she had always been, a broken and diseased woman foolishly clinging to a life that had overstayed its welcome.

Jack walked into the bedroom, saw her and smiled.

"Hey, you're awake," he said. "Wanna get breakfast? Or maybe order in?"

"Jack, stop," she said, her tone more firm than she had intended. He almost froze in his tracks, his smile transforming into a frown. A concerned frown.

"What's wrong?" he asked.

"I need you to go," she said. She couldn't force herself to smile, but she tried not to grimace. "I want to be alone."

"Are you okay? Tell me what's wrong." He took a step towards her. She couldn't allow him to come any closer.

"Jack, please, get out of here now." She held back the wracking sobs that desperately struggled to overwhelm her. She could just barely smell her urine. She had to get him to leave.

"Freddie, for God's sake, tell me what's wrong."

"Dammit Jack," she cried. "Get the hell out of here! Now!" She reached for a pillow and threw it at him. At least her arms still worked. "Now."

He batted the pillow out of the air effortlessly and took another step towards her.

"I'm not leaving until you tell me what's wrong. You're scaring me."

Another step.

She glared at him with all the hatred she felt for herself. "You just won't get the fucking hint, Jack. I don't want to see you anymore, okay? I'm done with you. You're overstaying your welcome. Now get the fuck out of here before I call security."

She had stabbed Casey with a sword, but she had missed his heart. The wound she inflicted on Jack had not. His face was blank, but his eyes burned. Without saying a word, he picked up his clothes and walked out of the bedroom, out of the apartment, out of her life.

First her father, then her husband and now Jack. The others had left on their own, she had not driven them away. Or had she?

After she heard the door slam, she wept, and the darkness consumed her.

Chapter 25

All fencers that look and wait on another's hews,
and will do nothing other than parry, they deserve
little joy in such art, since they thereby often become struck.
- Sigmund Ringeck, Ringeck Fechtbuch – 1440s

Jack stopped in the empty hallway and put his clothes on.

You just won't get the fucking hint, Jack. I'm done with you.

Once dressed, he walked aimlessly down the dismal corridors, trying to make sense of what had happened. He passed lobbies and foyers filled with people talking excitedly, eating, drinking. He paid them no heed.

What had he done wrong?

Had he said something? *Not* said something? He went over every detail in his mind, every conversation, everything she had done since the night before. There was nothing.

Had she seen him in the light of day, his tired old body, and been disgusted by him? She was so beautiful, so perfect, while he was a lumbering shaggy thing made of pale skin and wrinkles. That had to be it. But why had she not had that reaction before?

It didn't matter why, he would never know and that was something he would just have to accept. What mattered was that he had been given a taste of something wonderful and then had it cruelly taken away.

He thought of going back to her room, demanding to know her reasons, but he couldn't face her, not in such a pathetic way.

He passed a bar, almost walked right by, but regained enough of his senses to turn around.

"What would you like, sir?" the bartender asked, a thin man in his twenties with a thick moustache. Was *he* more her type?

"Whisky," Jack said. "Don't care what kind."

"Right away, sir." The young man took a bottle of Black Label and poured him a glass. Ah, good old Jack Daniel's, his familiar namesake.

"Leave the bottle. Hastings is paying for it."

The bartender smiled briefly. "Of course, sir. But Mr. Hastings owns the ship, he doesn't have to pay for anything."

"Does he? Good for him. Couldn't belong to a nicer guy." He swallowed the first glass in a single gulp, considered filling it again, then pushed it away from him and took the bottle.

"I'll just takc this with mc," hc said.

"As you wish. Is there anything else I can get you?"

"A new life," Jack said as he walked away. He wanted to go home, to forget all this had ever happened, but he was trapped. There was no way out. He had to ride this through to the end—so many more days. How could he stand being on the ship? With her?

The loss he felt was made more profound by Frederica's ready acceptance of the fact that he almost killed someone with a sword—no, not just acceptance, she had relished it. When Leyna shied away from him after he'd saved her life from Terrance, he knew that she was recoiling from the deepest and truest part of him, and that had hurt him more than he'd realized at the time. Freddie's acceptance had transformed him, freed him to be himself in a way he had never been able to do before. And now that was gone. Where in the world would he ever find another woman that would look upon the real Jack Fischer and not flinch away as Leyna had? Even Alison had never known that part of him.

He passed a wall clock and saw that it was a little past three in the afternoon, much later than he had thought when he woke up. When he woke up in her arms.

He ignored the clock at first—what did time matter to him now?—but then he remembered that the tournament was supposed to start at four.

Less than an hour, and then he could be distracted. If that couldn't take his mind off of her, nothing could. He wasn't scheduled to fight today, but—

But she was.

He went straight to his apartment and took off his fighter's uniform, tossing it on the floor by his bed. After putting on some normal clothes, he took a final swig of JD and put the bottle in one of the kitchen cabinets. He would need it later.

On his way out he glanced at the brass clock by the door. It was almost four. He practically ran down the hall to the elevator.

She would be there. He would get to see her. Maybe she would change her mind, maybe she would see him and realize that he wasn't as bad as she thought, or maybe—

He was being pathetic, and he had to stop. She had dumped him, it was as simple as that. Whatever he thought she felt for him, it was a lie. His own feelings, born so suddenly and with such fervor, would die in time. He had a life to live, and she had chosen not to be a part of it. Nothing to do now but move on. And yet, it didn't seem right. He couldn't help shake the feeling that there was something more going on.

How could someone say and do the things they had done, and then suddenly just decide it was over?

He continued on his way, slowly this time. He saw familiar faces as he got closer to the arena, but he ignored them.

He was the first at his table. He picked up a bottle of wine and wondered how he would open it when an attendant walked up behind him and extended his hand. Jack handed him the bottle, he opened it and handed it back. This time, Jack used a glass.

"Hey Jack," It was Logan. Boris was with him, and Rob would not be too far behind. "You were amazing last night. I just caught the end of it."

"Thanks. Sorry I missed your fight."

"It's okay man, there's video."

"Where's Frederica?" Boris asked. He was the one in a fighter's uniform this time, complete with his three pips. "She coming?"

"No." Of course they didn't know, couldn't know. In their minds, everything was still the same. In their minds, Jack's life hadn't been ripped apart.

"What's wrong, man?" Logan asked. "You look beat. Are you upset about Marrone? I went to visit him, he's doing okay. He was awake a little while ago. Couldn't talk yet, but the docs say he'll be fine."

"Yeah," Jack said, and now that he remembered, he was. Marrone was a jackass, but not in a bad way. He was a good martial artist too, an asset to the community. Jack had gone to see him, but he'd been unconscious at the time. He would have to go see him again before the night was over.

Logan was about to say something else, but Rob showed up, wearing a scowl to go with his tux.

"You were scheduled to fight today, Rob," Boris said. "Not going through with it?"

"You know I'm not," he said. "And don't worry, I won't try to talk you out of this idiocy. Since both of these other imbeciles did it, I know I don't have a bat's chance in hell of stopping you. I just hope you don't fucking kill someone."

"Stop being a dick, Rob," Logan said. "You made your choice, we made ours."

And Frederica had made hers.

Jack finished his wine, then poured another glass. The whisky was starting to kick in, but he needed more. They sat down, filling three of the remaining four chairs. The fourth had been brought for her, and no one knew to take it away. Jack wanted to call an attendant, to let him know that it wouldn't be needed, but he couldn't bring himself to do it.

"So you two got any pointers for me?" Boris asked.

"Just do what comes naturally," Logan said. "Don't think too much. It's just a bout, remember that. Nothing special."

"Thanks. Jack? You got anything for me?"

Jack considered leaving the table. He couldn't stand talking to them, not now, but these were his friends, and they needed him.

"Yeah," he said. "Don't just swing. Win first, then strike. The other guy is going to be scared, but you're not, because you're insane. He's going to make mistakes. See them. Use them."

"Thanks guys." He and Logan continued talking, but Jack tuned them out. Soon all the seats were full, and the old Japanese man, Saito, got up and started speaking. Everyone quieted down, and after he was done the drums began to beat. Junichi entered the field from the left while another kenjutsuka entered from the right. The drums stopped. They raised their swords.

Jack's awareness focused, tuning out everything else. The moment the blades were brought to bear, he came to life. His pain was not forgotten, but it was relegated to the depths of his awareness. He leaned forward in his chair and watched.

Junichi didn't hesitate, he all but ran towards his opponent and the moment he was in range he sprang forward, his sword a blur of motion. The other swordsman attempted to cut through the attack. Jack knew it was a mistake—Junichi was too powerful, too centered, too good. Junichi's cut finished, missing the other man's head, and ended up in his chest. The man stumbled back and dropped his sword while the doctors rushed towards him. Such a cut could have split his torso, but Junichi had pulled his strike and cut only with the very tip of his sword, opening the muscle down to the rib cage. A crimson river flowed from the man's cut kimono, but it was a superficial wound, almost surgical in its precision. Junichi was a true master.

"Jesus," Logan swore. "Why didn't he try to parry?"

"He did," Jack explained. "It's called kiri otoshi. You cut through the oncoming strike if you can keep your center better than the other guy. Just like the Zornhau in principle, at least the way I do it." It was amazing to him how he could view such a grisly spectacle and analyze it in such a detached manner. His experience on the field had changed him. What used to be nothing more than a mishmash of theories and ideas was now very real. He had been so wrapped up with what happened with Frederica that he hadn't stopped to see what had happened to him. Kanemori was right. His art had taken on an entirely new meaning.

"Well it didn't work," Boris said. Jack could sense his tension. That would be him down there all too soon.

"No," Jack said. "It didn't."

"I'm fucking scared, man," Boris said. "Do you think I'm making a mistake?"

Jack turned to face his friend. "No. This will change everything. Win or lose, you'll never be the same again."

"If you survive," Rob said, then cringed, expecting an angry retort.

"If you survive," Jack agreed.

"Ladies and Gentlemen," Hastings said. "I have the honor of announcing the second contest of the evening. Entering from the black gate, Mr. Arnold Montrose, who faced Mr. Eric Smith in honorable combat and came out the victor. Entering from the red gate, Miss Frederica Dragoste, who faced Mr. Kevin Casey and also emerged victorious. May God have mercy on them both."

Jack stared at the red gate as the drums beat their rising

cadence. When they died down, she entered the field. The sight of her brought all the pain back to the surface. She walked to her position looking straight ahead. He remembered how she had searched for him, her eyes desperate, filled with uncertainty, until she had spotted him. Could that have been just one day before?

It didn't make sense. She could lie to him with words, fool him in the bedroom, make him think she cared for him when in fact she was only toying with him for some twisted purpose, but she could not deceive him on the tournament field where all but the hard truth was cut away. That look, that had been real, and so had been the feelings behind it. He was certain of it.

After exchanging salutes, Montrose took his guard and started to advance. Frederica did the same. She was so graceful, each movement seemed so effortless, like gravity held no dominion over her. They touched swords, their blades moving subtly, then she lunged. Montrose's sword turned, deflecting her thrust, and his point sunk into her left arm. She leapt back, her face twisted with pain and shock.

Jack was on his feet. His wine glass shattered on the floor. She turned, and saw him. Her eyes betrayed the truth, just as he had suspected. She had withdrawn, Montrose had to wait. If he advanced before she was ready, Jack knew he would take the field and kill him.

"Jack, man, relax," Logan said. "She's okay. Come on, sit down."

"Miss Dragoste," Hastings's voice boomed through the silence. "Do you wish to continue?"

She nodded. The dark sleeve of her shirt had an even darker stain, slowly spreading, but she nodded.

Montrose wasted no time. He came at her fast, their swords touched, and she lunged again.

Why was she so careless?

Montrose's sword twisted for the counter. Jack leaned forward, fighting the impulse to leap onto the field. Montrose's point went through, but she wasn't there. She was under it, crouching, the point of her rapier behind Montrose's back. Had she missed?

Montrose stumbled, and the doctors were on him.

"The victor," Hastings said. "Is Miss Frederica Dragoste. Let us also honor Mr. Arnold Montrose for his sacrifice. Both fought well, bravely and with honor."

Frederica walked off the field without so much as a look back.

"That was amazing," Boris said. "She's really, really good."

"Yeah," Jack agreed, and suddenly wanted to be somewhere else, anywhere else. It was time for more whisky. "Guys, I'm gonna go for a bit. I'll be back."

"Come back to see me fight, man," Boris said. "I…I need you here."

"I will, of course I will."

He got up and made his way down the aisle, then drifted down the corridor and onto the elevator, walking without seeing where he was going. His mind was in turmoil, trying to rationalize what had happened between them. The look she had given him, just after she had been wounded, that was not the look of someone who had used him and thrown him away. That, and the night before, when she had found him in the aisles, those things did not mesh with what she had said to him in her bedroom. But what could he do?

The elevator door opened, he got out and turned towards his cabin. And saw Frederica. She was sitting on the floor next to his door.

He approached slowly. She heard him and turned. Her arm was bleeding.

Chapter 26

You shall drive all that you fence with the entire strength of your body
- Sigmund Ringeck, Ringeck Fechtbuch – 1440s

"Jack," she said, climbing to her feet.

"Frederica. You're bleeding. You need to see the doctors." He was tense, scared. What was she doing in front of his cabin?

"What I need," she said. "Is to give you what you deserve, and to try to make up for what I did to you this morning."

"What do I deserve?" She looked so subdued, so beaten, that his heart ached for her. Part of him wanted to hold her, to tell her everything would be alright, but the larger part was angry and would give her no comfort until she made right what she had done to him.

"You deserve the truth. Can I come in? I know I have no right to ask, but..."

"Come in," he said, touching his card to the lock. He pulled the door open and stood by while she walked into his room. He closed the door behind them.

"Can I get you something?" he asked.

She shook her head. "Just don't kill me." She glanced at his sword, which someone had delivered from the tournament field and left on his table. "Even though I deserve it."

"This is not the time for jokes, Freddie," he said with a trace of bitterness, thinking of the things she had said to him.

"I'm not joking." She walked over to the couch and sat down, her shoulders slumped. He sat on the opposite end, leaning away from her.

"What truth do I deserve?"

She sighed. "What I said to you...I didn't mean it." She wasn't looking at him. Her eyes were moist and distant.

"I don't understand."

"You will, I promise you." A drop of blood seeped from her sleeve onto the couch cushion.

"We should get you to the doctors," he said. "We can talk after."

"Dammit, Jack, just let me do what I came here to do."

"Fine. Tell me. You're right, I deserve to know."

"I'm so sorry." She reached for him, but he pulled back, without meaning to. He leaned back towards her, but she had already withdrawn her hand.

"Tell me why," he said. "I never thought I'd get the chance to ask you."

"I never meant to hurt you," she said, and turned completely away, leaving him to look at the back of her head. "But I knew I would. I told you, I warned you, from the very beginning, that I would hurt you, didn't I? But you didn't listen."

He remembered. "You did tell me." Did she think that made it alright?

"You have to understand why I'm here, for any of it to mean anything."

"Tell me."

"I came here to die, Jack."

He opened his mouth to speak, but no words came out.

"I wanted to enjoy my last few days," she said. "And, thanks to you, I did. Until…"

"Are you...are you dying?" Not this. Anything but this. Let her hate him, let her betray him, use him, dump him, anything , just not this. "What…how…how long?"

"I'm not dying," she said. "I want to die. There's a difference."

"Why? For crying out loud, why would you possibly want to die?" This was too confusing, an emotional sine wave with too many oscillations.

"I didn't come here for that, not at first." She turned back, and he saw that her face was wet, her eyes red. He so desperately wanted to hold her, but he didn't dare.

"But you said—"

"I'm sick, Jack."

"Sick? With what?" He silently prayed she would not say cancer.

"Have you heard of Multiple Sclerosis?"

"I've heard of it," he said. "But I don't know much about it. I know it's not fatal, someone I knew had it."

"Do you know what it does?"

He shook his head.

"It turns your body against you. It…a year ago I collapsed in my kitchen. Just like that, no warning, nothing. Couldn't move. My husband panicked, called 911. That's when I found out."

"Your husband?" He felt like a wretch as soon as the words left his mouth. The things she was telling him, and all he picked up was her husband. "I'm sorry, I…"

"My husband," she said, nodding. "He couldn't handle it. Maybe it was the responsibility…his job, his insurance, was the only way I could get the medicine I needed. I could never afford it on my own. My life was literally in his hands. Or maybe it was the way I walked at times, like a cripple, or maybe how sometimes I couldn't feel anything when we had sex. Perhaps it was that I embarrassed him in front of his friends, when I fell or dropped things."

"The night we met," Jack said, suddenly making sense of the myriad of small details he had missed. "That wasn't a cramp, was it?"

She shook her head and shuddered, wiping her eyes.

"And this morning," he continued. "When you yelled at me from the bed, you didn't get up…"

"I couldn't."

"Is it like paralysis?"

She nodded. "My immune system attacks my nervous system, damaging the connections. The attacks—they're called regressions—they come and go. It's different for everyone. Mine are bad, but brief."

"You said there's medication. It works?"

"Somewhat. I have to take a shot every day. It's very painful. Burns for hours. And it doesn't make me better, it's just supposed to keep me from getting worse."

"You feel like your body is failing you," he said, trying to understand.

"Yes," she said through her tears. "You have no idea, Jack. You don't know what it's like to live in fear of an attack, to never know when it will happen. To have people look at you with pity and disgust when you… I just couldn't handle it anymore. I came here to get money for the medicine, the Copaxone, but when I got here…"

"It was like a dream," he said. "You lived a life you never thought you could have."

"Yes. And I knew that it would be over. That I would have to go back to my own life, alone. To live knowing that no one gives a shit about me, that if I don't have enough money the world will just let me drown in my own filth while my body shuts down."

"What we shared," he said. He was afraid to ask, afraid of the answer, but he had to know. "What did it mean to you? Were you just using me to forget your pain?"

"At first," she said. "But then…"

"But then what?"

"It doesn't matter, Jack, don't you see that? What possible difference—"

"Tell me."

"You were the best part of the dream," she said, looking down at the floor. "The part I most wanted to last. It may be crazy, we've only known each other a few days, but I feel like…shit, I sound like a damned schoolgirl. It needs no excuses or explanations, and it doesn't matter, it doesn't change anything."

"Then no," he said, shaking his head emphatically.

"No what?"

"Never alone, Freddie, not if you don't want to be."

"Jack, that's nice of you to say, but…"

"I listened to you," he said, sliding up to her. "Now you listen to me. I don't care how long we've known each other either. This new life of yours, it never has to end."

"But you don't know," she protested. "You don't know what it's like to be with me. To tend to me when I have an episode. The first time I knock over a table at a restaurant, or soil myself in public…yes, Jack it happens. It happened in bed this morning, that's why…"

That's why she had been so desperate to get rid of him. Because she hadn't wanted him to see her shame.

He stood up, took her hands in his, and pulled her to her feet. "Freddie, you listen to me. I don't give a flying fuck about any of that. If you knock over a table at a restaurant, I'll knock over the one next to it, and the one next to that. If you wet your pants, I'll whip out my junk and piss all over everyone who notices. Do you understand me? I don't care about your disease. I just want to be with you."

She sobbed, fell into his arms, and put her head on his shoulder. "I don't dare believe you."

"You damned well better," he said. "Because I can't walk away from you again. I won't."

He kissed her, ardently, their lips clashing so hard that he could have described their movements with fencing terms.

"Just don't fight anymore," he said. "Okay? I know it's not fair to ask, but..."

"I won't. But you don't either."

"It's a deal. I don't need to, not anymore. I have everything I ever wanted. Now let's get you to a doctor. You're still bleeding."

Chapter 27

There are four causative elements which engender this discipline: reason, nature, art, and practice. Reason, as director of nature. Nature, as potent virtue. Art, as regulator and moderator of nature. Practice, as minister of art.
- Ridolfo Capoferro, Great Simulacrum of the Art and Use of Fencing – 1610

Everything was different. Jack had shattered her oppressive reality with his words, offering salvation, and she believed him. Instead of despair, there was hope, in place of solitude, companionship. The most challenging aspect was that she now had a future. There was nothing for her to go back to, she had thoroughly dismantled her old life, but there was somewhere for her to go.

It was strange, she had always been so independent, and now her life was in the hands of a man, the very sort of creature that had so terribly betrayed her. Prudence said she should doubt him, that in the heat of passion he was promising things he could not deliver. But this was no ordinary man, this was Jack, and that was enough.

She looked at him and saw his smile, a thing of pure warmth, and her eyes swelled with tears.

“Are you okay?” he asked. “We don’t have to do this if you’re not ready.”

“I’m better than okay,” she said. “And I want to.” She reached into the bathroom cabinet and fished the Autoject from behind the soap stack she had built when her pride had compelled her to hide it.

“This is what I use when I can’t reach a fatty spot,” she explained. “But it makes it worse. It jams the drug in, hurts like a bitch.”

“Well you won’t be needing it anymore.”

“You’re going to make me cry again.”

“You don’t have any fatty spots,” he said, running his hand along her thigh. “If this were me, it would be easy.”

She smiled. "I have plenty, trust me."

He slapped her butt. "Certainly not here." She laughed, enjoying his examination.

"There's a lot there, but try the back of the arm." She felt his hand squeezing her right arm, gently probing. The left, wrapped in gauze, was starting to feel sore, but the pain was mostly gone.

"Is this one?" he asked, feeling just above her right armpit.

"Yes, but it hurts too much there." She hesitated. "You know what, go ahead and do it. It will be better without the injector."

"Here goes," he said as he prepared the syringe. She felt a tiny prick and expected burning, but there was nothing. He did it very slowly, easing the medicine in.

"How was that?" he asked, withdrawing the needle.

"Perfect." She turned and put a hand on his cheek. "Just perfect." She started to tear up again, and he took her in his arms and held her tightly. "Thank you," she said, struggling to keep her voice steady. Could he have any idea what it meant to her? It was so ironic that the source of her shame now brought such comfort. Such a simple act, so small a gesture, and it changed everything. It had been Jack's idea to help, and her first impulse was to reject the offer, but she was glad she had not.

"It's nothing," he said, trying to smile away his fluster as he let her go and tossed the empty syringe into the waste basket. "What do you want to do now? We don't have to go back to the tournament if you don't want to."

"You have to see your friend fight," she said. "We should still have time. He was scheduled for nine o'clock."

"I guess so, but a real friend wouldn't make me watch him fight when I have something so much more interesting to do." He reached for her, but she slapped him with a towel.

They helped each other put on their fancy eveningwear and started towards the arena. As they walked, she noticed the beauty of the ship for the first time, the exquisite details in the workmanship, the artistry of the decorations. It was truly magnificent. They took a shortcut across the outer deck and she smelled the sea air, heard the rushing of the water. She asked Jack to stop for a moment.

She leaned over the rails, looking down at the waves, and took a hold of his hand.

"When I went to fight Montrose, I…I was going to…"

"I know," he said. "I saw it, but I didn't understand at the time." There was a long pause. "Why didn't you?" His voice was tight, his hand tense.

"Because of you. I heard the glass break. I turned, I saw you, and I knew I couldn't go through with it."

"It scares me to think how close I came to losing you."

She kissed him, then wiped her eyes. "Come on, let's go."

They entered the arena just as the drums began beating, and hastily made their way to their table.

"You made it," Logan said, raising his voice to contend with the taiko. "Boris will be glad. Hey Frederica, nice to see you again. That was great, with Montrose. How's your arm?"

"It's fine," she said, managing a smile. "Just a prick."

"Montrose or the wound?" Logan said with a chuckle.

She laughed as she took her seat.

"Rob," Jack said. "How are you holding up?"

"Fine."

"He's still being a little girl," Logan said. His words reminded her how young Logan was, almost ten years her junior, and it made her feel old.

"Lay off," Rob said sharply.

"Yeah, Logan," Jack said. "This is hard on everyone."

"Okay, sorry."

The drums died down and Ukrainian Boris entered the field from the left, the black gate, holding a longsword. His opponent entered from the opposite side, but it was no one she recognized.

"Who is that?" she asked Jack. "Do you know him?"

"He looks familiar. Holy crap, is that Andreas Hofland?" He sounded concerned, maybe even frightened.

"Yeah," Logan said, his voice grim. "I'm fucking scared for Boris, man."

"That name sounds familiar," she said.

"He was Europe's longsword champion for three years in a row," Jack explained. "One of the founders of modern tournaments."

"Here they go," Logan said, leaning forward.

Hofland advanced steadily, holding his sword low in an Italian longsword guard Frederica recognized as Dente di Chingale, or Boar's Tooth. Poor Boris seemed uncertain, perhaps unfamiliar with the position, and began to retreat, his sword held defensively in front of him.

Hofland's sword tip began to dance up and down, pressuring Boris, who continued to retreat. He was running out of space.

Giving up on his passive aggressive posture, Hofland raised his sword over his head and leapt forward with a powerful swing. Boris sprang to his right, his sword lashing out into a Zwerchhau, the same strike Marrone had attempted against Jack, but Boris used it correctly. His hilt held high, he caught Hofland's attack near his cross, the tip of his sword striking Hofland on the side of his head at the same time.

Hofland collapsed, instantly limp. His head was oddly shaped. A pool of dark blood spread quickly around his body. Boris stared down at him in horror, his face white, and dropped his sword. The doctors ran up to the body, but saw the split skull and stopped.

"Oh my god," Jack said, reaching out to take her hand. Frederica squeezed it tightly, trying to offer what little support she could. The chamber was deathly quiet. Several people in the rows behind them were on their feet. She had known that she faced death, they all had, but seeing it like this...

"I..." Boris stammered. "I killed him. Oh my God I killed him. I'm so sorry."

"I have to go to him," Jack said. Ukrainian Boris had joked about how he loved to kill people with swords, even though he'd never killed anything in his life. What people called the homicidal glee in his eyes when he fenced was just his love of the art expressing itself as pure joy. Would he ever be able to feel that joy again?

"Go," she said, urging him forward. He leapt over the ropes, Logan following close behind.

"The victor," Hastings said, his hand covering the microphone on his shoulder. He hardly needed it. "Is Mr. Boris Pyatkovskiy. He fought well, bravely and with honor. Let us bow our heads for Mr. Andreas Hofland, who gave his life in pursuit of his noble art. His name will always be remembered, and his family will receive the benefits of his sacrifice."

The room was quiet. Jack and Logan stood on either side of Boris, their arms wrapped around him. The only thing she heard were his sobs.

After a moment, sound returned. She heard murmurs, shuffling of feet, the sliding of chairs as people took their seats. Jack and Logan led Boris back to their table as the docs loaded Hofland's body onto a stretcher and slowly wheeled him off the field. They had draped him in a white sheet that turned red where it covered his head.

Frederica stood and made room for Boris, who walked with his swollen eyes downcast. They all sat down without saying anything and stayed quiet until Logan broke the silence.

"I'm sorry it happened like that man," he said to Boris. "But I'm glad it wasn't you."

"I killed him," Boris said weakly. "I fucking killed him." Seeing his face, hearing the strain in his voice, she started to feel foolish for her earlier elation. They had, until that point, experienced only the good aspects of the tournament. Death had revealed the darker side. The hardest part was accepting the fact that the tournament was about to continue. A man had been killed, but the show would go on.

Jack put his hand on Boris's shoulder. "You didn't mean to, you—" He was about to say more, but then he froze, staring at something. She followed his gaze, which led her to Rob. Jack was looking at his hands, in which he held a small black device with a single clear plastic button. It was about the size of a dime. She felt Jack's body tense.

"Rob," he said, his tone like ice. "Don't you fucking do it."

Rob started, jumping in his chair, and fumbled. He dropped the device on the table. Jack's hand was like a striking viper, snatching it off the white cloth before Rob could even attempt to reach for it.

"Give that back," Rob shouted, jumping to his feet.

"Sit down and shut up," Jack hissed, trying to keep his voice low.

"What the fuck?" Logan said, pushing his chair back as though the table were on fire. "You too?" He reached into his pocket and produced an identical device.

Moving too slow to force a reaction, Rob took it from Logan's hand.

"Hey," Logan shouted. He grabbed for the device, but it was too late.

"Rob don't," Boris pleaded. "Please."

Frederica was confused. What the hell was going on?

"No!" Jack shouted. Rob turned away from him and Jack seized him by the collar of his tux, but not in time to prevent him from pushing the button. A red LED blinked rapidly beneath the button's surface, then went dark.

"What's going on?" she demanded. Looking around, she noticed men were moving towards them from the aisles. Security, by the look of them. There was a murmur as the other attendees noticed the commotion.

"God no," Jack said, letting go of Rob's collar. "What have you done!"

"Jack," she said, grabbing his sleeve. "Tell me what just happened?"

He turned to her, and she let him go, almost taking a step back. She had seen real fear in the last few days, but this was something else.

"Do you trust me?" he asked, his voice shaky.

"With my life."

"Then we have to go."

"Where?"

"We have to get off this ship, and we have to do it now."

Chapter 28

The Noble War confuses him,
that he truthfully knows not
where he is without danger.
- Liechtenauer's Verses, Von Danzig Fechtbuch – 1452

He took Frederica's hand and led her down the aisle, away from the approaching men. People were looking at them strangely, exchanging nervous glances, but he ignored them. Damn Rob to hell. No, not Rob, damn that bastard Hick and his Eurotrash cohorts. It seemed he wasn't the only one duped by those sons of bitches.

"Mr. Fischer," Hastings's amplified voice called after him. "Mr. Fischer."

"Jack?" Logan said. "Where are you going?"

Jack stopped and looked over his shoulder. "Take Boris and come with us. Now. And you'd better keep up, because I won't wait for you." He looked for Kanemori in the crowd, thinking to take him as well, but he wasn't in sight.

Logan swallowed nervously, his eyes wide. He *knew*. They all knew, all except Freddie. How was it possible? How many people had Hick recruited?

Jack turned away and kept walking. No one stopped them, and as soon as they were in the hallway he stepped up his pace, almost running, dragging Frederica behind him.

"Do you want to tell me what's going on?" she asked.

"I'll explain later," he said. "Right now we have to go."

"Where? How can we get off the ship?"

"I depends where we are," he said. "If we're close enough to land, we can take one of the tenders, or maybe the pleasure boats. I saw some on the lower decks."

Suddenly she stopped, pulling him to a halt, and he turned to face her. They were near a glass door that led out onto the deck. Logan and Boris hadn't caught up yet, if they were even on their way.

"Jack," she said, her eyes narrowing. "You tell me what's going on, and you tell me right now."

He exhaled slowly, preparing for the inevitable. "Okay, okay. I don't know how long we have, but it's only a matter of time, maybe a few hours, maybe less, before this boat is crawling with FBI. And maybe worse. We have to go."

"What are you talking about? Explain it right now or I'm not going anywhere."

"Those things, those devices Rob and Logan had, they're transmitters. They send a signal that tells the feds where we are."

"How can you know that?" She was glaring at him, her brows furrowed. He knew she would be angry, maybe she would even hate him, but that didn't matter. What mattered was getting her to safety before they came and put her in prison. Such a shame, considering what they had both gone through to get to this point, but there was no helping it. He would not lie to her, not about something like this.

"Because I had one too."

She took a step back.

"You...you're an informant?"

He nodded. "I was." She took another step back, and he felt as though she had run him through with her rapier. A part of him wished she would.

"Where is your transmitter?" she asked, her voice devoid of emotion. "You said you *had* one."

"I threw it in the ocean," he said, looking down at the ground. "After we...after you told me you would fight." She seemed to consider his words for a moment. An eternity.

"Okay." Her expression softened, and she took a step towards him. "Let's go."

He blinked, taken aback. "What do you mean, let's go? Don't you want to know why? I mean I...I want to explain, I..."

She walked up to him, put her arms around him and kissed him. "No, you don't need to explain anything else, I understand. I was just surprised, that's all. I understand why you would come here looking to shut it down, and I get why you changed your mind. Both reasons."

"You understand?" That made one of them. "But I lied to you.

I mean I didn't tell you, which is the same thing. I didn't want to come here, I thought it would be different, like a bad horror movie, but…"

"I know," she said. "I felt the same way. I never thought it would be like this."

"I don't understand. You should be furious at me."

She smiled. "Would it make you feel better if I slapped you?"

"It might!"

She slapped him, so lightly it was almost a caress. "There. Can we go now?"

"But…"

She sighed. "Jack, you threw away your transmitter, and you did it for me, at least in part. So if you want to get us off this ship, or if you don't, I'm with you."

He stared at her, awestruck. She was remarkable. He knew that love was a thing of hormones, chemicals surging through the body triggering programmed responses, but he also knew that with her there was something else, a love of the mind. No matter what happened, no matter what the cost, he knew that he could not allow her to become collateral damage in a misguided campaign to enforce the will of an ignorant and apathetic society. There was only one thing to do now, and that was to get her off this ship and to safety, or die trying.

"Then let's get the hell out of here."

"Lead the way," she said.

"I have my phone with me. It's in my cabin. We can figure out where the ship is and go from there."

"Jack." It was Logan. He was running down the hall, Boris in tow. They both looked scared to death.

"Let's go, all of you," Jack said.

They made haste to his apartment, passing through nearly deserted corridors and lobbies. Just as they neared an elevator, they spotted a young man in a plain suit, obviously one of the guards. Jack tensed, ready for anything, but the man only eyed them warily as the doors slid shut between them.

"So far so good," he said. "It means they haven't figured out what the transmitter is yet, or haven't connected it to us."

"Why would they?" Freddie asked. "It wasn't yours. You tried to stop him. Oh, but that implies you knew what it was."

"Yeah."

"I can't believe Rob," Logan said. "How could he? Rat bastard."

"What were you doing with your transmitter?" Jack demanded. "I noticed you didn't exactly throw it away."

"I…"

"Yeah," Jack said bitterly.

"I threw mine away," Boris said softly.

The elevator chimed and the doors opened.

"Come on," Jack said. "We have to hurry."

They got to his cabin without seeing anyone else, and he went to his phone and turned it on. It was strange to see this relic of his old life, a thing he was usually never without. It was hard to believe he once thought it was so important.

"Come on," he said, waiting for it to power up. "Come on you piece of shit." It finally finished booting. He launched Google Maps and waited for the GPS to lock. After more than a minute of waiting he went out onto the balcony. "It should get a better signal out here."

Frederica followed him, while Logan and Boris remained inside, pacing nervously.

"Did you know?" Logan asked Boris. "Did you know other people had them? I thought I was the only one."

"No," Boris said. "I—"

Jack closed the veranda door, cutting off their conversation.

"It'll just be a few more seconds," he said. "Then we'll know where we are." He was starting to feel trapped. The situation was out of control. How the hell would they get off a cruise ship in the middle of the ocean? There were boats, and if they were close enough to land they could make it, but he didn't even know how to start a boat's engine, let alone lower it into the water. But there was no choice. Maybe once he was in the launch bay, saw the lift mechanism, he would be able to figure it out.

"There," he said. The GPS finally locked and showed their location. He played with the zoom controls until he got a good sense of scale. "We're in the Caribbean. About eighty miles north of Mayaguana, wherever the hell that is. Heading east. Hmm. We must be circling back towards Bermuda. "

"Mayaguana is a Bahamian island," she said. "If I'm remembering it right."

"Eighty miles. A small boat should be able to make it."

"Do you know how to…um…drive a boat? Sail it? What does one do with a boat?"

"Not a clue," he admitted. "Maybe Logan does. Or Boris." He opened the veranda door. "Hey, any of you know how to drive a boat?"

"I do," Logan said. "Sort of. My girlfriend's dad has a little speed boat we take out on the lake."

"Good enough." He started to say something more when he heard the door to his cabin swing open. There had been no chime.

Two men entered, the one in the lead gliding across the floor like a stalking wolf. Behind him was Teague, his cabin steward.

"Mr. Fischer," the lead man said. Jack recognized him from the gangway in Bermuda. Not the one he had spoken to, but one of the others. "All of you. You need to come with me."

"What if we don't want to?" Jack asked. He stepped into the apartment and started moving causally towards the dining table, towards his sword.

"Mr. Fischer, please," Teague said. His face was drawn, pale. He looked frightened.

"Stop," the younger man said. He reached into his jacket and produced a pistol, which he leveled at Jack.

Jack froze. He saw the gun, the sword, the severed arm falling to the floor.

"Don't," the gunman said, turning to point his weapon at someone else. "I don't want to shoot you, but I will."

Jack turned and saw that he was pointing the pistol at Frederica. She had been edging towards Jack's display cabinet where his other sword, the sword of war, hung on pegs behind a closed panel. In his mind's eye he saw the weapon discharge, saw the copper coated lead slam into Frederica's torso, tearing it open, destroying her.

When he heard Terrace threaten to rape Leyna, he had felt anger. Upon seeing Frederica threatened, whatever else he may have felt was eclipsed by terror that balanced on the edge of unimaginable loss.

The gunman looked at him, then back to her. Jack picked up a heavy crystal bowl and launched it at the man's head.

The gunman saw it and swatted it out of the air with his right hand, his pistol brought to bear against Jack in his left, but it was too late. Jack grabbed the gun hand as he lunged at the guard. The gun went off. A tremendous boom followed by silence and ear splitting pain. Keeping hold of the man's forearm, Jack struck him sharply at the elbow. He felt the snap of bone. The gunman's mouth opened, but Jack couldn't hear the scream over the ringing in his ears. The weapon fell to the floor, and Jack stooped to pick it up.

The gunman, his left arm broken, struck at Jack's head with his right fist, which slid off harmlessly, then kneed him in the head, which did not. The impact was like a hammer blow. Jack let go of the pistol, grabbed the man's leg with his left hand and pressed into his chest with his right as he lifted. The man tumbled over backwards, arms flailing. His head hit the edge of a chair and he lay still, the whites of his eyes glaring brightly.

Jack retrieved the weapon and pointed it at Teague while he fished a pair of spare magazines from the fallen man's belt.

"Don't!" Teague screamed. "Please!" Jack heard him. It was muffled, but his ears had recovered enough to make out words.

Jack turned to Frederica. "Are you alright?"

She nodded. He saw her shaking. Her eyes were wide open, looking from Jack to the man on the ground and back. Logan and Boris were staring at him with shocked expressions.

"Holy shit, man," Boris said. "Holy shit."

"You," Jack said to Teague. "See if he's alive." The cabin steward knelt over the fallen gunman.

"I…I think so."

"Boris, Logan," Jack said. "Search them for weapons, both of them, and then carry the unconscious guy to the Veranda. We're going to lock them out there."

Frederica came over to him while the others began frisking their captives.

"This," she said, her voice quivering. "This is real now."

"I'll get you out of here, Freddie, no matter what."

"Don't worry, I'm okay. I mean I'm scared, but somehow alright."

"Yeah, I know what you mean." Just a few days before he wouldn't have thought he was capable of doing what he had just done, but then he wouldn't have thought he could face a man in combat with a real sword either.

"How did you know how to do that?" she asked. "That man was…a professional."

"I didn't," he admitted. "I just used basic ringen—medieval German wrestling. I don't even do that much of it. Or maybe it was Aikido, but I haven't done that for twenty years. If you hadn't distracted him…"

"They're clean," Boris said. He and Logan lifted the unconscious man by his arms and legs and dragged him out onto the veranda.

"Join him," Jack commanded, pointing the gun at Teague. The steward almost ran through the glass door, and Jack locked it behind him. There was no way to open it from the outside, at least as far as he could see.

"That'll hold Teague," Jack said. "But as soon as the other one wakes up, he's going to break the door."

"How much time do we have?" Freddie asked.

"I have no idea, but someone must have heard the gun go off. Let's get the hell out of here." Remembering the gunshot, he looked around to see where it had hit but couldn't find the bullet hole.

"Where are we going, man?" Logan asked. His eyes were wide and he was breathing heavily. "We're on a ship. Where can we go?"

"To the pleasure boat launch," Jack said. "We're not far from the Bahamas."

"Pleasure boats?" Logan said. "Man, I can't drive a real boat. I was talking about a little sixteen foot runabout. That thing is huge!"

"You'll be fine."

"We'll need our passports," Freddie said.

"No time," Jack said. "We can always hit the embassy, make up a story."

“Good point,” she agreed.

“Let’s go.” Jack stuck the gun into his pants, hidden by the tux. They stepped out into the hall and locked the door behind them.

Chapter 29

In these times soldiers are a greater burden to Princes and to Lords, and more so to the populace in times of peace than in war, and because they are not trained in other studies than those of war, they hate peace, and much of the time they are the authors of turbulence and wretched counsel.
- Ridolfo Capoferro, Great Simulacrum of the Art and Use of Fencing – 1610

"The boat launch is on the lowest deck," Jack said. "I think it's in the middle of the ship, but I don't remember where." They made it to the elevator without seeing anyone. His head was pounding where the gunman had kneed him.

"Why isn't this place crawling with guards?" Logan asked. "The gunshot…"

"The veranda door was open," Jack said. "That channeled a lot of the sound outside. But still…"

The elevator chimed, the door opened, and they stepped out into the hallway. Several people, men and women in their twilight years, walked past them without giving them a second look. This was the main level, the one with the water fountain lobby.

"We need to get to the other elevator," Jack said. "The one to the..." He realized which elevator it was. "Shit."

"What's wrong?" Frederica asked.

"It's the same elevator to the arena. In fact the god damned boat launch is on the same level."

"Maybe there's another elevator," she suggested.

"Maybe."

They started walking towards the bow of the ship. Jack spotted a white uniformed attendant near a tastefully decorated ice cream stand.

"Excuse me," he said, trying his best to sound nonchalant. "How do I get to the lowest deck? Deck one?"

The attendant smiled and pointed behind them. "There's an

elevator just down the hall, sir. Not the main elevator, go about a hundred feet past that one. You can't miss it." He was a pleasant looking young man with a receding hairline and a Cockney accent.

Jack froze, uncertain how to ask for the information he wanted without arousing suspicion.

"All the way back there?" Frederica asked with a tilt of her head and a long sigh. "Isn't there another one the way we're going?" She pointed towards the bow.

"Yes ma'am," the attendant said. "There's an elevator that way. But it's a bit further, you might..."

"Thanks so much," she said.

"Yeah," Jack said. "Thanks."

"My pleasure."

They continued forward, passing through an indoor swimming pool and produce market sparsely packed with white and gray haired shoppers. Jack was surprised to see the market, but then remembered that it was a live-aboard ship. The elevator was just past a deserted hair salon. It came quickly, and in seconds they were on the lower level, heading back towards the center of the boat.

"There's no one here," Jack said. "I can't believe it's going to be this easy."

"There it is," Logan said, pointing to a sign that read *Pleasure Craft Launch*.

It was a large open bay that housed four speed boats, a bunch of jet skis and two rigid inflatables that looked like coast guard rescue craft without the markings. The outermost bulkhead was a big sliding door with a rubber seal around the edge, currently closed. Jack's eyes immediately focused on the rescue boats and their very large outboard motors.

"One of those should do," he said, pointing to the inflatables.

"They're huge," Logan said. "I don't know if I'll be able to drive them."

"You only have to drive one."

A young blond woman in a white uniform came out from an office in the back.

"Can I help you?"

"We'd like to take one of the boats out," Jack said. "Just for a little while."

She smiled apologetically. "I'm very sorry, sir, but the jet skis can't be launched while the ship is in motion."

"I was actually thinking about something bigger."

"Oh, well the larger boats definitely can't be launched either, they'd bang against the hull. But those boats are all privately owned. If you want, I can inquire about getting an owner's permission so you can take one out when we stop in Bermuda. You're with the…the um…tournament, right?"

"Yeah," Jack said. "What about those?" He motioned towards the inflatables.

"Oh, those aren't for passenger use, sir."

"I see," Jack said, then took out his pistol and pointed it at her. "How about now?"

Her eyes widened and she took a step back. She looked like she was about to scream.

"Jack…" Freddie said, but then shook her head. "Never mind."

"Take it easy," he said to the blond girl. "We don't want to hurt you. All we want is to get off this ship. Do you know how to work the crane?"

She nodded, her eyes locked on the gun. "Please don't hurt me." Tears began to roll down her face, and Jack felt like a world class scoundrel.

"I promise," he said. "I won't hurt you." He lowered the pistol. "There. Is that better? We don't want any trouble, we just need to get off the ship, okay?"

She nodded again.

"Good. This guy here is Boris, he'll go with you to get the door open. Then he'll take you to the crane, okay?"

"Okay," she said, her voice shaky. She was still crying, but seemed a bit more composed.

"Boris," Jack said.

"On it."

Jack watched them walk towards the office. It had a very big window facing the launch bay, making it easy to see that there was no one else in there.

"Come on," he said to the others. "Let's check out the boat."

"I can't believe we're really doing this," Logan said.

"Would you rather go to jail?" Jack could hardly believe it either. He didn't know what he was saying, didn't understand what he was doing. He felt like someone had taken over his body, leaving him a helpless observer. He understood such feelings were common in times of stress, but he had never experienced this sort of thing before, not even on the tournament field.

"No, of course not."

As they neared the boat, the outer bulkhead door buzzed to life and began to slide open. A breeze ruffled his hair as cool ocean air filled the bay. The sun was just starting to set, leaving an orange glow on the rushing waves. Spray leapt over the side, peppering the launch bay floor.

"We're going very fast," Frederica said, staring at the churning water.

"That's why I wanted the inflatables," Jack explained, looking at the one closest to the lift mechanism. "It's what they're made for. It doesn't matter if they bump against the side of the ship." The inflatable boat was about twenty five to thirty feet long with a small pilot house and two outboard motors, four hundred horsepower each.

"Did you see that on the Discovery channel?"

He smiled. "You caught me."

Boris and the young woman left the office and started towards the crane.

"You two figure out how to get the boat running, I'll be right back."

"Gotcha," Logan said.

"Be careful," Frederica said.

Jack ran up to the crane. "Boris, go back to the others. I'll take over here."

Boris nodded and took off.

"I did what you asked," the blond girl said. "Please, don't kill me."

Jack shook his head. "Don't worry, I told you, I'm not going to hurt you. I'm really sorry about all this, I just need to get those people off the ship, and I need to do it now. Do you understand?

"I think so."

"Good. Now…are all these boats topped off with gas?"

She nodded. "Yes."

"Good. How far will the inflatables get?"

She looked up, thinking. "Four hundred nautical miles at most, if you maintain cruising speed."

"Really?" Jack was surprised. He had figured they'd barely make it. "That's fantastic. Thank you."

"You're welcome." She looked uncertain, but somewhat relieved.

"You know how to work the crane? Can you get it in the water with the ship moving so fast?"

"I think so," she said. "I've never tried before. I mean while the ship was moving. I launch boats all the time when it's standing still." She seemed calmer now, which was good. He didn't want her making mistakes because she was scared.

"I'm going to trust you," he said. "We're all going to be in that boat. You could drop us in the ocean hard, or do god knows what else."

"I wouldn't," she said, eyes wide.

"I'm not going to threaten you," he said. "I wouldn't be able to carry it out." To emphasize this, he put the gun back in his waist band. "Please, we really, really need to get off the ship. Will you help us?"

"I guess so."

"Thank you. As soon as I'm aboard."

She nodded, and he started towards the boat. When he was about halfway there, he heard the pounding of feet.

"Shit." He raised his weapon just as three men, pistols drawn, ran into the launch bay. They spotted him right away and bolted to either side of the door as they leveled their guns at him, one going left, two right. The only thing close was one of the large speed boats to his left, so he ran behind it and knelt by one of the rubber cushioned steel supports that it rested on.

"Drop your weapon," one of them shouted. They had all taken cover behind crates of equipment by the door.

Jack turned back towards the crane and the blond woman and shouted, "Do it now! Get the boat in the water."

He saw her hesitate.

"Now!" he screamed. She flinched, then started working the

controls. Motors on the crane began to whir and the boat rose into the air. He saw one of the gunmen taking aim at someone or something on board.

Jack brought up his weapon and squeezed the trigger three times in rapid succession. The retorts slammed into his ears, but weren't as bad as the shot in the small apartment. The size of the room and the open bay door helped spread the sound. The man who had been aiming at the boat ducked behind the crate.

Jack heard several gunshots and felt the fiberglass hull of the speed boat vibrate as the bullets slapped into it.

"Stop shooting," someone shouted from the doorway. "Stop shooting, you imbeciles!" Jack looked and saw Hastings run into the bay. He was red faced, breathing heavy. He turned to the men behind the crates, his eyes filled with venom. "Have you lost your minds?" He turned to Jack. "Mr. Fischer, please put the gun down. We need to talk." He seemed to be completely unconcerned that he was directly in Jack's line of fire.

"I'm getting those people off the ship, Hastings," Jack shouted. "You might want to do the same. The feds, they're on their way."

"We know all about it, Mr. Fischer. Please, we need to talk."

"Not a chance," Jack said. "You can let us go, or you can have your men try to kill me, but I'm warning you, Hastings, if one of them takes a shot at that boat, I'm not leaving the ship until this gun is empty. Do you understand me?" He looked up at the boat as it moved closer to the ocean and saw Frederica watching him from the pilot house. She looked so frightened, and he knew it wasn't just for herself. If one of them took a shot at her, he would kill them all, no matter what it took.

Hastings hesitated. "Very well." He turned towards the gunmen. "Get out of here. Now."

All three stood and bolted through the door.

"Just like that?" Jack asked. Could it be so simple? His eyes tried to bore into the dark hallway beyond the open door, looking for signs of betrayal.

"Just like that," Hastings said. "You were never a prisoner here, Mr. Fischer. I just wish you would change your mind so that we could talk."

"Save it," Jack said and started towards the boat. It stopped moving when he got close and he climbed aboard with help from Freddie and Logan. It started to move again, and within seconds it was over the side, dangling above the open ocean, rocking in the wind. Jack was almost overcome by a momentary panic. What if she dropped them in after all? Was that why Hastings had sent his men away? Was it just easier to kill them this way?

The crane began to spool out cable, lowering the boat, slowly. As soon as it touched the water it lurched violently, slamming into the side of the ship, and Jack almost fell.

Logan started the motors while Jack and Frederica went to release the crane cables, but they were taut. Jack hesitated unsure of how to proceed.

"We need to match velocity with the ship," Freddie said.

"Right." He turned to the pilot house and shouted, "Logan, get it going, we need to match speeds with the ship to cut loose."

"Gotcha."

The outboards roared to life, and the cables slackened, then tightened, then slackened again while Logan struggled with the controls. Soon they were entirely slack as the boat moved under its own power alongside the behemoth cruise ship. To think that Jack had thought it was small when he first laid eyes on it.

They released the cable clamps and Logan gunned the motor. They pulled away from the ship, heading south towards Mayaguana, sea spray tickling their faces as the boat raced over the waves.

Jack reached out and took Frederica's hand, squeezing it.

"You did it," she shouted, trying to be heard above the roaring of the motors.

"We did it."

She stepped into his arms, and he held her tightly and kissed her. The boat leaped over a wave and they both fell on their butts, laughing. He felt incredible, a rush almost the equal of the one they had shared on the way to her cabin after they had both fought for the first time.

They were free.

Chapter 30

If you may not come to the Before,
then wait for the After.
- Sigmund Ringeck, Ringeck Fechtbuch – 1440s

"What's the matter?" Jack asked, coming to sit next to her. She had hoped he wouldn't notice her distress in the waning light, but Jack was Jack.

"Just thinking," she said. Logan had the boat moving at a steady speed and the ocean calmed enough to make for smooth running. They couldn't see the coast, but there was a GPS chart plotter that showed them exactly where they were. It would be a couple of hours before landfall, which gave her a bit too much time to think things through.

"So what's on your mind? You look…well…sad, I guess."

She sighed. "No, not sad, just introspective. This is all new to me."

"What is? Running from armed thugs and high seas piracy?" He smiled, but he looked worried, and she reached out to him, touched his cheek with her hand to reassure him.

"No, just us. You and me."

"I don't understand…"

"It's different. Back in the real world, a relationship is going to dinner, seeing movies, having sex in the back seat of SUVs. Drama is who forgot to take out the garbage, or how I caught you looking at some chick in a short skirt." She looked up him, her gaze intense. "Someone shot at you today. Yesterday someone tried to take you apart with a sword. You risked your life for me, you—"

"I only did what—" he began.

"Jack, shut up," she said, making sure to smile so he didn't mistake her words for a rebuke. "I'm trying to tell you something."

"Sorry."

"It scares me," she said, and felt his body tense. "It's too much to ask, it's as simple as that. I have no right. The fairy tale is over, Jack. We don't have our money, or we won't as soon as the feds put Hastings and the others in prison. Without that..."

"Uh uh," he said, shaking his head. "I don't care about the money, I never did."

"But that was in the heat of the moment, I won't hold you to that." That was a lie, she would hold him to it, and hated herself for playing this game. She had changed her life based on his promise, and she had no reason to doubt him, but he was giving her so much, and what was he getting in return? She was terrified that he would see the inequity of it all and resent her.

"Now you shut up," he said and put a finger to her lips. "I still have some money the FBI gave me, and they told me I wouldn't have to give that back if I failed, as long as I went along…I have that in writing. So that should buy us a couple of years. After that, we'll figure it out. I'll get a job…I used to do IT. Pays well, and I get big corporate insurance."

"Jack, listen to yourself. You're talking about changing your life. Going back to a meaningless job you used to hate. And for what?"

"Do you remember what you told me about what happened when you got to the ship? That you felt so alive, that you couldn't imagine going back to your old life? That you would rather die?"

"Yes."

"Well that's how I feel too."

She tried to speak, but couldn't.

"You think I'm doing you a favor, that I'm sacrificing something for you, but I'm not. You're the one that's giving me my life back, *you're* the one who's saving *me*. I'm sitting here right now, terrified, absolutely fucking terrified that you'll change your mind."

"I won't."

"So come live with me then, or I'll come live with you, or we'll get a new place together, wherever you like. I don't care."

She felt short of breath. "Jack, you don't have to…"

"Stop trying to get rid of me, or testing me, or whatever it is you're doing. It won't work. There's only one thing we have to decide. Your place or mine?"

She took a deep breath to compose herself. "I don't actually have a place to go back to. I sold everything, gave up my apartment and my school."

He slapped her thigh. "Good. It's settled. You'll come live with me. Right now. We'll go to the embassy, get them to let us into the country, and go straight there. You can start a new school. I own the building, and it's got plenty of space. Maybe we'll make a killing."

She let her tears flow and put her head on his shoulder. "Jack, I don't know what to say."

"How about yes?"

"Yes."

"Guys," Logan said from the pilot house. "I think we might have a problem."

Jack gave her a quick kiss and shuffled over to Logan. She followed, sparing a glance at Boris. He was sitting towards the back, oblivious to what was going on. Despite everything that happened, at least she could be glad she had been spared what he was going though.

"Shit," Jack said, staring at what looked like a radar screen. There was no circling line, but the screen refreshed periodically, revealing a large blip about ten nautical miles away, if she was reading the labels correctly. It seemed to be getting closer.

"What is it?" she asked. "The Invictus?"

"I don't think the Invictus can move that fast," Logan said. "And if I'm reading this right, it's coming from the coast."

"Can we outrun it?" Jack asked.

"Sure," Logan said. "This boat is fast as balls. But it's coming from the island, so we'd have to turn away and go somewhere else, but I don't know if we have enough gas to make it. We're down to less than half a tank."

"That bitch," Jack said. "She told me the tanks were topped off."

Logan shrugged, managing a grin. "You can hardly blame her."

"It's probably the Bahamian navy or coast guard or whatever," Frederica said. "They had to have picked us up on radar, and we didn't exactly announce ourselves."

"Well then," Jack said. "Shouldn't be a serious problem. We're not drug runners, and if they want to not let us in the country and escort us home, well, that'll save us the cost of plane tickets."

"Good point," Logan said.

"Unless Hastings reported this boat stolen..."

"Hastings has bigger problems," she said. She neglected to add that she didn't think he would do such a thing. Maybe it was the kindness with which he had treated her, but for some reason she trusted him.

"Good point," Jack said. "So we proceed on course. I guess I'd better get rid of this." He took out the pistol and spare magazines and tossed them over the side. She watched the weapon disappear beneath the waves and felt a strange sense of loss, as though her only remaining connection to that magical life on board the Invictus was finally gone.

They watched the horizon until they spotted the approaching ship's lights, barely visible amidst the rays of the setting sun that was almost touching the lip of the horizon. The ship grew steadily larger, until they could clearly see the gun turret on its bow. It was a gray military ship, its superstructure jutting with a mishmash of antennae and other protuberances. As it closed it began to turn to circle them, exposing its side. She guessed its length at about two hundred feet.

"P-60," Jack said, reading the white characters on the side of the hull. There was still just enough sunlight to make them out. Smaller black letters towards the stern spelled out *HMBS Bahamas*. Armed black men in woodland pattern camouflage stood on deck.

"You can tell these guys are on a budget," Jack said. "There aren't exactly a lot of trees out at sea."

One of the men on deck produced a loudspeaker and said, "Unidentified vessel, cut your engines and prepare to be boarded."

"Do it," Jack told Logan, and the motors spun down and died. The boat dropped off plane and rocked violently side to side. Her stomach started to feel uneasy.

The gray ship slowed down and drew up alongside them. Although small compared to the Invictus, the enormity of it next to their tiny boat scared her. It was an imposing thing, with its tall tower, armed soldiers and bow mounted turret, and it was right on top of them, looming in the twilight like a charging elephant.

Some of the soldiers lowered ropes, and Logan and Jack took them and tied them to their boat. Boris was on his feet, staring at the armed men with an expression of absolute terror. She couldn't blame him, he probably thought he would be brought to justice for what he had done.

The soldiers lowered a ladder over the side and a man with more stripes than his comrades said, "Come aboard, please." Jack stepped forward defensively and turned to give Frederica a reassuring look. She forced a smile, though she was almost as scared as Boris.

"What's the problem?" Jack asked.

"Just come aboard, sir," the soldier said. "Everything will be explained."

Jack boarded first, then extended his hand and helped Freddie up the ladder. She in turn helped Logan and finally Boris.

As soon as they were all on board, the soldiers shoved them away from the gunwale and patted them down, then forced their hands behind their backs and secured them with zip ties.

"Hey," Jack said. "What's going on? We're American citizens."

"You are under arrest," the stripe laden soldier said.

"For what?" Jack demanded, but all the fight seemed to drain from his voice as he noticed something in the direction of the superstructure. Frederica followed his gaze and saw a Caucasian man in dress slacks and a white shirt with a loosely tied necktie. He carried a blazer tucked under his arm, just above a holstered pistol and a small gold badge on his belt.

"We'll let your FBI explain that to you, man," the soldier said.

"Hick," Jack said, his voice almost a growl. She could tell by the look in his eyes that their adventure was at an end.

Chapter 31

...aim always at the openings of the man,
and fence not to the sword.
- Anonymous Commentaries on the Longsword,
Von Danzig Fechtbuch – 1452

It took them over an hour to get to shore, but it was an eternity. The flaking gray paint of their cell walls almost seemed to bubble from the stifling heat that the tiny porthole across the hall did little to relieve. The soldiers had separated the men from the women, leaving Jack to pace along the rust stained floor, tormented, not knowing what was happening to Frederica. Was Hick interrogating her? Were the Bahamians?

His rage had swelled and ebbed like a rapidly cycling tidal current, leaving behind uncertainty, fear and self loathing. He had failed them all, led them right into Hick's trap. They might as well have stayed on the Invictus, it would have been a lot more comfortable and equally fruitless. There would be no way he could talk his way out of it now that they had been caught running.

When the soldiers finally came to get them, Jack eagerly marched out of his cell and onto the deck, cringing away from the unbearably bright overhead spotlights. He saw Frederica right away and felt enormous relief, followed immediately by dread. They would soon be separated again, maybe for good. Once Hick fed them into the system, he would be completely helpless. There would be no one to reason with, no one to ask for mercy, no one to offer himself to so that they would spare her. The great American bureaucracy was an emotionless machine, turning its cold metal gears, blind to those caught in the teeth.

He heard the thrumming of rotor blades as they descended a gangway down onto the dock and saw a helicopter in the distance. The soldiers were leading them in its direction and he noticed Hick standing just outside. He certainly wasn't wasting any time.

It was a small, unimpressive machine, white and black with an open sliding door that led to a cabin with several uncomfortable looking seats. The wind from its rotors beat against his face, forcing him to squint and turn away. He looked back at Frederica and saw her hair dancing wildly.

"You should've played ball, Fischer," Hick shouted through an arrogant grin, his voice barely audible against the beating of the rotors. "Things would have been easier."

"Fuck you, Hick," Jack said. "Miserable bastard."

"Touchy touchy." Hick laughed, then motioned for the soldiers to load them into the chopper. Jack stumbled and collapsed into the nearest chair, unable to use his bound hands for balance. Frederica lowered herself into the seat next to his with a lot more grace. After Logan and Boris were seated, Hick boarded and closed the sliding door behind him, then motioned to the pilot who started talking into his radio. The Bahamians cleared the area quickly as the rotors spooled up.

Inside the helicopter the noise was almost as bad as it had been outside. Hick put on a headset that covered his ears, then took out a bag with a bunch of orange foam plugs and shoved one into each of their ears as the chopper rose into the air and headed into the darkness. By the absence of lights ahead, Jack guessed they were heading out over water.

He looked at Frederica and she met his gaze.

"I'm sorry," he said, but he knew she couldn't hear him.

She mouthed something back and smiled, and he wished he could reach out and squeeze her hand.

He stared out over the ocean, wishing he could be down there on a boat, running silently in the darkness, Freddie and his friends safely aboard. The sea was black, except for the occasional white swirl that showed up under the wan light of a crescent moon. He spotted several ship's lights in the distance, steady beacons in the night. One grew larger until they were almost on top of it.

The helicopter started to descend, and Jack realized that they were going to land on the ship. It was too garishly illuminated to be a Navy or Coast Guard vessel, which left only one option.

They were returning to the Invictus.

He turned to Frederica and saw that she recognized it as well. Her eyes were wide, either with fear or confusion, perhaps both. Jack couldn't be sure why they were coming back, but he had a pretty good idea. The feds had raided and seized the ship, and were combing it for evidence, on their way to Miami or some other US port to rendezvous with more of their ilk. Everyone he knew, his online friends, poor Marrone, all of the tournament organizers, Hastings, they would all be in custody, and there would be little their money could do to buy their way out of it. Despair overcame him. Would Frederica get the medication she needed in prison? Would she want to?

The chopper touched down on a pad on the ship's bow, and as the blades spun down, Hick opened the door, jumped out and offered his hand to guide the others. Jack went first, stepping onto the deck of a ship that had once felt like home.

A man was approaching the helicopter, kneeling away from the spinning blades even though they were well over his head. When Jack saw the man's face, his eyes widened.

"Mr. Fischer," Hastings shouted. "I'm glad to see you all unharmed. I was worried."

Jack stared, confused, swaying on uncertain feet.

"Agent Hick, please untie our guests. They're home now."

"Yes sir," Hick said, and Jack almost passed out.

* * *

Seated in Hastings's office, Jack held tightly onto Frederica's hand, afraid to let her go. He was confused, disoriented, but he did know one thing for certain. Somehow, by some miracle, they had been spared. It would all make sense, he was sure of it, but for the moment all he cared about was that they were free.

"First," Hastings said, glancing at each of them in turn. Jack and Frederica had taken the two chairs by the desk while Logan and Boris sat behind them on a small couch against the back wall. "I want you to know, you are completely free to leave, and we will take you to shore this instant if that is what you want, and arrange for travel to wherever you wish to go. You are not, and never have been, prisoners here."

"So why drag us back here in handcuffs?" Logan asked. Jack thought he understood, but it wouldn't hurt to hear it.

"You fled because you believed that you were in danger." He

hesitated, waiting for confirmation.

"Right," Logan said.

"At the time, because you were armed and on edge, I felt it best to allow you to leave so as to minimize the possibility of any of you being harmed. I tried to explain, but you were not in the right frame of mind, so I let you go. I knew that you would be more receptive once you were given time to consider and once you understood the full scope of our operation."

"You were right," Jack agreed. "I wouldn't have believed a word you said. But why the handcuffs?"

"Not everyone involved in your apprehension is sympathetic to our cause."

"That's what I figured."

"I suppose you have more questions," Hastings said. "I will, of course, answer them. But first, I want to sincerely apologize."

"For?" Jack asked.

"Those men who shot at you. They have been disciplined, and are spending the remainder of the voyage in the ship's brig. They exercised exceedingly poor judgment."

"I did break a guy's arm," Jack said. "And I pulled a gun on the poor girl in the boat launch."

Hastings nodded. "That was our fault, considering the nature of the way you were brought here."

"Speaking of which," Jack asked. "You said not everyone was sympathetic, but...Hick works for you? He called you 'sir.' He's on the take?"

"In a manner of speaking," Hastings said. "Though 'on the take' is a vulgar turn of phrase."

"What would you call it?"

"I may have mentioned before that our members comprise the upper echelons of society. Not the political leaders, those are but the hounds. Our membership comes from the ranks of those who hold their leashes. While this enterprise, this tournament, is our focus for the moment, our members engage in all manner of dealings that necessitate government compliance. Our influence is therefore firmly entrenched."

"That's..." Freddie said. "Frightening."

"I assure you, Ms. Dragoste, neither you nor anyone in his

room have anything to fear from us, not now or ever."

"So you control the FBI?" Jack asked. "That British thing, SOCA? All the others?"

"Of course not. Influence is a delicate game. However, this particular taskforce was our creation, its members handpicked for their loyalty, so in this instance, we are in direct control, as you witnessed."

"Wait a minute," Logan said. "So when we wouldn't go on our own, you had them try to recruit us as infiltrators?"

"That is correct, Mr. Holbrook. And when that didn't work…"

"The lawsuit?" Logan said. "That was your doing?"

Hastings nodded. "Indeed."

"Hold on," Jack said. "What lawsuit? I had a lawsuit too…Terrance...did you—"

Hastings's face turned dark for a moment. "That was very poorly handled. You have my sincerest apologies."

"But why would..." There was something odd he suddenly remembered. Terrance had held the revolver in his left hand, but he was a righty.

"He was planted in your school to provoke you into a fight," Hastings said.

"That's what happened to me," Logan said. "I injured him, and then he sued."

"Indeed," Hastings said. "That was how it was supposed to work. But you, Mr. Fischer, proved too difficult. When Mr. Calloway—Terrance—failed, the persons overseeing him took matters into their own hands and arranged for that fiasco." He scowled and his hands tightened into fists.

"Even so," Hastings continued. "Your life was never in danger. He was not permitted to harm you or anyone else."

Jack wasn't so sure about that. Thinking back, things fell into place. That first shot—Terrance should have hit him easily. He had been moving straight at him less than 20 feet away. An easy shot, especially for a combat veteran. He had missed that shot on purpose. But that second shot, something had changed in Terrance's eyes, and Jack now knew what it was. *He had changed his mind.* He had decided to save himself and kill Jack.

"Fortunately it turned out alright for all involved," Hastings said. "But I need you to know that it was not a sanctioned measure and it is not how we operate. You have my sincerest apologies."

"But he's in prison," Jack protested.

"No," Hastings said. "Not anymore. He is also quite well off now, if that makes any difference to you."

Jack nodded, his anger subsiding. His only feelings towards Terrance had been ones of guilt—he had failed him as a teacher, or so he'd thought. That guilt had just been relieved, and perhaps replaced with doubt.

He wondered if perhaps Hastings was lying just to mollify him, but Jack realized that he had no reason to do so. They were in his power, that much had been made very clear. Whatever he wanted from them, he would get. One way or another.

"Why go to such great lengths?" Jack asked. "I mean all that had to have cost a fortune."

"We've discussed cost in our previous conversation," Hastings said. "The amount of money involved is trivial. What is important is getting you here, despite the fact that none of you…" He turned to Frederica. "Almost none of you, would come here of your own free will. Not without understanding what we were trying to do, and seeing it for yourselves. Now that there are so many of you who have participated, beyond my expectations really, collective knowledge of the next such tournament will be seeded by your experiences here, and people will be able to make more informed decisions, hopefully without the need for such extraordinary coercion."

"The pips," Frederica said. "I noticed I was one of the only people with just one. I thought it was because…" She stopped herself, glancing back at Boris and Logan.

"Yes," Logan said. "What do the pips mean?"

Hastings smiled. "I believe Ms. Dragoste has figured it out. We needed a simple way for our security personnel to see which people needed more active monitoring. One pip indicates that you are here by your own choice. Two means you accepted the task force's request for assistance. Three indicates that you turned down the taskforce and required additional motivation."

"No wonder Rob pushed the button," Jack said. "He was a two…he agreed to be their spy right off the bat."

"Indeed," Hastings said. "The twos are the ones we were most concerned with."

"Is Rob okay?" Boris asked, breaking his silence. "What did you do to him?"

"Mr. Haugn is just fine," Hastings said. "Though he will be confined to his quarters for the remainder of the voyage." Once again, Hastings looked at each of them. "I would understand if you are angry at having been deceived."

"I should be," Jack said. "But I'm just glad it turned out the way it did, so I guess I'm not."

"I am," Logan said. "But I'm not going to cry about it. I thought we were done for just a few minutes ago, and now I'm a millionaire again. I am a millionaire, right?"

Hastings chuckled. "If by that you mean have we transferred the one million Euros to your account, then yes. That goes for all of you, except you, Ms. Dragoste."

"Why except her?" Jack demanded, instantly defensive.

"Her account now contains six million and one hundred thousand Euros."

Six million. She would never have to worry about being able to afford medication again.

"What?" Freddie said. "So much money? Why?"

"You won your division."

"But I only fought twice."

"There weren't that many in each category," Hastings explained. "We were able to arrange it so that each of you had to win two or three matches to win your division." He turned to Jack. "It is a shame, Mr. Fischer, that you are not likely to fight again. We had high hopes for you, but you have done your part, and we are satisfied, and proud."

"How do you know I won't be fighting?" Jack asked.

"I have some idea," Hastings said, glancing at Frederica.

"There's something I've been dying to know since I got here," Jack said. "Before that, even."

"Anything," Hastings said. " Just ask."

"How do you pick people? How do you know that all the costs, financial and otherwise, are worth it? How do you know you have the right people? Most people you picked ended up fighting, and I find that incredible. I mean…this is crazy, in a way, isn't it? To fight with sharp swords, no protection, little restraint? And yet…so many did. How?"

"It's a very good question," Hastings said. "It wasn't easy. To put it simply, we looked for people who matched a profile suggested by our Japanese friends, particularly those who have fought in the tournament, such as your friend Sasaki Kanemori."

"What sort of profile?"

"As you know, in the arts you have several kinds of people."

"Scholars," Jack said. "Martial artists, thugs, sport fencers and nerds."

Hastings laughed. "Indeed. We were not interested in scholars, despite how important they are to the growth of the arts, nor those with more eclectic interests, such as spirituality. Such persons would be ill suited to understanding the benefits of this tournament. We did not want those overly focused on competition because they seldom understand the true nature of the art, nor did we want individuals who were using the arts primarily as an extension of their interests in general escapism.

"Most importantly, we wanted people whose theories and views were closest to reality, which is another thing our Japanese cohorts helped us with. Certainly we wanted evidence of physical competence, such as tournament victories, which you all have in abundance, or videos demonstrating martial skill, such as Mr. Fischer's cutting videos, but the primary focus was on how you approach your studies. For each of you, the arts are a martial pursuit, and you work hard at them. Most importantly, you pursued your studies as though you would one day have to use them in earnest, despite the fact that you never believed you would need to do so until coming here. In short, you are the Western counterparts of the best of the Japanese swordsmen, and we value you to an extent that you cannot possibly comprehend at the moment. You are intangible cultural assets."

"I guess that makes sense," Logan said. "And I can't say it doesn't feel good to be recognized."

"Yeah," Jack said. "It certainly does." He shook his head and smiled. "This is all so crazy."

"If that takes care of the immediate questions," Hastings said, turning to Boris and Logan. "Gentlemen, if you will excuse us, I have a private matter to discuss with Mr. Fischer and Ms. Dragoste."

"Sure," Logan said, and he and Boris both got to their feet and headed for the door.

Boris stopped, looked over his shoulder and asked, "Am I in trouble? For killing that man? Am I going to—"

"No," Hastings said. "Of course not. We all regret it deeply, but we accept the inherent risks, just as you did when you stepped onto the field. Just as he did."

"He had a wife," Boris said. "Kids. I want you to give my million to them."

"No need. We have arranged a life insurance policy for him in the amount of ten million Euros. His wife and children will want for nothing."

"Thank you," Boris said.

"It was the least we could do."

Boris closed the door behind him, leaving Jack and Freddie alone with Hastings.

"So what did you want to talk about, Mr. Hastings?" Frederica asked. Jack saw her eyes sparkle and knew that she has been as deeply moved by Hastings's words as he was. He had called them intangible cultural assets.

"During the orientation, I mentioned exhibition matches. Do you perchance recall?"

"I do," she said.

"Me too," Jack said. "But I'm not sure what you meant."

"The tournament will be over tomorrow evening," Hastings said. "Junichi Kanazawa has already won the Japanese portion, Ms. Frederica the European Renaissance, leaving only the European medieval. Once that is over, we will have a grand ball to celebrate and there will be several exhibition matches, that is contests fought with sharp steel, but not a competition, merely a display of skill, matching swordsmen, and women, from different periods and cultures—"

"I'm not going to fight Frederica," Jack protested.

"Of course not," Hastings said, then turned to Freddie. "Junichi-san has asked for the honor of facing you in an exhibition match, Ms. Dragoste."

"Wow," Freddie said. "That guy is scary, but he's really good. I guess it's okay." She turned to Jack. "Unless you don't want me to?"

"No, it's fine, if that's what you want. I mean it's not a real fight, right? No one gets hurt?"

"Correct," Hastings said.

She nodded. "Okay, I'll do it."

"Splendid," Hastings said, then turned to Jack. "You, Mr. Fischer, have been selected for a singular honor. Mr. Sasaki, the greatest of the Japanese swordsmen, has asked for an exhibition match with you."

"Kanemori? But I didn't win my division. Shouldn't whoever wins fight him?"

"Ordinarily, yes, but Mr. Sasaki has stated that you are the only European swordsman he will fight, and we are happy to oblige him."

"Okay then. I'd be honored to fight an exhibition match with him."

"Excellent," Hastings said. "Now then, I'm sure you are very tired by your ordeal, and it is late." He stood up, and offered his hand, shaking each of theirs in turn. "I am very glad to have you all safely back aboard."

"Yeah," Jack said. "I'm glad to be back, as crazy as that sounds."

"Oh, before I forget," Hastings said. "Mr. Fischer, we are still working to repair the bullet hole in your apartment. Will you require temporary accommodations?"

"He will not," Frederica said, smiling.

"Splendid. Have a very good night."

They left Hastings's office and headed towards the elevator.

"What do you want to do?" Jack asked. "We're free."

"I'm exhausted," she said. "Let's go to my place and sleep like logs."

"Sounds like a plan."

When they got to her apartment, they found her dining table set with a grand feast, the hot plates still steaming.

"Oh wow," she said. "I'm so tired I forgot how hungry I was."

"Me too." His eyes found a plate of jumbo shrimp, the same kind from the reception where they'd met, and he smiled, letting out a deep contented breath. Being an intangible cultural asset was going to be interesting.

Chapter 32

...when you have the advantage, it is much better to proceed without waiting for anything else, reassured by the fact that the opponent cannot harm you from his current position. Also, this way the opponent will not have time to realize the danger and change his strategy.
- Salvatore Fabris, Lo Schermo, overo Scienza d'Arme – 1606.

They lounged in the spa pool, watching the early afternoon sunlight trickle through the tinted glass roof where its reflection from the water's surface danced in scintillating waves. The spa pool was much like the regular pool except for some tastefully placed plants and the subdued décor, but it was indoors, and they didn't feel like baking under the hot Caribbean sun.

They were alone, sitting along the edge of the shallow area. Frederica leaned against Jack, her head resting on his shoulders. He held her around her waist with one hand, the other stroking the goose bumps on her arm and shoulder. The cool water was soothing, relaxing. A far cry from the tension and anxiety of the day before. She wished she could swim, but she wasn't supposed to get the bandages on her left arm wet.

"If I told you I was madly in love with you," Jack said. "Would you get scared and run away?"

She laughed. "That depends. How long have we known each other now?" She took a sip of her drink, some sort of lightly alcoholic concoction with a fruity flavor. Drinking in the spa was probably not allowed, but if Jack could shoot up the ship, take hostages and steal a boat, she could drink in the pool.

"Lemme see..." She felt him tapping on her arm, counting. "Five days?"

"Sounds right. If a man I've been dating for five days tells me he loves me, I usually call the police."

"Ouch. It's a good thing you left your phone in your room."

"Well, you'd get a reprieve anyway."

"Oh?"

"I'd have to call them on myself too, and we can hardly have that."

He took a deep breath and she rode his expanding chest.

"So are you mad?" she asked. "I know yesterday you said you weren't, but…"

"At what? Oh, being tricked into coming here? No, not at all."

She found that hard to believe. "How can you not be? I mean they put you through all that."

"Because they had to. I would never have come on my own, and then I would never have fought. Do you know how different everything is now?"

She was about to answer, but he chuckled and said, "Of course you do. When we go back to teaching, back to practicing, it will never be the same again. We won't ever question what we're doing, wonder if we're wasting time, wonder if we would have had what it takes had we lived in those days. I feel like my life's work means something now, and then of course there's the way these guys treat us. I talked to Hastings before I fought…they have plans for us. This is not the end of it, just the beginning."

"It's a little bit wonderful," she agreed.

"But all that isn't what really matters to me."

"Oh?"

"If they hadn't tricked me into coming here, I never would have met you. So am I mad at them? Fuck no. If I could, I'd help them fool my dumb ass all over again just to make doubly sure I'd end up here."

"Did you know that when you say very romantic things you tend to curse?" He also tended to make her choke up, but she wasn't about to tell him that.

"Really? I say very romantic things?"

She spurted the fruity blend into the pool water, laughing so hard she almost fell off of him and barely managed to save her bandaged shoulder from a dunking.

"So should we get going?" he asked when she finally got herself under control. "We don't have much time." They had slept through the night and half the day, waking up briefly in the morning to make love before going back to sleep. The spa pool's wall clock read two in the afternoon, which gave them an hour to get ready and get to the arena.

"If we must," she said.

They climbed out of the pool, dried off and headed to her cabin, where their dry cleaned evening wear was waiting for them. In another situation, she might have found it creepy how their hosts seemed to know everything they were about to do. Well, almost everything–Jack had surprised them the day before. But their attentions made her feel taken care of, and that was something she'd had entirely too little of before coming to the tournament, meeting Jack and becoming an intangible cultural asset. That last part made her laugh.

"What's so funny now?" he asked. She hadn't realized she'd laughed out loud.

"The things Hastings said last night. About us being cultural assets." She turned her back to him. "Zip me up." She felt a tingle as his hands touched her spine. She wished they had time to fool around, but she didn't want to miss Logan's fight. It was the division championship, the one Jack was supposed to win. The fact that he wasn't going to did not disappoint her as it might have before. After the things she had seen him do, even the primordial beast woman that lived in her subconscious was satisfied.

"Yeah," he said. "It feels so weird, doesn't it? We fool around with swords and these people treat us like dignitaries."

She chuckled. "It's good to be appreciated."

Once dressed, they made their way to the arena, passing familiar faces. She couldn't help but feel a sense of depressing finality. Today would be the last day of the tournament, and though they had many days left on the ship as it returned to Bermuda, this would be the last night of an event that had changed her life forever in a way she could never have hoped for. She reached out to Jack, grabbing his hand, and he turned to her, puzzled.

"Everything okay?"

"Yes, I'm just…you know, it's the last day."

"I know." He squeezed her hand and held it as they walked.

"Excuse me," someone said in a thick Japanese accent. She turned and saw Junichi walking towards them.

"Hello," she said, extending her hand. The Japanese man took it awkwardly and bowed. She returned the gesture, though she didn't know how long to hold it or how low to go. It would have to be good enough.

"Hello," he said, then turned to Jack and exchanged quick bows.

"I want to say," he said. "I am looking forward to our…how do you say…exhi…" His English was pretty good despite the accent.

"Exhibition match," she said.

"Yes, thank you. I am looking forward to our exhibition match."

"I am also," she said, though in truth she was more than a bit nervous. Junichi wasn't as imposing in a tuxedo as he was on the tournament field, but there was something about him, the way he carried himself. He was like a lion lounging lazily under the sun. He seemed passive, but that was a façade.

Junichi turned to Jack. "I understand you will also have exhibition match. With Sasaki-san."

"Yes," Jack said. "It was Kanemori's…Sasaki-san's idea." She could tell he was uneasy around Junichi, though he wasn't intimidated, at least not as far as she could tell.

"Sasaki-san should fight tournament winner, or division winner. You will not fight again? Try to win division?"

"I will not."

"Why?"

"Personal reasons."

"I see. Sasaki-san, he is good friend to you?"

"Yes, he is."

"I see." He turned away from Jack, dismissively, and faced Frederica. "Good day."

"Good day," she said, then watched him walk away.

"Charming guy," Jack said.

"He's an asshole." She was angry, partly at Junichi, but also at herself. There was more than just her feelings at stake. What if Jack needed to fight?

"Nah, he just doesn't understand. He probably thinks I'm scared to fight again."

"But you're not. Jack, I have no right to deny you. If you want to fight, then—"

"But I *am* scared," he said, keeping his voice low so that others in the hall didn't hear. "I'm terrified, actually, just not for the reasons he thinks. I have so much to lose this time around...too much. And so little to gain, it's just not worth it. I wanted to face the reality, and I did. I'm satisfied."

"Five million Euros? That's so little to gain? Winning your division?"

"Compared to the chance of losing you? Of leaving you alone? None of that is worth anything."

She looked away. "Stop it, you're going to make me cry again. My eyeliner will run."

He smiled. "Did I say something romantic? At least I didn't curse this time." He always managed to make her laugh when it counted.

They found their way to their table, now with only three chairs. Logan was there, wearing his fighter's uniform.

"Where's Boris?" Jack asked.

"He's going to sit this one out," Logan said. "He's bummed about what happened."

"I guess I can't blame him."

"I can," Logan said. "He's going to miss my fight. What if I…"

"You won't," Jack said. "You're going to kick ass and take names. You're the best longsword fencer in the world." He grinned. "After me, of course."

"Thanks."

"Hey, speaking of which," Jack said. "Why are you here? Shouldn't you be getting ready?"

"No need," he said. "They'll get me from here when it's time. I wanted to see you guys first."

"We're here for you," Jack said.

"Yes," Frederica said. "We'll be rooting."

"Thanks guys."

They took their seats and waited while others filled the room. Frederica watched the back rows, wondering what kind of people their patrons were. She'd never been overly curious about them before, but after the things Hastings had said, it was hard not to want to learn all she could about them. Why did they go to such great lengths? How could it possibly matter so much to them?

All too soon the lights dimmed and an attendant came and fetched Logan.

"Ladies and Gentlemen," Hastings said, and Frederica warmed at the sound of this voice. She realized she was growing quite fond of Hastings, like a father figure to fill the void left when her own walked out on her. "We are about to conclude this tournament with a final contest between two medieval German stylists, but before I announce them, I want to take a few minutes and thank everyone for what has been an extraordinary event. To the men and women who took up arms, and to those who chose not to but offered their support to their fellows, I extend our deepest gratitude and respect."

"How many women fighters are there?" Jack asked her. "I hadn't noticed." Hastings continued talking, thanking people and expressing his delight at the way things had turned out.

She smiled. "Besides me? Not many, maybe two or three others. There was a longsword chick that fought while you were getting ready." The tone of Hastings's speech changed as he discussed the tournament's two fatalities. She had apparently missed the other one, a fact for which she was grateful.

"Really?"

"Yup. Maybe you want to meet her."

"Nah, I have all the dangerous women I can handle."

"Shush, he's announcing the fighters."

"Entering from the black gate," Hastings said. "Mr. Tyler O'Neil, who faced Mr. Samuel Windham in honorable combat and came out the victor. Entering from the red gate, Mr. Logan Holbrook, who faced Mr. Tim Parker and also emerged victorious. God have mercy on them both."

"The red gate," Jack said. "That's our gate." The drums beat and died, and the two fighters came onto the field.

"He's, um, very tall," she said. Indeed, O'Neil was huge, towering over Logan even from across the field.

"Shit," Jack said. "That's going to be tough." She heard the fear in his voice and reached out and took his hand.

Logan wasted no time and started right towards O'Neil, who

held his sword on his shoulder. Logan raised his sword behind his head, transitioning through the aggressive Zornhut guard and struck at O'Neil as soon as he was close enough.

The big man took a small step back and Logan missed, but brought his sword up in time to stop O'Neil's chasing cut. Logan was too shaken to follow up and leapt back. Both fighters started edging away, regaining composure.

"Come on Logan," Jack said. "Don't just attack, make an opening."

Logan leaped forward again and cut, or so it seemed. O'Neil stepped back and raised his sword, ready for the chasing, but Logan's sword was still held high. It had been a feint. His friend's blade lashed out, scoring against O'Neil's forearm. Blood showed through the gash in the fabric of the big man's sleeve.

Both fighters retreated, and Hastings said, "Mr. O'Neil?"

O'Neil nodded, and Jack saw Logan deflate slightly.

"Damn, I thought that would be it," Jack said. "He must have pulled it back in time so only the tip got him."

Logan lowered his sword until the point was on the ground and advanced slowly.

"The Fool," Jack muttered.

"Why? What's he doing wrong?"

"No, that's what that guard is called."

"Oh, right, I'm used to the German name."

"He better know what he's doing. He's playing the losing role, either gambling that O'Neil won't go deep enough into the play or he wants to reverse the slice. Goddammit, Logan. Play it safe!"

O'Neil advanced slowly, his sword back up on his shoulder.

"Shit, he's going to do the textbook counter, but O'Neil is too tall."

The big man leapt forward, his sword arcing over Logan's head, hands held high. Logan raised his sword to catch the attack. O'Neil immediately pushed his pommel forward, shoving Logan's hands aside as the smaller man tried to slice at his arms.

"Shit," Jack cursed, pressing forward so hard their table's legs scraped against the floor.

There was a faint tapping sound as O'Neil's pommel smashed into Logan's forehead.

Logan crumpled to the floor as O'Neil raised his sword for a finishing strike, then seemed to realize what he was doing and backed away. The rushing doctors knelt before Logan.

One of them held out his hand, thumbs up.

"Oh thank god," Jack said.

The docs helped Logan up and onto a stretcher as Hastings announced the victor. He was bleeding profusely and wobbled on his feet, but he was alive, and the docs didn't seem overly concerned.

"It's done," Frederica said, and felt herself tearing up. It was over, she and her new friends were alive, and she was, beyond all hope, happy.

Chapter 33

Under the sword lifted high,
there is hell making you tremble.
- Miyamoto Musashi, Go Rin No Sho
(Book of Five Rings), 1645

Jack knelt down, his hands on his knees, sword hilt pressing painfully into his leg. The spectator's cheers drowned out his labored breaths as he looked at all the horrible nicks in the blade of the longsword they had lent him for the fight. He was thankful he had not been asked to use his own.

Kanemori clapped him on the back, then helped him up. "Awesome." He wore a goofy grin that made Jack smile.

"That was…intense," Jack said. "I was fucking terrified, man." Sharp blades, moving faster than the eyes could see just inches from their faces. It was one of the most nerve wracking and amazing experiences of his life, almost as much so as the real fight had been.

"You didn't show it."

"Just don't smell my pants," Jack said, smiling.

Kanemori stopped for a moment and shook with silent laughter.

"Ladies and Gentlemen," Hastings said from his usual table. "A final round of applause for Sasaki Kanemori and Jack Fischer. A splendid display of martial prowess." The blue blooded crowd did not hoot and holler in the way a more plebian assembly would have, but they made their satisfaction known in their own way.

"Come," Kanemori said. "Let's get our jackets and get a drink."

"Can't, gotta watch Freddie." Fighting in tuxedos was weird, even without the jacket. Jack felt a bit like James Bond.

"Right. I'll bring you a drink and we'll watch together."

"Sounds good."

They walked out of the arena as Hastings announced Frederica's match with Junichi. She approached in the same glittering black dress he had zipped her into earlier, carrying her rapier like an evening accessory. She looked so beautiful that Jack felt an almost painful love for her. He wanted to scream, to jump through the roof or pound his fists on his chest. Something, anything to express what he was feeling.

As she passed them, she stopped and kissed him. "That was fantastic. You're amazing." She turned to Kanemori. "Both of you."

"Thank you," Kanemori said, blushing.

"You'll be even better," Jack said, and squeezed her hand. "Good luck, and be safe." He wondered how she would fight in that dress and heels, but he was sure their sponsors had it all figured out.

He watched her walk onto the field, where Junichi was already waiting. He was also wearing a tux, sans jacket, though he had removed his bow tie.

"He won't hurt her, will he?" Jack asked.

"No way," Kanemori said. "He's fantastic."

"As good as you?"

"Maybe. But I'll never find out. They won't let me fight any more tournaments. Don't worry, the guy has amazing control, I've seen it. You have nothing to fear. He's ballsy as hell too, with that samurai haircut. You sport something like that in a place like this, you better be able to back it up, and he did."

"That's a lot coming from you, man. I'm glad it's him in there then."

Kanemori nodded. "He won't touch a hair on her body, if for no other reason than that to do so would bring great shame on him. Lemme go get our drinks."

Jack found his usual table, though it was depressingly empty. Rob was confined, Boris was sulking in his cabin and Logan lay in the recovery room next to Todd Marrone. So much had happened in so short a time.

"...something I'm sure many of you have wondered, just as I have," Hastings said. "Can the deadly and elegant rapier triumph against the legendary katana? Although this is an exhibition match, it is not truly anachronistic, as accounts of such duels do in fact exist, though both their authenticity and bias remain in question.

What we have here is an extraordinary contest between two masters of their respective weapons…"

Jack turned his attention to Frederica, who had taken off her shoes and unbuttoned one side of her dress, revealing a long slit all the way up her slender thigh. She stretched on bent knees, going from one to the other. Jack looked around, noticing how some of the men were looking at her. He found such attention especially disturbing from some of the old men in the top rows. They had the money and influence to—

No, there was no point in thinking like that. These people had done right by them so far, and they didn't deserve his suspicions.

"Here you go," Kanemori said, handing him a glass of champagne. "I tried to find you some whisky, but I got bored."

Jack chuckled. "Annoyingly honest as usual."

"At least I'm not a racist."

"Like hell. You're twice the racist I am. Why do you assume I want to drink whisky?"

"Because you're Irish."

"But I'm not Irish."

Kanemori shrugged. "All whites look the same."

"I should have cut you out there."

"Too late now." Kanemori put a hand on his arm. "Relax, man, don't be so nervous. She's going to be fine."

Jack nodded, suddenly realizing he was trembling. All the banter had been to cover up his fear.

"You really love her don't you?" Kanemori asked. "After so short a time?"

"I really do."

Kanemori nodded. "I'm glad for you. It's about time you found someone again."

The taiko drums exploded into action as Junichi and Frederica approached each other, exchanged handshakes and bows, and returned to their starting positions.

"Shit," Jack said, shaking. "This is it man. This is it."

"Relax."

"How would you feel if it was your girlfriend out there?"

Kanemori laughed. "I'd be scared as hell…for Junichi."

The drums died and they took their guards and began to

approach. Frederica stood in the forward guard, called Quarta if he remembered correctly, with her waist tucked in and her upper body leaning forward. Her rapier's wicked point menaced Junichi from a considerable distance, rendering Chudan almost useless. He tried it anyway, attempting to beat her sword aside. With a twirl of the point she effortlessly changed through to the other side of his blade and lunged. He was wickedly fast, striking back to center, but he was in a losing battle. The rapier's complex hilt protected his closest target, so all he could do was defend against her clever twists and turns until he made a mistake and got stabbed. He came dangerously close to her arm, and it wasn't clear whether he would have been able to cut her there, but neither was it clear if she could have stabbed him.

Suddenly he stepped out to the side and forward, moving past her point, but she knocked his cut aside with the hilt and swiped at him with one of her slicing cuts. He retreated, and Frederica let him go. He didn't look happy. There was no decisive victory, it could have gone either way.

Approaching again, he tried a different strategy and raised his sword over his head in Dai Jodan, posturing, pressing forward aggressively. Freddie didn't hesitate, she held her guard and walked towards him. He stepped forward suddenly and powerfully, moving around her point and cut hard at her head. She raised her hilt and for a moment Jack was terrified that the delicate rapier would not be able to stop the cut, but as the katana's blade struck the hilt it stopped cold with a high pitched clang as Frederica pressed her blade forward and over Junichi's shoulder. She could have scored. The spectators clapped and cheered, recognizing the victory.

"Out-fucking-standing," Kanemori said. "Man, your woman is dangerous."

"Yeah," Jack said, too nervous to say more. Junichi had underestimated the rapier, but he wouldn't make that mistake again.

The combatants withdrew.

"Dude, he looks pissed," Jack said. "When is this going to be over?"

"Don't worry, he's a hot head but he won't do anything stupid.

He's not an idiot."

They clashed again, Junichi's blade a blur of motion as he tried to get past the rapier's point. He succeeded and struck at her head.

Jack would have leapt to his feet but Kanemori grabbed his sleeve.

The sword stopped short and Freddie stumbled back, clearly unnerved. The crowd cheered again, recognizing Junichi's point.

"Damn," Kanemori said. "He's really good. Wicked fast. He's figured her out now. Probably never faced a different weapon before, but now he's over it."

"For a second I thought…"

"I told you man, you need to relax. It'll be fine."

Once again they closed, and blades began to dance, too fast for Jack to follow in his state. Freddie lunged, Junichi parried and tried to press to the arm but she stopped it with her hilt. He pulled back, she followed and she stumbled. She fell forward and Junichi, instead of retreating, stepped towards her. Her sword pierced his leg.

Junichi screamed as he sprang away, a furious sound, his eyes flaring with anger. Jack felt the world pressing in on him, making it hard to breathe. She had had an attack. A small one, but the timing—

"I'm so sor—" Frederica began.

Junichi lifted his sword and roared a thunderous kiai as he lashed out in his rage. The blade swung in a blur, past her head and ended near the floor.

Jack was on his feet. That sort of menacing was uncalled for. That sword had come too close to her. It—

She stumbled and dropped to her knees, her rapier falling to the dirt at her feet. A torrent of blood welled down the front of her dress. She turned as she fell and Jack saw her shoulder, her chest. Junichi's sword had not missed.

It had cleaved her left shoulder near her collarbone, impossibly deep, all the way through. Her flesh between her neck and arm was split open, a cleft so massive it evoked a primal recognition. A mortal wound.

The arena was chocked with silence.

Jack was running towards her, but he felt like he was flying—

nothing below registered. He looked into her eyes as she fell and saw wonder, confusion. There was motion in his periphery. Doctors?

She fell onto her back atop a spreading island of blood. He was at her side, she looked up at him, but all he could see was the gaping wound, a savage thing like the workings of a butcher. It was so deep. There was severed bone and a frighteningly thick artery that spurted blood in rhythmic pulses that grew farther apart as her heart faltered under the strain.

She tried to speak, but air hissed from the terrible gash and her eyes rolled in her head as the blood left her. He knelt over her, closed his eyes, tried to blink away the ghastly vision. Alison on the morgue table, a broken thing.

"No," he whispered. "Not again."

"Out of the way," a doctor screamed and knocked him aside so hard he tripped on the blood slicked dirt and fell.

Three of them hovered over her as Jack lifted his head.

"Give me a clamp," one of them shouted. "He's cut the subclavian."

"Wait," one of them said. "We have a DNT for this one."

"What?" another demanded. "We don't have time for this she's bleeding out."

"It says right here, we're not supposed to…"

"Do it," a familiar voice commanded. Jack looked up and saw Hastings. "You get her in that OR or so help me God—"

Jack got to his knees and watched helplessly as they picked her up, got her onto the stretcher and started to wheel her away. There was so much blood. He looked around, dazed, looking for something to do, some way he could help—

He saw Junichi. He was standing still, watching without emotion, his bloody sword held casually in one hand. Jack looked into the man's eyes, and saw…satisfaction. Everything around him turned red.

He looked around and noticed the hilt of Frederica's rapier from behind a doctor's leg. He got to his feet, grabbed the weapon and turned to Junichi, leveling the point at the man's heart.

He tried to scream, but what came out was more like a roar.

"*Bastard!*"

Junichi saw him, his face contorted with anger and he raised his sword over his head and bellowed a kiai almost as fierce as the one he had used on Frederica.

Anger, rage, wrath, they were just words, and none of them could come close to describing the primordial fury that overcame Jack. He needed to rip Junichi apart and wallow in his remains until his pores were clogged with blood. He needed to cut the heart out of his body and shred it with his fingernails.

And yet, as he closed with Junichi, some part of his mind that was still capable of reason knew that he was about to die. The weapon he held felt awkward, alien, and the man he wanted to kill was a master of his art—and of his sword. A born and made killer, drenched in the blood of the woman Jack loved.

It didn't matter. There was killing to do, no excuses, no way out. Only when he realized that it was no longer Junichi in front of him did he stop.

Kanemori raised his sword and stood between them, his back to Jack.

Junichi didn't flinch. He moved forward, once more posturing in Dai Jodan. Kanemori's explosive kiai made Jack cringe, and Junichi stopped dead in his tracks, but did not lower his weapon.

"Out of the way," Jack said, his voice barely above a growl.

"He'll kill you," Kanemori screamed. "You don't even know how to use that thing."

"Out of my way."

"*Yamae!*" The familiar voice was like the tolling of a massive bell. Junichi lowered his sword and stepped back. Saito, the old Japanese man who had announced the fights, stood between the three of them, his outspread arms like a stone wall. His presence was so intense that even Jack hesitated. Kanemori grabbed Jack's rapier blade.

"Stop."

Jack dropped the sword, turned around and saw the bloody trail left by the stretcher. His fury drained out of him, leaving only agony. He ran, following the blood to the operating room.

Chapter 34

The way of the warrior is the resolute acceptance of death.
- Miyamoto Musashi, Go Rin No Sho
(Book of Five Rings), 1645

The monitors beeped, steel instruments clinked and the doctor's voices murmured. Jack stared at her face. So pale, so haggard. The overhead lights banished all shadows, leaving her breathing tube to rise from her mouth in solitude. One of the surgeons shifted position and her face disappeared behind green cloth.

The observation room was small, with cold metal walls and three padded chairs he could not bring himself to use. He stood pressed to the glass wall, eyes fixed on the operating table. He didn't know, didn't care how long he'd been there. Minutes, hours, days. It was all the same.

The surgeons, their hands covered in blood, worked tirelessly. They had been at it for so long, and there was nothing to indicate how much longer they had to go. They had placed a whiteboard next to the operating table and drawn a complex diagram of lines with labels like MC, M and T1. One of the surgeons referred to it frequently.

The doctor who had stepped in the way moved aside, giving him back her face. She was alive now, and so as he looked at her he cherished every second, every particle of light reflected from that living face. He had known pain before, but this was different. He was immersed in a cold fire, every ounce of him in unrelenting agony. He would not survive her death. He didn't want to.

Twice now he had found happiness and had it taken from him in the most gruesome way. Both of the women he loved had ended up on stainless steel tables, their bodies broken. Only Frederica was being put back together by the untiring labors of the world's best and brightest. Slowly, methodically, they worked their tools, their magic, while he watched and prayed and hoped that it would be enough. But the wound had been so *deep*.

The observation room door opened and a doctor walked in. His hands were clean but his smock was drenched in blood. Too much blood. Freddie looked so small on the table. How could she have enough left inside her?

"Mr. Fischer," he said, approaching. Jack looked his way briefly to acknowledge him, then turned back to look at her face. So pale, so haggard. So fragile.

"Tell me the truth," Jack said. "Don't you bullshit me."

He heard the doctor swallow. "I won't."

"Will she live?"

"It's hard to say."

Jack's knees buckled, and he braced himself against the glass as he lost control, tears flowing unchecked.

"The sword severed the clavicle and part of the scapula, transecting the subclavian artery. We managed to clamp it in time and repair it, and so far the sutures are holding. Also, the wound was deep enough to perforate the top of her left lung, but we've got that under control. What we're working on now is her brachial plexus, which was completely transected across all connections."

"I don't know what that is."

"The brachial plexus is a nerve cluster. It contains the neural connections between the neck and brachial nerves." He saw that Jack was still confused. "It's how her brain talks to her arm, how she's able to move it. I don't think anyone's ever seen an injury this extensive, where every connection is severed…at least not where the patient was still alive. Unrepaired, or repaired poorly, it would cause total paralysis of the left arm. There are maybe two people in the world who can handle something like this, but on the positive side, we're not waiting, we're doing it right now, which gives us the best possible chance to fix it."

"Can…can you do it? Can you fix it?" He was horrified. So much damage from a simple stroke of a sword. Did he really devote his life to the practice of such butchery?

"I mentioned there were two people who could do this. One of them is here. Dr. Epstein is the best neurosurgeon in Great Britain, and probably the world. I think he can repair it, yes. If anyone can, he can."

"Is that what the diagram is for?" Jack motioned towards the whiteboard.

"Yes. It helps him focus."

"But you said you fixed the artery, right? So she'll live?"

"If I had to guess, I'd say yes. But that's a lot of trauma for the body to deal with, and the surgery isn't helping in that respect. Her body has its limits, and the most we can do is hope that we will not cross them. Honestly her best chance at life is to close her up right now and leave the arm paralyzed."

"That's not an option, not for her."

The doctor nodded. "That's the same thing Mr. Hastings said. So we're doing what we can, and hoping for the best. So far she shows no signs of succumbing. She's strong, and she wants to live, and that's important."

"If there's anything you need," Jack said. "Blood, organs, nerve tissue, take mine. I mean that, anything."

"We have more than enough blood. As for the rest, we're not there yet, but I will keep your offer in mind."

"Good, thank you. And thank you for being honest with me."

The doctor nodded, then put a hand on Jack's arm. "Hang in there, Mr. Fischer. She's in good hands." He turned and walked out of the observation room, leaving Jack alone.

The doctor's words had brought equal parts relief and doubt. His grief was like a turbulent ocean, waves cresting and falling between periods of bearable despair and intolerable anguish, and as the relief softened one peak the doubt deepened the other. If he lost her now....

He realized that he had never actually told her he loved her. He had put it in the form of a question, said things that implied it, but he had never actually said the words. She must know, she had implied it in much the same way he did, but at that moment it didn't matter. The fact that he had never told her, that there was still a chance he might never get to tell her, was a new kind of torment.

The door opened again and Hastings walked in. His face was drawn, he looked tired.

"Mr. Fischer," he said as he came to stand next to him. Jack wanted to be alone, but he couldn't bring himself to send the old man away, not after everything he'd done for her.

"Mr. Hastings."

"I'm so terribly sorry. I never—"

"Thank you," Jack said. "For everything you're doing. I'll never forget it."

Hastings nodded. "I could do no less." Jack sensed his pain, his guilt. He had arranged the match, but he hadn't swung the sword.

"It's not your fault."

"That's kind of you to say."

"You know I have to kill him," Jack said. When it came to the man who had done this, he had moved beyond fury to a cold place where there was no anger or hatred, only death.

To his surprise, Hastings nodded. "I do." Nothing more needed to be said between them.

The surgeons continued their work, some of them trading places to rest, though one of them, presumably Epstein, stayed at his post throughout. He never wavered, never faltered, and Jack loved him for it.

Hastings stayed by his side for a long time, then finally excused himself and left. Jack hoped he was going to arrange what needed to be arranged.

At long last, the surgeons were finished. Other doctors and nurses came and carefully wheeled her out of the OR. Jack left the observation room and intercepted them in the hall.

"Where are you taking her now?" he asked.

"To an intensive care room," one of the doctors said with a heavy German accent. "We are keeping her under for forty eight hours."

"I'm going too," Jack said.

"No. It is important that— "

"I wasn't asking."

The doctor opened his mouth to say something, but then seemed to reconsider. "If you insist. But do not touch her. Not at all. She cannot be moved. You understand?"

"I understand."

They took her to a plain room filled with assorted medical equipment and prepared to clean the blood without moving her from the wheeled table. One of the nurses, a red headed woman with intense green eyes, started to cut away what was left of Frederica's black dress but then stopped and stared at Jack.

"It's fine," he said.

She didn't seem satisfied, but shrugged and proceeded. Jack knew that in a real hospital he would have been thrown out or arrested, and he was grateful to Hastings for whatever it was he must have said to get them to accept his presence.

They quickly cut away her dress, wiped her down with a wet sponge that smelled faintly of alcohol and covered her in a white gown. They weren't able to clean all of the blood without moving her, but they did what they could.

Before leaving, the nurse turned to Jack and said, "Just because we bathed her doesn't mean you can touch her. The slightest push in the wrong place and…" He had noticed how they shied away from her shoulder, which was encased in some sort of rigid plastic contraption.

"I know. I won't."

She nodded and, hovering in the doorway, said, "She's not out of the woods, but the worst is behind her. She's strong, good pulse, everything's steady."

"Thank you."

She left the room and closed the door behind her. Jack pulled up a chair and sat down, never taking his eyes off of Frederica's face. So pale, so haggard. So lovely.

* * *

When he woke he wasn't sure where he was, then remembered and jumped to his feet in a panic. His eyes desperately cast about the room until he found her, resting in her bed. The monitor that showed her heart rate displayed a steady pulse accompanied by a reassuring beep for every blessed beat.

The knock repeated itself, though he only realized when he heard it again that it had been what woke him.

"Uh…come in."

The door opened and Kanemori entered, carrying a tray of food.

"I brought you something to eat."

"Thanks, but I'm not hungry."

"Jack, I'm so sorry, I told you that it would be fine, I—"

"Don't," Jack said. "You don't have to. It's not your fault."

"They say she should recover," he said. "I'm sure she will. No doubt."

"Thanks for trying to reassure me." If only he could have no doubts, but then life had never been that kind.

"I spoke to Epstein, the guy's a wizard, man. He knows more about neurosurgery than you and I combined know about swordsmanship. He said it went extremely well, that everything came together like it was supposed to. He said…" He stopped, a faint smile at the corners of his mouth.

"What? What did he say?"

"He said she has beautiful nerves."

Jack took a deep breath, holding back his tears. "She has beautiful everything."

"Look, Jack, you know I dropped out of med school, but I still know how to read between the lines. All of the surgeries went well, the only question as far as I'm concerned is her arm. Brachial plexus repair is hard, it's like black magic, but Epstein is the fucking dark lord of Mordor. I could tell by talking to him that the cocky fuck knows he pulled it off, he just doesn't want to be seen counting his chickens."

"Thank you."

"So eat something. The worst is over."

"They said she could still…" He couldn't bring himself to say it. He whirled on Kanemori and grabbed his shirt with both hands. His friend's eyes widened in surprise. "You tell me, you tell me the truth. She can still die, can't she?"

"It's possible," Kanemori admitted. "I don't think—"

"The truth."

Kanemori slumped. "I don't think she will, but…man, that was a big gash. I've never seen anything like it. If this had happened anywhere but this ship, she wouldn't have made it. When he swung that sword, he wasn't trying to wound her, he was…"

"Say it." He felt his rage returning.

"He was trying to kill her. The human body, it just wasn't made to take that kind of trauma. But…I mean, considering, where she is, what Hastings did getting all those surgeons…"

Jack let him go and turned away, once again looking at Frederica. Five days ago, he didn't know what she looked like. Today, he loved her as intensely as he had ever loved anyone. Someone had tried to cut her in half like she was a slab of meat hanging on a hook. And that someone was walking around, breathing.

"You're going to challenge him, aren't you?"

Jack nodded. "He has to die."

"If I tell you to let this one go, is there any chance you will listen to me?"

"Would you? If that were Aiko on that table?" Jack saw Kanemori tense and regretted his words. He had no right to take his misery out on his friend. "I'm sorry, I didn't mean to—"

"No, it was a fair question. And you're right, I wouldn't let it go. Not until I brought her his head."

"Then you can't expect me to do anything less."

"No, I can't. But Jack…" He took a deep breath rubbed his temples. "Jack, you're my friend, and I'm going to tell you the truth."

"I'm listening."

"You're good, Jack, real good. Of all the Western martial artists here, you're among the best, if not *the* best. But Junichi, well, he's better." He shook his head, as though saying it was distasteful. "Man, he's just better. The guy is faster, more skilled and has better reflexes. He's not human...cold as ice and he doesn't blink or falter. When I faced him, after you picked up that rapier, I saw it. I couldn't faze him, couldn't unbalance him. He's the best I've ever seen."

"So you're telling me I can't win?" Jack knew as much already, but he also knew that he had no choice, just as he had had no choice about fighting in the tournament, not after Hastings gave him the answers he wanted to hear. He had lied to Frederica after all, she would be alone.

"No," Kanemori said, surprising him. "No, I'm not saying that at all."

"But—"

"Logan is a lot better than O'Neil, but O'Neil won because

Logan made a mistake, underestimated his size and strength. What we have to do is get Junichi to make mistakes, and that's how we're going to take him down."

"We?"

Kanemori nodded. "I'm with you for this one, Jack. All the way. We don't have much time, but I'm going to train you, and I'm going to help you mind fuck that son of a bitch before the fight ever begins."

"Won't that cause problems for you? I mean with the other Japanese? You being one of them, but training me?"

Kanemori shrugged. "Not with most. There is a lot of hate for Junichi right now. But some, yeah, especially Saito. But, really, fuck those guys. I'm not Japanese. I mean not like the others...I was born in Florida. Now do you want my help or not?"

"I would be grateful."

"Then come with me now Jack. Eat that food, and let's go. They're keeping her out for forty eight hours, give those nerves a chance to fuse. All you're doing here is sitting down, and that's not doing her any good. When she wakes up, she's going to see you kill Junichi, or she's going to see him kill you. If you sit here on your ass while you should be getting ready, it's going to be the latter."

Jack knew that Kanemori was right. If he had any chance to keep his word, he had to make the most of what little time he had left. But he couldn't leave. The machines, they were watching her, and he had to watch them. What if something happened? What if he wasn't there and she were to...*there's been an accident, Mr. Fischer. You're wife's car...it...well, we need you to come with us. To the hospital? No, sir, not the hospital.*

"I can't," he said, fighting back tears. "I'm sorry, I just can't leave."

"I thought you might say that," Kanemori said, and reached into his pocket. He pulled out a small black device with a belt clip and handed it to Jack.

"What is it?"

"A pager. If any of these instruments detect even the start of something wrong, they will page all the doctors, and you. The machines are set way too sensitive, it will probably go off five times a day for no reason, but they'll all come running. Hastings will skin them alive if they don't. Two of them are across the hall in a lounge right now, on standby. Did you know that? Hastings's orders."

"Thank you." What had he done to deserve such a friend? Or such a benefactor?

"So are you coming? The training room is just down the hall. You don't have to go far."

"Yes," he said. "We have work to do."

Chapter 35

. . . unless you experience cutting with a real sword,
you will never begin to taste true sword technique.
- Nakamura Taizaburo

"What the hell do you mean he won't fight me?" Jack demanded.

"He says it is beneath him to fight someone who is not a winner of his division," Hastings said.

"Beneath him?" Jack said, feeling himself start to tremble. "Was it beneath him to strike down a woman who wasn't defending herself?"

"It's a bullshit excuse," Kanemori said. "Tell him I challenge him then."

"I'm afraid that's what he wants."

"What?" Jack said, standing up. "I don't understand…"

"I'm afraid you do," Hastings said. "Or soon will." His eyes were cold and hard. Gone was the friendly old man that had comforted them, guided them. This Hastings was a dangerous man, used to the wielding of power.

Jack concentrated, trying to get past his anger at Junichi's refusal long enough to figure it out.

"No," Kanemori said, eyes alight with sudden understanding. "It can't be true."

"What are you two talking about?"

"Think," Hastings said.

Suddenly it came together. The way Junichi had asked Jack about trying for the division, making sure that he wouldn't.

A tear rolled down his cheek. "That absolute bastard."

"I am deeply sorry for my part in this," Hastings said. "I didn't know."

"But how could he have known that she would…" Jack hesitated, unsure if he should share her secret with them.

"Trip?" Hastings said quickly, but a slight narrowing of his eyes betrayed the truth. He knew. "He couldn't, but I doubt that would have been necessary."

Kanemori nodded. "It shouldn't have mattered if she stumbled, Junichi is too good to get accidentally hit with a sword. He would have arranged it, stumble or no. Remember how he stepped forward into her sword?"

"He can't get away with this," Jack said, his fists clenched so tightly he was crushing his own fingers. "He has to be dealt with." The idea that Junichi had deliberately set up a situation in which he would have an excuse to cut down Frederica just to get a shot at Kanemori was too much. It was a kind of evil Jack had never before experienced.

"I have spoken to Saito," Hastings said. "About the possibility of dealing with him by less direct means, but he refuses to accept my conclusion. He said…" Hastings broke off suddenly and swallowed, looking away.

"What did he say?" Jack said.

"It's not important, what's important is—"

"Tell me," Jack said. "Please."

Hastings narrowed his eyes, but not at Jack. "He said the clumsy woman deserved what she got."

Jack kicked the chair behind him. It toppled over and crashed into the small coffee table next to the couch. "Is that how they all feel?"

"No," Kanemori said. "The others are outraged. They think Junichi should be banished from the society. Some of them think he should be arrested and put in jail."

"No," Jack said. "He has to die, and he has to die in the ring. I mean he didn't just try to kill Freddie. He dishonored the tournament. What he did...it undermines everything you did here." Jack was surprised to hear himself say it, but it was true. It was the least of his reasons for wanting to fight, but it did matter. This tournament didn't just belong to Hastings or Kanemori, not anymore. It was his, it was hers. He would fight for Frederica, but also for the institution that had given their lives meaning and brought them together.

"Everything *we* did, Mr. Fischer," Hastings said, and briefly put a hand on Jack's arm.

Kanemori looked at him and nodded. He looked pleased.

"I will deal with Saito," Hastings said. "He may be the big fish here, but this is a small pond."

"I'll deal with Junichi then," Kanemori said. "He wants me? He's got me. Only I'm not going to play nice, Mr. Hastings, I'm going to put him in the ground."

"No," Jack said. "I have to do this."

"What difference does it make?" Kanemori said. "Dead is dead."

"And if he kills you? What chance is there for justice then? If I fight him, and I die, then you can still take him down. There is no way he will fight me if he beats you."

Kanemori frowned. "I see your point."

"There has to be a way," Jack said.

"There is," Hastings said.

"What?"

"You will win your division. Mr. O'Neil has already agreed to fight you."

"He has? Why? I mean he has nothing to gain, he's already won."

"The society committee offered him another five million Euros," Hastings said. "Win or lose. Can you beat him?"

"If it gets me closer to killing Junichi," Jack said. "I can beat anyone. But what if he still says no?"

"Then," Kanemori said. "I'm going to tell him I will not fight a coward who refuses a challenge from a worthy opponent."

Jack put a hand on his friend's shoulder. "Thank you." He turned to Hastings. "Both of you."

Kanemori looked away, his eyes betraying his uncertainty. "I'm not so sure I'm doing you a favor."

* * *

It was strange to be back in the arena, wearing his fighter's uniform. He had told Frederica he wouldn't fight again and it felt wrong to betray his promise, but everything was different now. The spot where she had fallen was clean of blood, though he thought he could just make out a darker patch of dirt. Or maybe it was his imagination.

He saw Junichi, alone at his table, watching him from across the field where the Japanese fighters were seated. He looked so ordinary, like a normal man in a tuxedo holding a glass of red wine. There was nothing sinister about his appearance at all. How could he have done it? How could he look at Frederica and think of her as nothing but a thing to use to get what he wanted? How could he cut her down without a second thought, and then watch the doctors haul her broken body away without so much as a hint of remorse? Jack saw Junichi's sword swing, he felt it bite into her body with savage force. He saw the gleam in Junichi's eye, the satisfaction of unleashing his power on living flesh without restraint.

Tormented by these conjured images, his awareness of self grew hazy. Something deep within him stirred, a sentient darkness that sent tendrils of hatred weaving up from the depths. Jack had never been a violent man, never been quick to anger or to wish ill on another human being, but the man whose body he now occupied was a savage creature, and it wanted to bathe in an ocean of Junichi's blood.

"Jack," Logan said as he and Boris approached the table. "Can we sit with you?"

Jack, startled out of his thoughts, looked up. Logan's head was bandaged where the pommel strike had chipped his skull, but he seemed otherwise okay.

"Of course. Please. Why would you even ask?"

Logan shrugged. "You looked…I dunno. I'm being an idiot. Jack, man, I'm so sorry. I'm praying for her. All the time. I know you don't believe in God. I don't either. Or I didn't. I don't know anymore."

"There are no atheists in the trenches," Jack said.

"I'm sorry too," Boris said. "It's horrible, what happened."

"Thanks guys. Logan, you okay? You took a pretty good shot."

"Don't worry about me, I'm fine. Just don't make the same mistake I did. That son of a bitch is strong."

Jack nodded. "How about you, Boris?"

"Stop asking about us," Boris said. "We're fine. We're here for you, Jack."

"Mr. Fischer," someone said, and Jack turned and saw an

attendant, the same man who had come to fetch Logan the day before. Coincidence, or an ill omen?

"It's time, huh?"

"Yes sir."

Jack got to his feet and felt an apprehensive jitter.

"Take him down," Logan said. "You can do it."

"We'll be rooting for you," Boris said.

"Thank you," Jack said, then followed the attendant to the dark area behind the red gate. Their gate.

"A very special circumstance brings us here tonight," Hastings's amplified voice said. The murmurs of the gathered crowd subsided. "A challenge has been issued, and accepted. Mr. Tyler O'Neil has agreed to surrender his division victory and face another challenger, Mr. Jack Fischer, who faced Mr. Todd Marrone and emerged victorious.

"Many of you," Hastings continued. "Know the real reason this match is being fought, and know who will be responsible for the blood spilled here today." Saito cleared his throat, but Hastings ignored him. "The rest of you will learn the truth soon enough. Let the fighters take their places, and God have mercy on them both."

The taiko drums beat, and Jack entered the field and saw O'Neil. He was even bigger than he looked from the table. Six feet and seven inches tall to Jack's five ten, with powerful arms and thick legs that bulged under his black jacket. Jack would have to avoid binding swords with him. Binding with his hands held high would leave his lower openings too exposed, but every bind they could conceivably end up in would have Jack raising his hands to compensate for the height difference.

The drums stopped and O'Neil practically ran forward. Jack was taken off guard. He wasn't ready for this. He wanted to pressure O'Neil, to test his openings, to slowly figure out his weakness, but he couldn't do that if the man charged him.

Jack backed away, but he sensed that he was almost on the ropes and O'Neil was still advancing. He had given up his most important tactical asset, the ability to control distance. There was nothing to do now but to fight, ready or not.

O'Neil stepped into range and struck immediately. Almost too late Jack saw that it was the Zwerchhau and brought his sword up to parry, his hands high, almost over his head. Too high. If he had not retreated like a fool, he would have had room to void the strike, and O'Neil would have been his.

Their swords met with a jarring clang and Jack knew he was done for. The Zwerchhau and his foolish retreat to the ropes had forced a bad parry, and O'Neil's height made it worse.

Time seemed to slow as the giant's sword took off, headed down to Jack's unprotected stomach. Two layers of linen, one of wool, then naked flesh. How could it end like this?

Jack didn't have time to think and reacted instinctively. He cut down into O'Neil's abdomen just as the man was cutting into his. If he was going to die, then so would the son of a bitch who was robbing him of his chance at vengeance.

O'Neil's sword hit first.

Jack felt the burning of the edge biting into his skin, and then felt his own sword cut into the big man's gut. He felt the parting cloth and the spatter of warm blood on his face as O'Neil's stomach split open, intestines falling into the dirt at his feet like a burst sack at a butcher's shop spilling links of bloody sausage.

The big man screamed, a horrible agonized shriek, and Jack stumbled back, dropping his sword, clutching at his stomach to hold in his own guts. He felt the parted cloth, the blood.

O'Neil collapsed, and the doctors surrounded him.

"What about me?" Jack said, and looked down at his wound. He saw only blood.

Curious, he spread the parted layers of his uniform. The last layer wouldn't come apart. It was cut in places, and those places were soaked red, but it had held. Jack couldn't believe it.

O'Neil's cut had failed.

Chapter 36

Fence with the entire body,
so that you most strongly drive.
- Liechtenauer's Verses, Von Danzig Fechtbuch – 1452

"That was stupid," Kanemori said, glaring angrily. "Fucking stupid. If you fight like that with Junichi he'll take you apart. You might as well go up on deck and jump over the side."

"I know, I know, I'm sorry. I just wasn't ready for him to come at me like that." They entered the training room, which was empty except for an attendant cleaning the mirrors. Jack's stomach felt sore, but that only served to remind him how much worse it could have been.

"You know why you weren't ready? Because your head is full of shit. You have to stop thinking about her, Jack, stop thinking about revenge. You think your anger gives you strength? It doesn't. It clouds your judgment, makes you weak and stupid."

Jack felt himself getting mad, but he forced it back. Kanemori was right, and if he didn't listen to him, he would die. "I know."

He had spent the night sitting with Frederica. She didn't move, didn't so much as twitch, but then that was the idea. Her rhythmic breathing through the plastic tube had reassured him, lulling him into a few hours of fitful sleep. How could he stop thinking about her?

"You're lucky that fucking guy doesn't know how to cut, or you would have been in the OR getting your gut stitched back together right next to him."

Jack nodded. "I—"

"Yes, yes, you know, I get it. You know." Kanemori shook his head. "What am I going to do with you?"

"At least I won, now we can focus on Junichi."

"You didn't win, Jack. Your theories won."

"I know, okay? I fucked up. I got it. Now stop badgering me and let's get to training."

Kanemori smiled. "That's the spirit. I heard from Hastings

before I came to get you. Junichi has accepted your challenge, it's scheduled for tomorrow afternoon, but..."

"But what? I wish people would start finishing their god damned sentences"

Kanemori looked away. "He didn't say it, but Hastings read between the lines. If he wins, not even Epstein will be able to sew you back together."

"Humpty dumpty," Jack said.

"Pretty much. You still in?"

"I died the moment the sword hit her. He can't kill me twice."

Kanemori stared at him a moment, as if measuring him. "You mean that?"

"The woman I love is lying on a hospital bed stained with her own blood because they can't move her to clean it. She may never wake up. You think I'm afraid to die? The only thing I'm afraid of is that you and I will both fail. And…"

"And you're afraid to leave her alone."

Jack nodded. "I suppose that's the same as fear of death."

"No. It isn't." Kanemori reached into his duffel bag and pulled out a hakama and kimono. "Put these on."

"Why?"

"Just do it."

Jack went into the changing room, where he fumbled with the obi and hakama straps, having completely forgotten how to tie them. It was hard to concentrate on such minutia and his attention drifted to the pager. He kept picking it up, looking at it, making sure it was still on. He ended up settling for double knots and tucking the ends out of sight. When he emerged, feeling awkward, he saw that Logan had joined them, and several Japanese men stood outside, looking in through the glass panels on both sides of the door.

"Hey Logan," Jack said. "Thanks for coming. Boris can't make it?"

"No," Logan said, shaking his head. "I don't think Boris will pick up a sword for a long time, and I can't blame him."

Jack nodded, understanding. The reality of the sword was a far cry from the fantasy. Boris had stared it in the face in a way Jack and Logan had not. Jack wondered how he would have felt if he had taken a life. But then, God willing, he would soon find out.

"You sure I can't talk you out of this?" Logan asked. "If this guy is as good as your friend here says…"

Jack shook his head. "There's no choice, never was. You know that."

"The part of me that's about reason says there is a choice, and that this is the wrong one, for all the reasons you already know. But, in here…" Logan put his hand over his heart. "In here I feel a part of what you feel. What that bastard did. It just can't stand. So yeah, I know that."

"Thank you."

Logan turned to Kanemori and said,"What makes him so good anyway? I mean I saw him fight, he's amazing, but why?" He hesitated. "Are the Japanese arts…are they better?" Jack saw the tension in his eyes. It was a difficult question for him to ask.

Kanemori shook his head. "No. The Japanese arts, the Western arts, they are the same. Different approach to the same thing. Junichi is so good because he lives in a different world than you do. He trains as many hours a day as most people sit in a chair in a cubicle. He has sponsors, supporters who give him everything he needs. And most importantly, he's spent most of his life knowing that he would be here, fighting for his life and his honor."

Logan nodded, satisfied. "Makes sense. Let's get started then. We don't want to waste any time."

"Indeed."

"Why am I wearing this?" Jack asked, turning to Kanemori.

"Psychological warfare," Kanemori said. "Junichi doesn't know the first thing about German longsword. When word of this gets back to him and he realizes you know how he fights it's going to make him nervous. That, and you need to remember what you learned, so that your understanding isn't a bluff."

"That's going to be hard. It's been a long time."

"Take this," he said, giving Jack a blunt steel katana.

"This feels weird," Jack said, hefting the weapon. The silk wrapped tsuka felt too thick, too knotty. A longsword's handle was smooth to facilitate a fluid, constantly changing grip. Yet there was an undeniable familiarity to the katana.

"Logan," Kanemori said. "Pick up your longsword, face Jack.

We're going to do some drills."

"Gotcha," Logan said, hefting his federschwert.

"Jack, get in Chudan. Come on, do it now."

Jack held the sword out in front of him, point roughly at face level, and sank into a comfortable stance.

"Have you forgotten so much?" Kanemori said, shaking his head. "Hands lower, point at throat level. Lower. A bit more. That's right. Make it strong, but stay relaxed."

"Why are we going into such detail?" Jack asked. "Shouldn't I be the one with the longsword? I mean I get the psychological stuff, but—"

"You can't beat him if you don't know how he fights. You need to know what he's going to see when he sees you. What he's going to do when you raise your sword against him."

"Makes sense I guess," Jack watched Logan, nervous about the greater length of the longsword. His katana, at just under thirty inches, gave up almost a foot to its European counterpart.

"Logan is about to attack. Remember how we fight, Jack. Control the center. If he cuts, you cut. If your technique is stronger, your foundation more solid, then you will succeed and he will fail. This is how Junichi fights, how he thinks. Remember the mountain, its foundation rooted to the earth, solid, unwavering, its peak high above clouds, looking down, seeing everything. Get into his mind."

"Control the center," Jack said. "I remember. It's the same as what we do, now that I think about it."

"Yes, it is. Get in to Jodan."

Jack obeyed, raising his sword above his head.

"Good. Logan…cut kesa giri. Jack, kiri otoshi."

"Cut what?" Logan asked, confused.

"Diagonal oberhau," Jack translated.

"Oh." Logan approached and cut in a fluid motion. Jack cut into his strike and his sword stopped an inch above Logan's head, while the longsword arced harmlessly over his shoulder.

"Very good," Kanemori said. "So you do remember after all."

"How'd you do that?" Logan asked.

"It's like Zornhau Ort," Jack explained.

"Good," Kanemori said. "The shorter sword gives you more

leverage, and the structural connection to your body makes you strong. Control the center, and you will succeed. Don't forget the curvature, he will use it against you. You see how his sword went flying away instead of ending up in a bind?"

"Yeah."

"That's the curvature. What you did was more suriage then kiri otoshi. Okay then, Logan, start from one step away, give Jack any strike you want. Jack, take any guard you want."

Logan took a few steps back and raised his sword over his head in high Vom Tag. Jack held his sword by his right shoulder in Hasso. Logan advanced and struck a Zwerchhau into the side of Jack's head.

Jack, driven by memories of his training, stepped back and cut into Logan's arms, the point of his sword striking the hilt between Logan's hands.

"That's a double kill," Logan said. "My sword would finish its arc if I strike with force."

"Maybe," Kanemori said. "Maybe not. Junichi won't think so, so he'll try it. A double hit is not always a double kill. Logan, what do you have to do to avoid it?"

"I don't know, maybe step more out to the side, keep the hands back until the last minute." He gave it a try. Jack repeated his defense but this time ended up striking the cross guard.

"Now what?" Kanemori asked.

Logan pushed his pommel to the right, winding his point over to Jack's face and attempted to thrust. Jack pushed down on the sword, pressing his blade into Logan's arms and pushing his sword away before he could score.

"Shit," Logan said. "Where are you getting the leverage to do that?"

"Try the same thing again," Jack suggested. "This time turn your cross to stop my pressing."

They repeated the sequence, and this time the cross got in the way, just as his own cross had when he fought Kanemori. Had that been just a few months ago?

Logan, seeing his advantage, thrust, just as Jack had, and scored on Jack's neck.

"Ouch?"

"Sorry man," Logan said, pulling away.

"Good," Kanemori said. "Are you starting to see?"

"Yeah," Jack said. "Now I understand why I can't always out leverage you…keeping centered, using your entire body, it makes you strong. Also, the range is not as big a factor as I thought. The cross guard though, that is a big advantage, if you know how to use it."

"The range thing is true, but, tell me, why don't you aim for the legs when you attack from wide measure unless you set it up really well?"

Jack shrugged. "You know why…attacks to high targets outreach attacks to low targets. So if I attack low, he can step back to void and still be able to hit my head."

"Yes," Kanemori said, and grinned. "When the swords are the same length."

Jack's eyebrows raised with sudden understanding. "Holy shit, you're right. I start an attack, you go to kiri otoshi but instead of stepping forward I step back and cut your leg."

"With one hand," Kanemori said. "Otherwise he'll cut your arms."

"Let's try it."

"Not now. Too many people watching. Save this one for when we're alone."

Jack turned and saw that the number of spectators had grown considerably. Junichi was nowhere to be seen, but he had no doubt that word would reach him soon enough, if it hadn't already.

"Let's keep going."

After an hour of trying various actions and reactions, Kanemori had Jack change back into his sweats and t-shirt and they did the same thing in reverse, this time with Kanemori wielding the katana and Jack with the longsword. Logan took turns, letting Jack see what it looked like from the outside. He finally got why it had been so important to approach this from both sides—there was no way he could have understood the strategy he needed otherwise.

Some attendants wheeled in a cart of tatami and a cutting stand, and Kanemori had Jack do some cutting, with both swords. The katana, stiffer and curved just enough to matter, was the better cutter, but the longsword had more reach and felt more nimble in the hand. Jack remembered the mentality of a Japanese swordsman, his reliance on a powerful cut, and his understanding deepened. He actually started to believe he had a chance.

"Let's do some pell work," Kanemori said. "We don't use a pell, and seeing someone smacking away at it can be intimidating." He noticed something over Jack's shoulder and his eyes narrowed slightly. "Don't look. He's here." He leaned closer. "Do you think you could break one of these steel blunts on the pell?"

"Don't know. I've done it before, though not on purpose."

"Good, do it right now, while he's here."

"It's not like I can do it on command. These things are through hardened steel."

"Just try."

Jack picked up a blunt longsword and stood facing the pell. He had no idea how he was going to break the sword, but he was willing to give it a shot. Maybe if he kept hitting it over and over again it would snap. He certainly had enough anger to give it a good go.

He got ready to swing and glanced over his shoulder—and saw Junichi. He was standing in front of the glass panel, watching. The corners of his mouth were turned up in the hint of a smirk.

Jack turned back to the pell, raised his sword over his head and let out a bestial roar as he swung with all the strength of his body. A high pitched metallic clang rang in his ears as the last third of the blade snapped off against the pell and flew into a nearby wall before clattering to the floor.

"Holy shit," Logan said.

Jack turned to Junichi. He wasn't smirking anymore.

"Jack, that was fucking amazing," Kanemori said softly. "You should've seen the look on his face."

Jack started to say something, but he heard a series of beeps and felt a buzzing in his pocket. At first he was confused, but then he remembered the pager.

The pager that monitored Frederica's heartbeat.

Chapter 37

But it is time at last, that, gathering up all that we have said to this point in brief words, we come to lay the foundation of this discipline, which is its true and proper definition, following the rule from which we will guide and direct the rest of all its precepts.

- Ridolfo Capoferro, Great Simulacrum of the Art and Use of Fencing – 1610

He dropped the sword and ran out of the room, almost knocking over a few startled Japanese men that had been standing near the door. Kanemori ran after him.

All he could think of was getting to her, doing something, anything. Maybe Kanemori was right, maybe the monitors were too sensitive, maybe it was just a false alarm.

But what if it wasn't?

The hallway seemed impossibly long, each step took forever. Absolute panic overcame him and he ran faster, his feet pounding into the wooden floor like jackhammers. He finally rounded the turn, ran past the arena and glimpsed inside. He saw her walking onto the field in her dark blue uniform, so graceful, so elegant.

He kept running, past the operating rooms. He heard the monitors beep, the steel instruments clink and the doctor's voices murmur. So deep, so savage, how could she survive? He finally turned the last corner and ran through the open doorway.

A group of nurses were clustered around her, one of them was pumping one side of her chest, careful not to disturb her shoulder. The monitor that displayed her heart rate showed a flat line with tiny occasional blips. An alarm blared.

"She's asystolic," one of the nurses said as she saw them enter.

"Oh no," Kanemori said, his voice barely audible. Jack moved closer until he could see her face. She looked so peaceful. Asystolic, no heartbeat. He knew little about medicine, but he knew what that meant. No defibrillator, her heart was already depolarized. She was dying.

"What do we have?" a doctor said as he rushed in behind them. "Watch that shoulder." Jack recognized him: it was Epstein, the neurosurgeon. Another doctor was on his heels.

"Asystole," the nurse said. "We're about to do epi and atropine."

"How long?"

"One minute and…twenty two seconds."

Jack knew that they were losing her—most people did not survive true flatlining. She would never wake up again. It was over, everything was over. Everything that she was, everything he loved, was about to be extinguished. It would only take a few more minutes before her brain suffocated.

You were the best part of the dream.

He should have stayed with her, never left her side. How could he abandon her? He had dared to hope that she would wake. She had survived such a horrid wound, and then the surgery. It wasn't fair that she should die like this, lying in a bed.

"Take me," Jack whispered. "Please God, let her live and take me."

One of the nurses brought a pair of large syringes. Epstein took them in one hand and probed Frederica's arm with the other.

"Take me," he said again, even fainter.

"Stop compression," Epstein shouted.

The nurse that pumping her chest was moved away quickly, her expression quizzical.

"Why?" Jack asked faintly. "Why stop?" Were they giving up so soon?

The nurse felt Frederica's other arm.

"Holy shit." she said.

"Find it," the other doctor ordered. He sounded angry.

"What's going on?" Jack demanded.

"She's got a pulse," Epstein said. He glared at the nurse. "I know I said not to touch her, but for god's sake." He set down the syringes and looked at Frederica's chest, his eyes roving over her body, looking for something. "There." He grabbed a wire with a small round pad at the end and pressed it firmly into her skin.

The alarm stopped. The monitor showed a steady, regular rhythm.

"A fucking lose connection," the other doctor said. "But there was activity. Maybe radio interference?"

"It would have to be RF," Epstein said. "Who makes these bloody monitors?"

Jack stared at the monitor, then at Frederica and felt himself getting lightheaded as a tremendous wave of relief washed over him.

"Thank you," he whispered. "Thank you."

* * *

It wasn't like waking up, not exactly. She was dreaming of lying on a bed in a small room. Hastings was there. The dream crystallized, becoming more and more real, until it wasn't a dream anymore.

"Jack?" she tried to say, but the only sound she heard was a raspy croak. Hastings brought her a plastic bottle with a straw and put it to her lips. She drank, and as soon as the water touched her throat she realized how thirsty she was, how dry everything felt.

"Where is Jack?" she asked. "What happened? Where am I?" Her voice was weak, gravely, but it was improving with each word. Hastings gave her another sip of water.

"Shh," he said. "Don't try to talk. Just relax for a few minutes, everything will come back to you."

She tried to sit up, but something held her down, some sort of restraint, and she couldn't feel her left arm. Another attack? It felt the same, but it had never happened to her arm before.

"I can't feel my arm," she said as her confusion slowly lifted its veil from her eyes. "Why can't I feel my arm?"

"That's to be expected," Hastings said. "They say it will take a while for the sensation to return"

"What's going on?" she asked. "Where is Jack?"

"You don't remember?" There was something about the way he looked at her, a kind of disturbing concern that made her think something terrible had happened. The last thing she remembered was lying in the pool with Jack. They had been laughing. He had told her he loved her, in a manner of speaking, and she had done the same. It was a wonderful moment.

"No, I..." There was more. They were going to the arena. Junichi came up to them. Yes, she was supposed to fight him. An exhibition match. She remembered that now. She'd felt so self conscious with that big slit up the side of her dress. The fight had gone well, until her foot had gotten numb and she stumbled and—

She recoiled from the memory, trying to turn away from Hastings, away from the overhead lights. Better to drown in darkness than to remember.

"Please," Hastings said. "You shouldn't try to move. You remember now, don't you?"

She did remember. She remembered the sword striking her shoulder. It was an ice cold thwack that had *unwound* her. She remembered losing balance, and looking down. Down at her broken body, so horribly misshapen. Bones, muscles, nerves, hacked apart. How could she have survived?

"I'm so terribly sorry," Hastings said. "I feel responsible. But Dr. Epstein believes the surgery went well. He is confident you will regain full mobility and sensation very quickly."

"Why isn't Jack here?" She remembered him running to her, the horror on his face as he looked at her. Had he abandoned her, after seeing her broken body? No, he would never do that, not Jack. Would he?

"Mr. Fischer, Jack, he was here almost the whole time. He never wanted to leave your side. But, the time came when he had to."

"Why?" She looked around the room for the first time and noticed a large flat panel television on a wheeled cart by the foot of her bed. It looked out of place. "Is he alright?"

"At the moment, yes," Hastings said, his tone conveying his concern, and his uncertainty.

"What do you mean at the moment? Where is he? What is he doing?"

"Don't worry, Miss Dragoste, he is attending to something very important, and we will be able to see him shortly." He motioned to the monitor. "That is why I had that brought here. First, however, there is something about which I need to speak with you."

Her confusion intensified, blurring the edges of her awareness.

Where was Jack? "I don't understand. I…I'm still very groggy."

"I need your consent. You don't have to sign anything, but I do need you to agree. An opportunity arose at the last minute, and I don't want to waste it."

"Consent? For what?"

"There is a treatment center in Bonn that has developed an experimental cure for Multiple Sclerosis. It is a gene therapy, a bit too complicated for me to understand, I'm afraid, but something about adding generic markers to your myelin sheaths."

"What? MS can't be cured." The conversation had taken an obscure twist and her brain was barely able to keep up, so she fell back on the familiar. "I mean there's experimental stuff, like wiping out the immune system and using stem cells from marrow to reset it, but no one knows if that will work."

"There are actually several genetic treatments available, but this facility's success rate has been almost one hundred percent. However, the treatment has not yet been approved for human trials, and because of genetic patents, it is absurdly expensive."

"I don't understand. If it's not approved for trials, how can they have a success rate?"

Hastings smiled. "There are certain people who do not care to wait for the wheels of government and have the resources to not have to. The treatment will not repair the damage already done, but it will stop the disease from doing more, and you will no longer need any sort of medication."

"So this really works?" she asked, feeling some small twinge of hope amidst the fog in her head. "And I have enough money to pay for it now?"

"Indeed, and more so shortly, I pray."

"What do you mean, more so shortly?"

He ignored her question. "A helicopter is on its way here now. It will meet us before we dock in Bermuda and transport you to the airport where a private jet will take you to Germany."

"But what about Jack?" Could it be true? Could she dare hope?

Hastings nodded, turned to the television and pushed a button. The picture came on, and it took her a second or two to recognize what was on the screen.

"Why are we looking at the arena?"

Hastings looked down at the ground.

"God forgive me if I'm wrong," he said softly.

Chapter 38

If you frighten readily, then you shall not learn
the Art of Fencing since a sheepish despondent heart
does no good as it becomes struck by all art.
- Sigmund Ringeck, Ringeck Fechtbuch – 1440s

The arena was packed with spectators, but Jack didn't pay any attention to them. His awareness was focused, withdrawn. He felt the sword in his hand, the air in his lungs, the steady beating of his heart. There was no excitement, no anxiety, only a steady sense of purpose.

"I told Hastings that you wanted to bet on yourself," Kanemori said. "Everything. He said they wouldn't pay you the division prize because they had to use that to get O'Neil to fight you, but they did give you the standard fight award, for this fight too, so you have over three million Euros. He placed your bet at four to one odds."

Jack shrugged. "You shouldn't have done that. I wanted that money to go to Frederica."

"You can give it to her yourself, after you kill the son of a bitch."

They stood in darkness, just before the red gate. Saito was speaking Japanese over the loudspeaker.

"Do you want to know what he's saying?" Kanemori asked.

"Not really."

"Good. You wouldn't like it anyway. I really don't like that guy."

Jack saw Logan and Boris at their usual table. He was surprised to see Rob there also. Jack turned to the other side and saw Marrone watching him, his neck bundled in white bandages. Marrone noticed him looking and nodded. In this, it seemed, even Todd was on his side. Jack was grateful.

"Where's Hastings?" Jack asked. "I thought he would be here."

"He's watching," Kanemori said. "I'm not supposed to tell you this, but..."

"What?"

"He's with Frederica. She's awake, and they're watching you with that camera." He pointed to a spot on the ceiling.

"She's awake?" The excitement of that sudden realization threatened to disrupt his serenity, but he fought against the urge to go to her. What he was doing, it had to be done, and it would not be right to ask another to do it for him.

"I probably shouldn't have told you, but you were getting fatalistic on me. I don't know what's gotten into you, but the plan is not for you to die, it's for you to win. Got it? Then you can go to her."

Jack nodded. "I understand." He allowed himself to feel relief. She was awake, and she would live. It was up to him to make sure she could do so in peace.

Saito stopped talking and the taiko drums began to beat. Jack saw Junichi emerge from the black gate and he started forward, but felt a hand on his shoulder and stopped.

"Wait," Kanemori said.

"But the drums…I'm supposed to go."

"No," Kanemori said. "Make him wait."

"Why?"

"Just wait."

The drums died and Junichi stood around, looking annoyed. He was shifting his weight back and forth, eager to fight.

"What am I doing?" Jack asked.

"We don't play his game, Jack, remember that. Don't let him control you. Own him, make him dance to your tune. Swordsmanship is not about techniques. You don't win or lose with your body, you win or lose with your mind. Got it?"

"Got it."

"Look at me," Kanemori said, and Jack turned to face him. "Under the sword lifted high, there is hell making you tremble."

"What?"

"Musashi. Book of Five Rings. Under the sword lifted high, there is hell making you tremble. But press onward, and you shall have the land of bliss. Do you understand?"

Jack nodded. "I think I do."

"Good. Now walk out there. Slowly." Kanemori shoved him

forward and he walked out onto the arena floor, fighting the impulse to hasten his steps. "You've already won, Jack. Remember that."

The drums started again as he stepped into the light then died abruptly, and he found himself alone on the field with Junichi, who drew his sword and raised it over his head.

This was it. His whole life, with all its twists and turns, had led him to this place, this moment. A final glory. He could never have imagined, sitting back in his apartment in Kingston, what it felt like to shed the fallacies of civilization and truly embrace life. And death.

Junichi screamed and started to run forward, just as O'Neil had. Only this time Jack's fear was distant, numb, as though it belonged to someone else. He held his sword out in front of him in Langenort, the Longpoint, and moved forward quickly, putting as much space between him and the ropes as he could. He didn't expect Junichi to stop, but he did. Well out of distance.

"You can't win," Junichi said. "You are weak, fat. I will kill you."

"Maybe," Jack said, his voice devoid of emotion. "But I'll take you with me."

Junichi blinked, then immediately attacked with kesa giri, leaping forward like an uncoiling viper.

Jack voided, then struck a Zwerchhau to the head. Junichi stepped forward to meet his strike and Jack realized too late he hadn't moved out far enough. The katana struck, almost invisible, and just missed Jack's arms, stopping near his cross and arresting his strike. Junichi had miscalculated his timing, failing to factor in the cross guard. If he hadn't, Jack would have ended up like Terrance.

Jack wound his point around instantly, trying to thrust, but his opponent was too quick and too strong. Junichi pressed upwards, moving Jack's point offline, and then wound his blade under the cross. Jack felt the edge of the katana bite into his forearms. In a fit of desperation, he kicked Junichi in the stomach and jumped back.

He looked down at his arms and saw severed cloth and blood. He lowered his sword, but the blood flowed towards his palm, so he raised it back over his head. Too late. Blood had welled onto the sword's hilt. Disaster.

Only the hilt wasn't slippery. The leather felt tacky, helping his grip. His hands were weaker, particularly the right, but he was still strong enough to hold his sword.

"Just a little bit longer," he prayed. "Please."

Junichi smiled and raised his sword, posturing in Jodan. Jack saw his arms and chest ripple. Kanemori had often spoken of the manifestations of overconfidence, and this was one of them.

Jack raised his sword over his head and stepped forward aggressively.

Junichi shouted and moved closer, a hair out of Jack's reach.

Jack dipped his sword slightly to the right. Junichi noticed. Jack started to cut and Junichi, confident he could cut through, stepped forward and attempted kiri otoshi.

Only Jack didn't step forward, he stepped backwards, just as he and Kanemori had practiced. He let go of the hilt with his right hand and cut down at Junichi's leg with the sword in his left, barely able to hold onto the blood soaked grip.

Junichi's kiri otoshi sailed past Jack's face, eerily close. He was too far away, out of distance, but with the greater reach of the longsword, Jack wasn't. He felt the tip of his blade strike Junichi's leg. It cut though and hit the dirt at his feet. Jack leapt back, brought the sword up and returned his right hand to the grip.

Junichi also retreated and looked down at his leg in disbelief. There was a tear in his hakama and a dark red spot appeared by his right foot. A very small spot. Junichi looked up at Jack and smiled.

"That is last trick you play on me." He bounced up and down on the balls of his feet, as if to emphasize that the cut hadn't hurt him.

Jack leaped at him, hoping to catch him off guard, and threw a fast cut at his head. Junichi didn't flinch. He dropped his weight into a deep and solid stance and struck Jack's sword so hard he knocked it completely offline. Jack bent backwards as he stumbled away from the riposte, but the katana caught his arm just below his left shoulder. Stinging pain, but that was good. He would not have felt a deep cut. Leaping away from Junichi, he dared a glimpse at the wound and saw a gash that opened and closed like a mouth as he moved. It wasn't deep, but neither was it shallow.

And that was that. Everything that Jack could think of to try, he had tried. Kanemori had been right, the first time. Junichi was just too good. Eastern, Western, it didn't matter. It was always about the swordsman, the skill of the individual, and Junichi's skill was greater than his own.

The blood flowed from his arms, and his hands grew weaker with every passing breath. Soon he wouldn't be able to hold his sword at all—already his grip was faltering, his fingers numb. Now Frederica would watch him die, and she would be left alone and unavenged. How much more could he have done for her if he had lived?

But it was never in the cards. He had made a deal, and it was time to pay.

He turned to the camera and said, "I love you." Though he had spoken of accepting death, it wasn't until that moment that he knew for certain that a God he barely believed in would claim his end of their bargain. If that had to happen, if he had to die, then let it be for her.

He started to walk towards Junichi, his sword in one hand at his side, no guard, no posturing. Junichi moved to meet him, his eyes eager for blood. He would have it.

Jack took his sword in both hands, but held it loosely in front of him. Junichi's eyes twitched in confusion. He didn't understand, and wouldn't.

It is almost impossible to defeat a man who is willing to sacrifice his own life to kill you.

Junichi didn't hesitate, he stepped into measure and cut at Jack's head. Jack didn't bother to parry or void. Instead, he raised his sword under Junichi's arms and thrust it into his heart.

He saw the katana's point moving towards his face on a perfect trajectory that would split his skull, and he smiled. No regrets. To die for love and honor, with a sword in hand, what more could any man ask for?

* * *

"Jack no," she screamed and tried to sit up, but the restraints held her down.

"Forgive me," the old man said. "I should never have done this."

Jack was walking towards Junichi, not even bothering to hold a guard, his hands red with his own blood. How could he even hold on to that sword? She couldn't hear what he had said, but the movement of his lips made everything clear. She was about to watch him die.

It should have been her. She should have been the one to die on the arena floor, not him. She had had no right to drag him into her life, a life that was never meant to last. She had killed him, as surely as if she were the one holding the sword that would end his life, and she wouldn't even be given the chance to die in his place.

Junichi leapt at Jack and swung his katana at his head, and Jack didn't even bother to defend himself. Instead he raised his own weapon and thrust, and she realized in that split second what he was doing, giving his life to kill Junichi. And she knew with a terrible certainty that he was doing it for her.

How could she live with what she had done?

* * *

Jack started to close his eyes, waiting for the fatal strike. The katana smashed into his skull and he felt the splitting skin and the flow of blood down his face. It continued its ark to strike his longsword as it sunk into Junichi's chest, causing the thrust to miss the heart. If he didn't hit Junichi's heart, they would be able to fix him. Junichi was backing away, his eyes wide with terror. That was when Jack realized it.

He *felt* his blood flowing down his face. He wasn't dead. Junichi had pulled his strike to save his own life.

Jack raised his sword to Langenort and pressed forward, going after him. Junichi stopped retreating and struck up at Jack's blade with terrible ferocity, knocking the point off line. He then dipped his own point to cut Jack's neck and Jack let him, bringing the longsword's point back online and thrusting at Junichi's face. Once more Junichi faltered and acted to save himself, knocking Jack's sword down and pressing into his arms, this time from above. Once again Jack caught him on his cross, and once again Junichi was too strong and his blade found Jack's forearms. But this time Jack didn't care, didn't try to get away. Jack's grip was so weak he was about to drop his sword but he pushed it forward, feeling the katana's razor edge slide along his arms and into his throat, then thrust his own point deep into Junichi's chest.

Junichi dropped his sword from limp hands and stumbled backwards. In his periphery, Jack saw the doctors rushing towards him. They would try to fix him. His grip had almost failed, but he had the strength for just one more cut.

He raised his sword over his left shoulder, locked his eyes onto Junichi's neck and struck with all his might.

The sword hit right below Junichi's chin and Jack felt a thump as the blade passed through the vertebrae. Junichi's head, eyes mad with terror, toppled off of his shoulders and fell to the dirt floor, where it blinked three times, then died. The doctors stopped running.

Jack stumbled back, his sword dropping from fingers too weak to hold themselves closed. Kanemori ran towards him from the gate. Logan and Boris jumped over the ropes, on their way to the arena floor. They were screaming, triumphant sounds of joy and relief, though they were barely audible above the cheers of the crowd.

He had won. The doctors started moving again, but not towards Junichi. He looked at them, puzzled, and suddenly felt the warm wetness spreading down his chest and back, and remembered that Junichi's sword had touched his neck as he had lifted it on his cross for the finishing thrust. Arterial blood flowed in pulses, timed to the beating of his heart.

He looked up at the ceiling where the camera was and tried to speak but couldn't get the words out. He dropped onto the blood soaked dirt, and then the blackness took him.

* * *

Frederica's tears flowed freely, washing away the dreaded certainty that she would have to watch the man she loved die the same brutal death she had barely been spared.

She watched Jack push his blade into Junichi's chest, then pull it free. Once the katana had fallen, it was over, but not for Jack. She saw the cut, saw the head fly off, and at that moment, she knew that she would love that man until the day she died, with all of her heart.

But then he fell to the ground and didn't move. His blood slowly spread onto the dirt.

Chapter 39

Under the sword lifted high,
there is hell making you tremble.
But press onward,
and you shall have the land of bliss.
- Miyamoto Musashi, Go Rin No Sho
(Book of Five Rings), 1645

Hastings walked him to the gangway, a final honor.

"You could have waited for me to wake up," Jack said, rubbing the bandage on his neck where Junichi's sword had nicked his carotid artery. He had never actually seen Frederica regain consciousness. He knew she was alright, but he was tormented by uncertainty that only seeing her could cure.

"I'm terribly sorry," Hastings said. "All of the resources were lined up in Bonn. I didn't want to have to wait."

"Yes, of course. I just really want to go to her, to be with her."

"This is something she needs to do on her own, I'm sure you can understand that."

"I do. But I don't even have a way to contact her. I mean I could message her on Facebook, but…"

"You need not worry, Mr. Fischer, everything will be taken care of. I want to say, before you go, that it is an honor and a privilege to know such a skilled fighter, and such a brave and honorable man. Few believed you would triumph over Junichi."

"I didn't, I lost. He defeated himself in the end."

"If you say so," Hastings said with a smile.

"Thank you, Mr. Hastings. For everything."

"Please, call me Reginald."

"Really?"

Hastings smiled. "I prefer Reg, actually, but only when we're among friends."

"Okay, but only if you call me Jack." Jack extended his hand. Hastings shook it.

"That will be fine, Jack. Oh, before I forget." He handed him a piece of paper. "Your account balance."

Jack took the paper and looked at it and almost dropped it. He had never imagined having so much money. Four to one odds indeed.

"Wow."

"Enjoy it, Mr. Fi…Jack."

"Thanks. See you later, Reg."

"Indeed you will."

Jack walked down the gangplank where Kanemori waited for him next to the same Jaguar that had brought him to the ship.

"How are you holding up?" Kanemori asked.

Jack shrugged. "I'm fine, but I miss her. I'm worried."

"Don't be. Hastings will take care of everything, you have my word. I just wanted to say before you go, I'm proud of you. Very, very proud, and I'm not the only one."

Jack frowned, not understanding. "Why would you be proud of me? I tried to suicide to kill him. It was only because he didn't want to die that he lost."

"Exactly," Kanemori said. "I know you don't understand yet, but you will." He grinned. "It's a Japanese thing."

"If you say so," Jack said, echoing Hastings's words. He embraced his friend and bid him farewell, then got in the car.

He tried not to look back as they pulled away, but the urge proved too powerful. The Invictus was a magnificent ship, a place where his life had changed forever. It was comforting to know that he would see it again one day.

"Did you have a nice trip, sir?" the driver asked. He was the same man who had taken him to the ship.

"Incredible."

"Glad to hear it, man."

Instead of taking him to King's Wharf, the driver took him to Bermuda International, where he boarded a plane to JFK. Jack was glad, he wasn't sure he could deal with being on a cruise ship without Frederica.

As soon as he got on the plane he felt the depression set in. It was over. The greatest adventure of his life, gone. It was said that every man has his time, and he'd had his, and he would never have it again. The worst part was, he was going home alone.

He found his seat in first class, next to a pretty blond in a business suit.

"Hi," she said, noticing the bandages on his neck and arms. "That looks painful. If you don't mind my asking, what happened?"

"I was injured in a sword fight," Jack said with a barely suppressed grin. "But you should see the other guy."

"Really," she said, but her tone conveyed boredom. She either didn't believe him or, more likely, thought he was some role player who swung sticks around for kicks. Either way, she would leave him alone now, and that was what he wanted. The flight was uneventful but dreadfully long. He tried to drink, to watch television, but he couldn't escape the growing sense of loss that was eating away at him.

There was another car waiting for him at Kennedy, with the same young Swedish man that had taken him to Bayonne.

"Hey Anders," Jack said.

"Good to see you again, Mr. Fischer. Did you have a nice trip?"

Jack nodded. "You could say that."

"Great. I have your luggage, including your swords."

"Really? That was fast." Jack wondered how they had gotten there before he did.

"Straight home, sir?" Anders asked. "Or is there someplace else you would like to go?"

"Bonn," Jack said. "If you can manage it."

Anders looked confused. "I'm sorry sir, did you want me to get you a plane ticket?"

"Forget it, bad joke. Just take me home."

"Yes sir."

The drive seemed longer than the flight as the oppressive reality of a lonely homecoming drew ever closer. Twice he had thought he lost her, and twice he had been spared, but what about now? Would time accomplish what the stroke of a sword had not?

The sun was still high overhead when they pulled up in front of the school.

"What day is it?" Jack asked.

"Saturday, sir. Let me help you with your bags."

"No, that's okay. I'll take it from here. You have a safe ride back to…well, wherever it is you're going."

"Thank you, sir."

Anders unloaded his sword case and duffel bag onto the sidewalk and drove away. Jack watched him go, the last remnant of a life he didn't want to leave behind. He had always been so happy to come home from trips. His school, his apartment, they had greeted him with a promise of comfort and a return to a familiar routine. Now they were an empty shell, a reminder of what was missing.

He hoped that Will had cancelled Saturday's class, but as he climbed the stairs and heard the sounds of training he knew that he would be deprived of even that small relief. Still, it would be good to see Will again, even if he wasn't quite ready to face him.

He walked onto the training floor and headed for the door to his office.

"Jack," Will shouted. "Everybody keep doing what you're doing." Jack turned as Will ran up to him. The students had ignored his orders and were staring at Jack.

"Will," Jack said. "It's good to see you again." He didn't need to force himself to smile.

Will grabbed him and lifted him off his feet.

"Whoah," Jack said. "Watch the stitches."

"Holy crap man," Will said. "You're back. What the hell happened to you?"

"It's a long story."

"It's good to see you. Do you even know what's been going on?"

Jack shrugged. "I've been out of touch."

"You gotta tell me what the hell happened, man. It's crazy what's going on in the community. It's a fucking mad house."

Jack wasn't in the mood for face book bullshit, but Will wasn't one to exaggerate. "What's going on?"

"The IHFF."

"What about them?"

Will blinked. "You mean you don't know?"

"Will, just tell me, will you?"

"They named *masters*, man. And you're one of them, a god

damned Meister des Langen Schwertes. So is Logan Holbrook, and Ukrainian Boris. Even that asshole Marrone. The community went buck wild."

"Marrone's okay," Jack said. "Not a bad guy at all." He remembered Hastings telling him about it, but he had other things on his mind. "What about…" He found it hard to say her name. "Frederica Dragoste?"

"Her too, Maestro d'armi in rapier. Wait…she was there?"

"Yeah."

"So…" Will hesitated. "This thing you went to…was it what we thought?"

"It was, and it wasn't. It's hard to explain."

Will looked at Jack's stitched neck and arms. "Holy shit man. You…you fought, didn't you?"

"We'll talk about it later, okay? I'm exhausted." He saw the hurt in his friend's eyes. "It's great to see you again, Will, it really is. And I will tell you everything, I promise. Everything is different now, everything. And don't worry, your turn will come."

"My turn?"

Jack smiled, picked up his bags and went upstairs, leaving Will to gawk after him.

Compared to where he had been sleeping for the last week and a half, his apartment seemed too small, and too shabby. Cracks in the ceiling, blemishes on the walls, uneven lines and a worn floor were something he had gotten unused to quite thoroughly. He would have to hire some contractors to give the place a serious make over, no expense spared. Perhaps a nautical theme, or better yet, English country house.

He set his bags down in the middle of the living room and wondered how he was supposed to live there alone.

Walking over to his kitchen, he reached into the cabinet and pulled out Alison's photo. He unfolded its stand and set it on the counter, took a few steps back and took a good look.

It was just Alison, as lovely as he remembered her. There was no broken corpse, no dark feelings, only pleasant memories of a happy time together.

The cupboard was still open, revealing a bottle of Black Label. Jack took it and unscrewed the cap. He thought about getting a glass but then closed the bottle and put it back. There would be time for drinking later.

* * *

"Swordsmanship isn't about techniques," Jack said. "You don't win with your body, you win with your mind."

"Yes, meister," Will said, and tried again.

"Good. Much tighter that time. Keep your center low, your movements will be stronger if your body supports them. And stop calling me meister, it gets on my nerves."

The advanced class was small, just Will and three others, and that was a relief. His regular classes had swelled considerably. The IHFF had engaged in a massive advertising campaign and his school was listed prominently on their website. People were coming from all over the country to train with him. It was ironic that now that he had more money than he knew what to do with, his school was finally making a profit. At least Will was happy with his new salary. He had even wanted to drop out of college until Jack threatened to fire him if he didn't finish his degree.

Three weeks had passed, and he had heard nothing. He'd messaged her on Facebook and sent her an email, but she had not replied. Jack understood about her needing to go through the treatment on her own, but why couldn't she at least contact him to let him know she was alright? His fears were growing every day. Had something happened to her? Had they lied about her waking up?

He had no way to contract Hastings, but he had pinged the URL from the invitation letter several hundred times, so if anyone was watching it, they must know he wanted something. That had been a week ago and there was no reply. He'd gotten Kanemori to help, but Hastings hadn't responded to him either.

"I think we'll call it a day," Jack said. "I wanna get some rest before afternoon classes."

"Okay guys," Will said. "You heard the man. Let's wrap it up."

Jack went upstairs and powered up his new laptop. Plenty of residual chatter from the master fiasco, but no messages. Nothing of consequence in his email either. With nothing else to do, he read through the master threads. The community was, as usual, divided. There were those who supported the IHFF and those who tried to discredit it in an attempt to hold on to their fading prominence. It was the same old bullshit, and he had little use for it.

Students started to pour in around an hour before class, and Jack decided to watch them practice. He was on his way down the stairs when he saw something odd in the sword rack—a rapier. He had ordered a couple, along with a bunch of new longswords, but no one had told him that any had arrived. If Will opened his box without permission, he would have to give him a proper beating on the training floor.

It probably was one he had ordered, it looked oddly familiar.

He headed for the rack to take a closer look and turned the corner. Frederica was sitting on the floor next to a large green duffle bag, wearing dark blue jeans and a white sleeveless top. Her left arm was immobilized in a rigid plastic cast. She saw him and smiled, climbing to her feet.

He was running towards her before he realized his feet were moving. He slowed himself just in time to avoid smashing into her and grabbed her gently in his arms. He pressed her close, burying his face in her hair. It was the same scent of strawberries that he remembered.

For several long seconds he said nothing, clutching her tightly as his body trembled with relief. The clouds above his sky had parted, letting in the sunshine. Finally he pulled away just enough to kiss her. She returned his kiss with the same passion they had shared the first night after their fights. Students were staring at them, but he couldn't care less.

"Oh Jack," she said, pulling away from him. "It's so good to see you."

Jack took her right hand and led her into his office, closing the door behind them.

"I should be furious," he said, unable to get the grin off his face. "I was so worried."

"I'm sorry," she said. "But I had to…"

"To do it on your own, I know."

"I wanted to call you," she said. "More than anything, but I knew that if I heard your voice I would have to go to you, and I needed to finish that treatment. I think it was the hardest thing I've ever done. Oh, and Hastings asked me to apologize on his behalf. He felt bad about ignoring your attempts to reach him, but he did it for me."

"Was it painful?"

"Yes."

"So you're…cured?"

She nodded, her tears flowing down to her smile. "So they tell me. I'll still have regressions, but I won't get worse. If you can still live with that?"

"Do you even have to ask?"

She looked away. "I'm assuming a lot by coming here, Jack. It's been a long time since you said…what you said."

"Stop it," he said. "I don't want to hear any of that. I thought I would never get to tell you. When you were lying in that bed, I didn't know if you would ever wake up, and I begged God or the universe or whatever you want to call it for just a chance to tell you how I feel. So here it is. I love you, Frederica, and there's nothing I want more than to be with you."

"I love you too, Jack," she said, and started to cry again. "Oh god, you have a way of making me do that." She wiped at her tears.

"Then it's settled." He looked at her left arm, immobilized in a contraption made of white plastic and stainless steel. "How is…it?"

"Getting better. I can't move it for another month, but I'm feeling more of it every day. Those doctors were something else."

"That's just incredible." He remembered what she had looked like when Junichi's sword struck her and shuddered.

"Jack, I want to say, about what you did, facing Junichi…I wouldn't have let you do it, not if I was awake, but now that it's done…I have nightmares sometimes, but then I wake up, and I know he's dead, that you killed him, and it makes it alright. What you did was the most any human being could ever do for another, and I will never forget it. Not ever."

"I did what I had to do, but no more of that, it's in the past," he said. "How about we go out there and tell everyone that the

Kingston Academy of Arms will soon be offering seventeenth century Italian rapier, taught by the eminent Maestro d'armi Frederica Dragoste?"

She took his hand. "Nothing would make me happier."

Jack reached for the door knob and hesitated, savoring the moment. The end of one journey, and the beginning of another. The world didn't seem so evil anymore, or so ugly. He looked at her face, her genuine smile, her eyes aglow with the joy of life, and felt an overwhelming love.

"What is it?" she asked. A ray of sunlight lanced through his cracked office window and illuminated the tiny dust motes that floated around her head like an angel's halo.

"The land of bliss," he said.

They walked out of the office to the waiting students, to their new life, together.

About the Author

Michael Edelson is the director and principal instructor of the New York Historical Fencing Association, a world renowned school of Historical European Martial Arts (HEMA). He is an accomplished tournament fighter with fourteen medals in assorted longsword competitions both in the United States and abroad, including open longsword, cutting and paired technique. In 2013, he was Mexico's national champion, winning gold in that country's premier longsword tournament. He also took first place in Gekken (Japanese fencing) at the 2013 East Coast Tai Kai.

Michael lives in rural New York state with his wife, two kids and too many pets. At present, he is a firefighter with the Andes Fire Department. In his past, he was a soldier, a sailor and a failed "dot com millionaire." His hobbies include traveling (mostly to compete in and teach historical fencing), shooting, collecting mechanical watches and arguing on Facebook.

Made in the USA
Lexington, KY
05 September 2016